The light shines in the darkness, but the darkness has not understood it.

John 1:5

Novels by W. F. Rogers

<u>The Mirror and the Prism Series</u>

Silhouette
Point of Refraction

Visit the author's website: https://wfrogers.com

The Mirror and the Prism

Book 2

Point of Refraction

W. F. Rogers

W/P WAYRIDGE PRESS

This One Is For Fran

CONTENTS

1. Principle Uncertainty.................................1

2. Inverse 19

3. On Edge 40

4. Harkless...56

5. The North End of the House 70

6. Prisoner on the Moor..................................80

7. Invitations and Incantations.........................92

8. Lost 110

9. Dartrun 126

10. Twists and Turns..137

11. Caught in the Current 156

12. Parries and Pirouettes.................................169

13. A Cascade of Shards....................................185

14. Mirror..198

    Epilogue 213

A Mirror and Prism Novelette:

    Saving the City of Light.............................217

Hi Paige and Lara,

It's been raining. It does that a lot here. I've been busy with school but managed to take another trip to Devon. I have Gwen's next diary! It was in a cabinet on the library's third floor rather than on the first floor with the other Maham family records. Since you have trouble reading her cursive, I'll transcribe this one and send entries as I finish typing them.

My cousin William and his wife Patricia will be staying in London for the next few months, but they told me I'm welcome to visit Maham House on my own. I just have to let Connor, the butler, know in advance. I'm going to search for Lady Buckleigh's journal (Cecilia Maham's winter/spring 1918 journal, that is). I've been frustrated by gaps in the housekeeping records. There were details of the War Cabinet dinner party that Lady Buckleigh apparently didn't want recorded. I want those details.

You've been asking how Maham House is laid out. I've attached a rough floor plan.

More soon,

Kirk

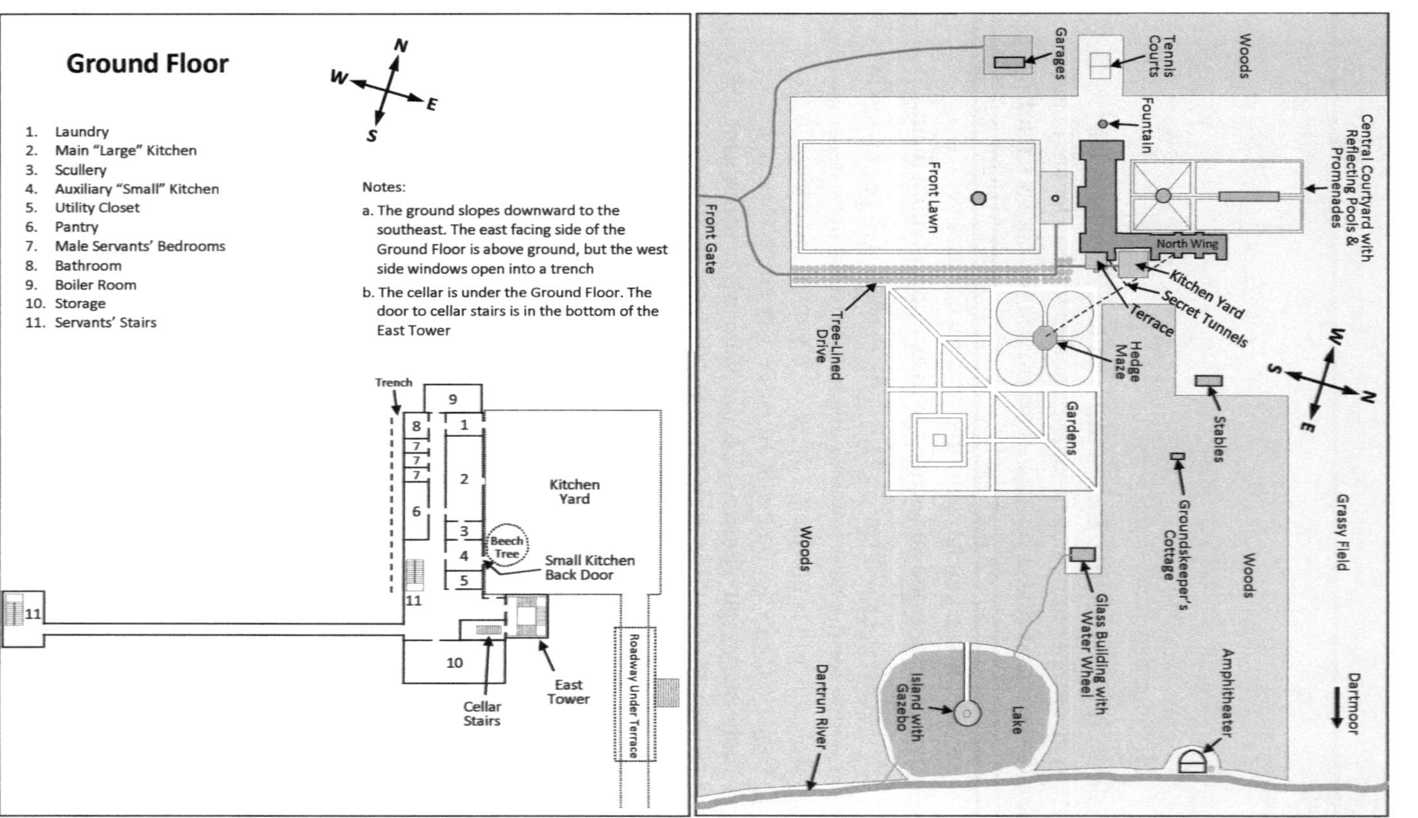
Ground Floor
N
W
E
S
1. Laundry
2. Main "Large" Kitchen
3. Scullery
4. Auxiliary "Small" Kitchen
5. Utility Closet
6. Pantry
7. Male Servants' Bedrooms
8. Bathroom
9. Boiler Room
10. Storage
11. Servants' Stairs
Notes:
a. The ground slopes downward to the southeast. The east facing side of the Ground Floor is above ground, but the west side windows open into a trench
b. The cellar is under the Ground Floor. The door to cellar stairs is in the bottom of the East Tower
Trench
9
8
7
7
7
1
2
6
3
4
5
11
Beech Tree
Kitchen Yard
Small Kitchen Back Door
10
Cellar Stairs
East Tower
Roadway Under Terrace
Central Courtyard with Reflecting Pools & Promenades
Woods
Garages
Tennis Courts
Fountain
Front Lawn
North Wing
Kitchen Yard
Secret Tunnels
Terrace
Front Gate
Tree-Lined Drive
Hedge Maze
Gardens
Stables
Groundskeeper's Cottage
Woods
Glass Building with Water Wheel
Woods
Island with Gazebo
Lake
Dartrun River
Amphitheater
Grassy Field
Dartmoor

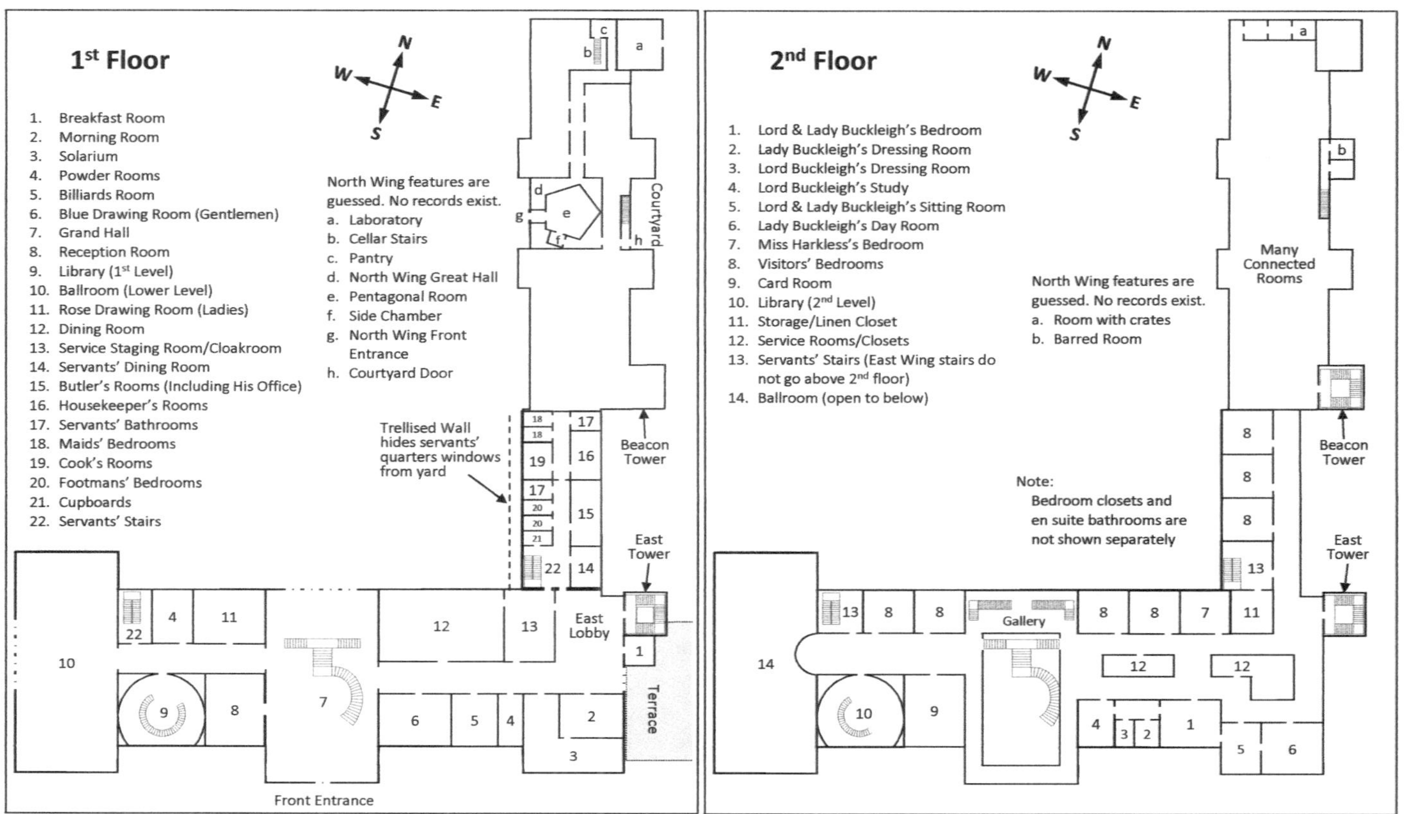

1st Floor
N
W
E
S
1. Breakfast Room
2. Morning Room
3. Solarium
4. Powder Rooms
5. Billiards Room
6. Blue Drawing Room (Gentlemen)
7. Grand Hall
8. Reception Room
9. Library (1st Level)
10. Ballroom (Lower Level)
11. Rose Drawing Room (Ladies)
12. Dining Room
13. Service Staging Room/Cloakroom
14. Servants' Dining Room
15. Butler's Rooms (Including His Office)
16. Housekeeper's Rooms
17. Servants' Bathrooms
18. Maids' Bedrooms
19. Cook's Rooms
20. Footmans' Bedrooms
21. Cupboards
22. Servants' Stairs
North Wing features are guessed. No records exist.
a. Laboratory
b. Cellar Stairs
c. Pantry
d. North Wing Great Hall
e. Pentagonal Room
f. Side Chamber
g. North Wing Front Entrance
h. Courtyard Door
Courtyard
Trellised Wall hides servants' quarters windows from yard
Beacon Tower
East Tower
East Lobby
Terrace
Front Entrance
2nd Floor
N
W
E
S
1. Lord & Lady Buckleigh's Bedroom
2. Lady Buckleigh's Dressing Room
3. Lord Buckleigh's Dressing Room
4. Lord Buckleigh's Study
5. Lord & Lady Buckleigh's Sitting Room
6. Lady Buckleigh's Day Room
7. Miss Harkless's Bedroom
8. Visitors' Bedrooms
9. Card Room
10. Library (2nd Level)
11. Storage/Linen Closet
12. Service Rooms/Closets
13. Servants' Stairs (East Wing stairs do not go above 2nd floor)
14. Ballroom (open to below)
North Wing features are guessed. No records exist.
a. Room with crates
b. Barred Room
Note:
Bedroom closets and en suite bathrooms are not shown separately
Many Connected Rooms
Beacon Tower
East Tower
Gallery

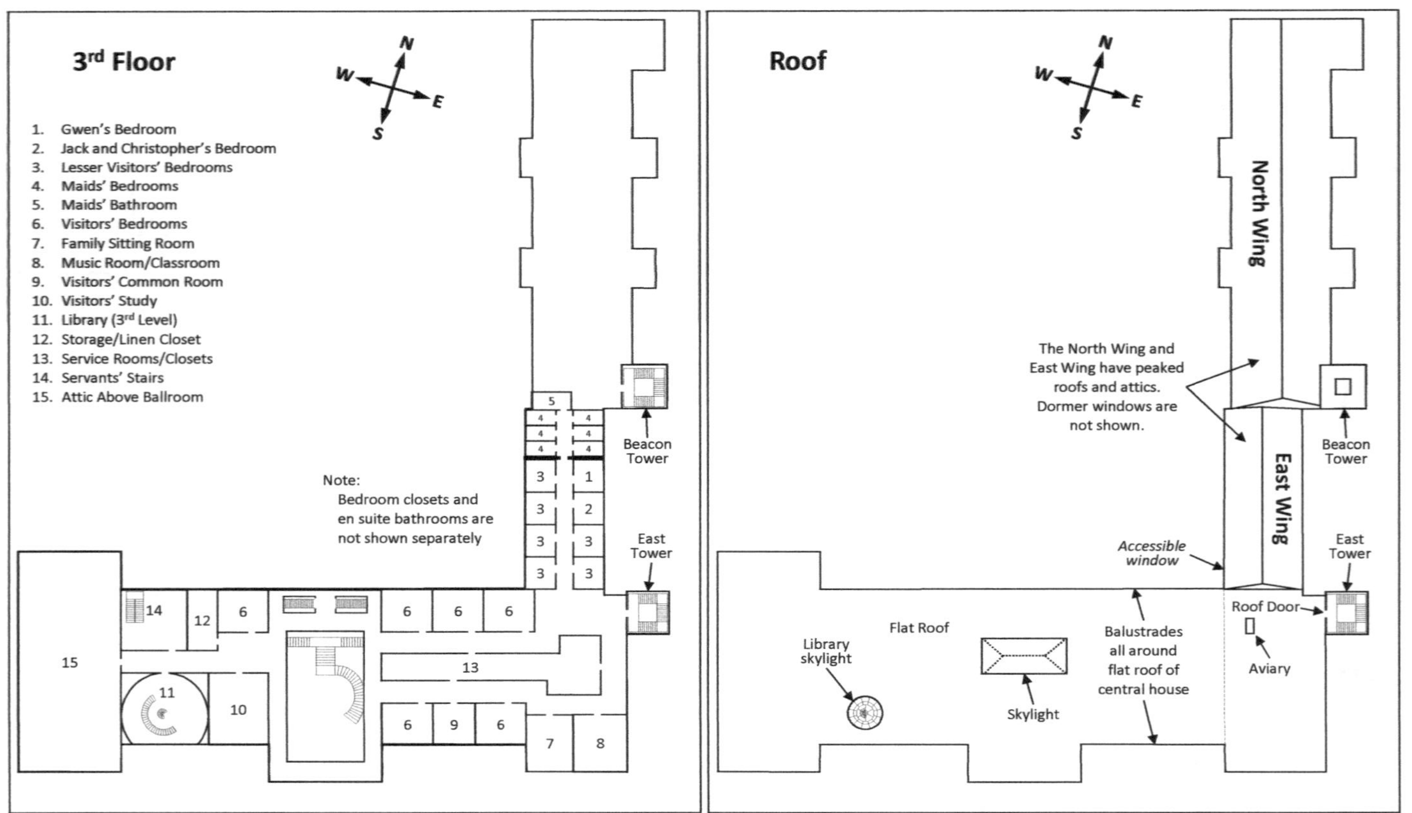

3rd Floor
1. Gwen's Bedroom
2. Jack and Christopher's Bedroom
3. Lesser Visitors' Bedrooms
4. Maids' Bedrooms
5. Maids' Bathroom
6. Visitors' Bedrooms
7. Family Sitting Room
8. Music Room/Classroom
9. Visitors' Common Room
10. Visitors' Study
11. Library (3rd Level)
12. Storage/Linen Closet
13. Service Rooms/Closets
14. Servants' Stairs
15. Attic Above Ballroom
N
W
E
S
Note:
Bedroom closets and en suite bathrooms are not shown separately
Beacon Tower
East Tower
Roof
N
W
E
S
North Wing
East Wing
Beacon Tower
East Tower
The North Wing and East Wing have peaked roofs and attics. Dormer windows are not shown.
Accessible window
Roof Door
Aviary
Flat Roof
Library skylight
Skylight
Balustrades all around flat roof of central house

CHAPTER 1

Principle Uncertainty

4-1-10

Gwen watched the angel soldiers go. They didn't appear to be walking fast but were out of sight in moments. Her heart sank. Memories of the people she had met and the things she had seen the previous day were scattering like dry, crumpled newspaper pages blown down a windy street. She felt much older than her fifteen years.

"Are we going to re-anchor ourselves to silhouette?" Christopher asked.

Jack contemplated the prism. "Yes." He glanced eastward. The bright sun was high above the jagged, snowcapped mountains. Tentatively, as if handling a strange organism, he exposed the prism to light. The result was a small, faint spectrum cast on the ground.

He took a breath. "Father, God, re-anchor us."

There was no dazzling beam, distortion of space, or transformation of anything.

The others waited, anticipating.

Jack licked his lips and repeated: "Re-anchor us."

Christopher shifted to get a better view.

Jack closed his eyes and willed. "Put us right."

Nothing happened.

"Restore us…Right us…Return us…In Jesus's name, transfer, transmute, transmogrify!"

Christopher folded his arms and tapped a foot. "It sounds like you're trying to cast a spell."

Jack became very still. "Holy Spirit, we beg you to intercede for us. Jesus, please, *please* restore us to our rightful condition."

The prism glinted primary colors. That was all.

"Perhaps if we were in silhouette space..." Patrick indicated the end of the clearing where his airplane was parked. "There's a stretch of mundane Dartmoor over that way."

They gathered their things and crossed the windswept field.

Gwen buttoned her overcoat to the top. She wished her cotton blouse were thicker. Thankfully, the torn seam of her borrowed skirt had been mended, so cold air didn't blow around her legs the way it had when she and the boys were trudging through the forest. Her legs had been rather exposed, then. She glanced self-consciously at Patrick. Patrick...he was slightly taller than Jack, but a little thinner. The two boys were the same age—almost adults, now. In some cultures, they would already be considered adults. And she was only a year behind.

Standing beside the F.B.5, Jack repeated his performance, alternately commanding, imploring, and pleading. Ultimately, he gave up. "It's no good."

Gwen looked at the prism in her brother's hand. Everything had seemed so clear and straightforward when the angels were with them. But suddenly the way ahead was obscured.

Jack gritted his teeth. "Someone else give it a try." It was an angry challenge, not a request for help.

The other boys took the prism and prayed. Gwen observed. She felt entirely disconnected from everything. *I've wandered onto a stage in the middle of a play and don't know the script.*

Neither Patrick nor Christopher achieved anything.

Gwen thought for a minute, then gazed at Jack. "What did you do when you put the prism on my desk? That was when you started everything, wasn't it?"

Jack glanced sideways at her. "I'm not sure I was the one..." He looked at the ground. He held out the prism, indicating that Gwen should take it. He didn't meet her eyes.

For a startled moment she imagined he was resentful. She took the prism, but her only thought was that the Lord was gone. Everything was gone.

The object between her thumb and forefinger did no more than project a weak spectrum.

Watching Gwen try and fail, Jack's expression evolved from puzzlement to dismay to anguish. He ran his fingers through his hair. "The lieutenant said something about Gwen's mirror…offhand. Does anyone remember what it was?"

No one did.

"I'm going after the soldiers."

Gwen looked at the empty trail. "They're long gone."

Jack pressed his palms against the sides of his head. "Let's…catch mice and vault to Maham House. We'll figure something out when we get there."

Patrick shifted his weight uncomfortably from his left foot to his right. "M'lord…we'd be leaping blindly through mountains. And have to cross miles of open moor."

"Uncle Geoffrey and Mrs. Holliwell will know what to do," Gwen said. "We should go to Buckton."

Jack scrutinized the landscape to the northeast: a variegated contrast of dark ravines, shadowed valleys, and snow-crowned mountains glistening in the sun. Buckton lay somewhere beyond. "How do you propose we do that? If we can't get to our house, we positively can't get to Buckton."

"We have an airplane," Christopher pointed out.

They all turned to gaze at the F.B.5 which, while newly repaired by the best aircrew of all time, could not be considered anything but dangerous.

Patrick studied the ground between the spot they stood on and the rim of the canyon. "There's about three hundred yards of runway. It should be enough."

Jack stared at the Irish boy. "Yesterday you said we couldn't get back to Buckton."

"The winds are favorable today."

"The angels repaired Patrick's airplane for a reason," Gwen said. "We should fly."

Jack glared at her. "You've never ridden on a wing!"

"You can sit up front this time," Patrick offered.

Jack scowled at the airplane for twenty seconds. "Hang it! *Hang* it! All right. We'll fly to Buckton." He turned to Patrick. "How soon can you have the blasted contraption ready?"

"It's ready now."

Jack took a long, deep breath.

Patrick went to the Lewis gun and began loosening its mount.

"What are you doing?"

"I'm going to leave this behind. We don't have any use for a machine gun and could do without extra weight."

Jack waved him off. "We're taking it."

Patrick glanced at the chasm at the end of the short runway. He chewed his lower lip.

Jack retightened the gun mount. "I suppose I'll have to be the one to start the blasted engine?"

"You were very good at it before." Patrick rummaged in a compartment and found an extra pair of goggles. He gave them to Jack. "You may want these."

Jack took the goggles and beckoned to Gwen. "Come here." He helped her into the forward cockpit.

"You'll be with me in the back," Patrick told Christopher.

"Excellent! Can I help with the controls?"

Eagerly, the boy climbed aboard. But when Patrick joined him inside the small aft cockpit, Christopher was squished to immobility and had no view of anything except Patrick's shoulder. And a flare gun in a holster secured to the starboard sidewall dug into his thigh.

Patrick checked the controls. He couldn't pull the stick all the way back. It pressed into his chest when he tried. That was because the human pillow beside him forced him to sit skewed in his seat. He twisted around to see Jack. "Switch is off. If you please, m'lord, pull the propeller around a few times to prepare the engine."

Jack did as requested.

Patrick handed Christopher a waxed paper bag. "I saved this from the breakfast packaging. Use it if you become ill."

Gwen gathered her long hair in a loose braid, secured it with a ribbon, and tucked it into her coat. She felt like a sack of mail. She had no role in any of this. She prayed for God's guidance but wondered if He was listening.

"Well then." Patrick licked a finger and held it up to test the breeze. The wind was light but blowing directly at them. "Should be enough…" He turned the magneto knob and yelled, "Switch is on!"

Jack swung the propeller.

The engine burst to life, its exhaust deafening but smoother than it had ever been.

Jack darted under the wire-braced booms, kicked away the rock serving as a chock, sprang up into the gunner's position, and squeezed down beside Gwen.

The weird biplane began its takeoff run across the meadow, lurching and shaking, its rotary engine roaring and spinning madly.

Patrick had not considered that his airplane would need extra runway in the thin, high-altitude air. He pulled back on the control stick when the craft was a dozen yards from the rim of the Defile of Ash, but the Gunbus was not ready to fly. "Uh oh."

They dropped into the jagged canyon.

Jack gripped the Lewis gun as if it would keep him from falling. The airplane nosed almost straight down. Air whistled past the open cockpit.

Gwen's heart raced. But she didn't die. The plane accelerated out of its stall and pulled up sharply. Centripetal force crushed her down in her seat.

The F.B.5 missed the ground by twenty feet.

Gwen's heart continued to pound. Her stomach was still back on the runway. God had summoned her, sworn her into His service, and flung her off a cliff. In her imagination, she still had the sword and shield with her, but they were wooden toys. The racket of the engine was so tremendous she could hardly think. She hunched down to escape the arctic slipstream.

Climbing, the airplane banked to the right and headed northeast. Today there were no updrafts to carry it over ridges; however, it sailed above the first snowy razorback without difficulty. The machine had been tuned to perfection. The ground crew had even installed an upgrade: a voice tube for communication between the two cockpits.

Patrick pulled the signal cord to raise the flag that alerted his passengers to listen. "It's a fine day to be flying. We're doing splendidly." He thought it would encourage them.

It didn't.

They had a tailwind and made good progress. Patrick navigated through a realm of deep gorges and towering pinnacles. The scenery was breathtaking: a hyperreality where rocks blazed with color and shadows moved in complex, unexpected ways.

Gwen gazed at the amazing world. Perhaps God hadn't cast her adrift. Perhaps He had set her on a horse and given her the reins.

Jack might as well have been in a cave. Victories over demons had not raised his self-confidence. He was not so foolish as to believe he and Patrick had overcome a single one of the demons they had fought by their own strength or skill. It was God's doing—the Lord had delivered them. Nor was there any solace in knowing that God had done so. Jack was being carefully watched by a strict, unsleeping master who might withdraw His support at any time.

He fiddled with the machine gun to comfort himself. Jack Maham was no more than an average student. He was strong for his size but not a spectacular athlete. He rivaled his father for lack of charm. But he was a fantastic shot. When he was thirteen, he had accompanied his brother Fredrick to a pheasant hunt at Waddesdon Manor and amazed everyone by using a rifle instead of a shotgun and never missing. For Jack, holding a large automatic weapon was reassuring.

A quivering white blotch rose from a hollow in the narrow, steep-walled valley they were entering.

Jack gestured to Patrick. He bent and yelled into the voice tube, "What's *that*?"

Patrick stiffened. He stared at the strange, rippling matter. "I haven't the foggiest…"

Christopher, feeling the sudden tension in Patrick's back, struggled to lift himself to see out of the cockpit.

Gwen watched the fluttering shape emerge from mist and separate into four pale-skinned demons flying in formation. If she had possessed Colonel Sir Geoffrey's black notebook, she would have found pages captioned *Pterothert* with sketches approximating what she saw: sinewy spirits with enormous wings formed of leathery membranes stretched between splayed-out spines.

Oddly, Patrick's first thought was that Lady Gwendolyn must think him a complete fool for saying they had no use for a machine gun. He veered his plane away from the spirits.

The demons flapped madly, climbing until they were above the F.B.5. Then they swung across Patrick's course and cut him off.

Blocked by a soaring mountain on his left, Patrick could not steer anywhere but toward the pasty-white pterotherts. When they were within a thousand yards, he watched helplessly as they feathered their wings and dove at his airplane.

Jack fumbled with the Lewis gun. He released the safety and yanked the bolt to chamber a round. His arms trembled badly, but he got the incoming demons squarely in his gunsight. He did not wait to fire—the diving spirits were already so close he couldn't miss. He pulled the trigger and held it, spraying bullets.

The pterotherts broke in all directions, swerving to evade the airplane. But none of them were hurt. Not a single one of Jack's shots had had any effect.

The demons wheeled in the sky and chased the airplane.

Patrick kept the F.B.5's engine running at full power and pulled away from the demons. But the mountains soon forced him into a zig-zagging river valley. With each turn, the maniacally thrusting pterotherts drew closer.

A broad strip of silhouette territory ran like a fence along the east bank of the winding river. The interstitial boundaries were discernable to Patrick as walls of faint aurora extending upward into space. He drifted to the right to avoid them and their unpredictable atmospheric transitions.

But the demons converged on his airplane. When the nearest pterothert grabbed at the starboard wingtip, Patrick instinctively banked left and, as an unintended consequence, flew straight through an interstitial boundary. The strong headwind changed instantly to a tailwind. The F.B.5 stalled, fell like a plank, and spun. It plummeted for nine and a half revolutions before Patrick regained control.

Gwen and Jack had not been ready for the violent maneuver. They had not seen the interstitial boundary and did not know an airplane could spin in midair.

All Christopher knew was that something awful had been done to his stomach.

But the spin saved them. They dropped below the demons and slipped behind them.

The pterotherts reoriented.

Patrick watched the turning creatures. He looked at the Lewis gun, then at the demons, and then shouted into the voice tube: "Change magazines! The other one has tracers!"

Jack had no idea why he should use bullets that glowed, but he snatched up the second ammunition drum and, after some fumbling, got it locked on top of the machine gun.

The pterotherts joined once again in formation. Patrick did not run. He turned to attack.

Gwen focused on the person of the Lord. She closed her eyes and blocked out the crazy rotations of terrain and sky, the deafening noise of the engine, the reek of petrol and castor oil, the frigid and chafing wind, the violent jostling, and her nausea.

The demons lost their synchronization. Two of them got too close in their formation, accidentally smacked wingtips, and screeched angrily at each other.

Jack pulled the trigger. The fiery bullets passed well ahead of their targets. Patrick had guessed correctly. The problem was not supernatural. It was conventional physics. Jack had never fired from an airplane moving at seventy miles per hour. He had overshot his obliquely approaching targets. His error graphically revealed to him by the tracers, he slewed the stream of bullets into the lead demon.

It turned out that British .303 rounds anchored to the Primary World had the same effect on evil spirits as they did on mortals. With five ragged holes blown in its body and more through its wings, the lead pterothert dropped away convulsing and spewing thick, dark fluids. The others scattered. They ignored their fallen comrade—although it would have made for a tasty hors d'oeuvre—and continued chasing the F.B.5.

Jack couldn't point his gun to the rear—it wouldn't swivel that far. He could only grip the handle and pray for Patrick to set up another shot.

Patrick banked hard, pressing everyone down in their seats with the force of the maneuver.

Christopher felt like kneaded dough.

It was no use. Twist and turn as he might, Patrick couldn't shake the pursuers or get them into Jack's sights. The demons' movements were too erratic. Coming from both sides, they closed on the airplane.

Gwen continued to pray.

Patrick steered the F.B.5 between two rock formations. There, the strip of silhouette bent sharply to the right. He purposely flew at an interstitial boundary. The airplane passed through west to east. This time, the wind on the far side of the transition was blowing toward them; the F.B.5's wings were buoyed by sudden extra lift. Patrick hauled back on the stick. The nose came up violently. Like a marble rolling in a mixing bowl, the airplane went straight up, stopped in midair, turned completely around, and dove down on the demons.

Jack had a perfect head-on shot. He held the machine gun trigger for three seconds, riddling two of the demons. They fell convulsing and cartwheeling. But the last pterothert peeled off, pivoted in midair, and scooted into Jack's blind spot.

Patrick banked hard left, slamming the control stick as far as it would go, thinking he would use an interstitial boundary to pivot again. But this time the demon anticipated his move. It pulled inside his turn and zoomed above the F.B.5.

The plane's wild gyrations and thunderous machine gunfire had registered only vaguely in Gwen's consciousness. The Lord was with her, and she paid no attention to anything but her prayers.

Patrick veered into a slice of silhouette and slipped his plane as it met the shear. The Gunbus was buffeted and hurled sideways.

Then the young pilot made a mistake. He was looking behind himself and inadvertently flew through another interstitial boundary. The air currents swirled in a vortex; they grabbed the left wing and shoved it down.

The world whirled. Patrick managed to regain control and pull out of the dive, but the demon had followed them down. Gwen and Jack had a perfect view of the pterothert's long claws as it latched onto the upper wing.

Patrick tilted his head up and came face-to-face with six infinitely black eye sockets. He was transfixed. A monster's gaze really could turn a man to stone. The demon's snarl was so vicious that Patrick momentarily lost control of his muscles.

Jack fumbled frantically with the Lewis gun. If he could dismount the weapon and hold it in his hands, he could point it up at the demon. But no, he couldn't free the gun.

The demon unhinged its jaw and opened its mouth. Patrick stared into a huge, fang-filled maw wider than his head.

But the pterothert had overlooked the little boy behind the pilot. Christopher pulled the flare gun from its holster and, as the demon extended itself to bite Patrick's head off, fired a magnesium flare point-blank into the monster's throat.

The demon tumbled off the wing and was swept backward, almost missing the propeller. Almost. A leg failed to miss the whirling tips.

A spray of ghastly bits blew behind in the slipstream as the writhing, burning pterothert fell away.

Patrick threw his plane into a series of tight turns, first to the left and then to the right, scanning the sky, twisting his neck and body to see in all directions.

Jack did the same, gripping the Lewis gun, pointing it every which way, searching for his next target.

Gwen, head down and eyes closed, was still absorbed entirely in her prayers. She continued to sense the Lord's subtle changing of her world.

At last, Patrick accepted that the sky was clear. He leveled the wings and flew the F.B.5 straight ahead until his pulse slowed. When he had relaxed as much as he was able, he tilted the control stick and set a course for Buckton.

Christopher threw up into the wax-lined bag.

Patrick followed the river to the interstitial sea. Once out of the mountains, he flew due east across the blue water. He and Jack searched the sky, but there was no sign of enemies.

Half an hour after their dogfight, they descended into a field alongside Old Mill Road, practically in Mrs. Holliwell's backyard.

A hundred yards above the ground, Patrick killed the spark and the engine stopped. "Hold tight!" he called.

They glided down to the field, bounced hard, settled, bounced twice again, lurched, and, after a bumpy roll, came to a jolting halt. The silence was jarring, the engine's roar still ringing in their ears.

"Thank you, Patrick," came Christopher's muffled voice from deep down in the cockpit. "Now would you please get off me?"

They climbed out of the airplane. Jack contemplated taking the machine gun into town but decided it might attract attention and settled for Gwen's dagger.

They hurried to the lane beside Mrs. Holliwell's house and let themselves through the gate into the yard. By silent consensus, they paused at the kitchen door, listening. All was quiet. They knocked. There was no answer.

"Mrs. Holliwell?" Gwen called.

No one came.

"What's *that*?" Jack stared at a weird, wound-like hole in the wall. Peering into it was like looking through an excessively cracked pane of smoked glass.

"Something interstitial?" Patrick guessed.

"This place is wholly open to attack!" Jack stared at the hole. "Mrs. Holliwell must have known. How could she have sent us to bed without keeping watch!" He rapped on the door. "Mrs. Holliwell? It's us!"

Christopher tried the knob. "It's not locked."

They went inside. The kitchen was cold.

"Mrs. Holliwell? Uncle Geoffrey?" Gwen's soft voice sounded unnaturally loud in the silence. A drop of water fell from the kitchen faucet into the sink.

Jack stood still, holding Gwen's dagger at the ready.

Patrick hunted in drawers until he found a carving knife. Seeing that, Christopher took one also. Gwen appropriated a cleaver.

Jack inspected the remains of a burned-down candle in a holder. "No one has been here for a while." He stepped cautiously into the parlor. "Mrs. Holliwell?"

They searched the ground floor, moving as a group.

If there were grades of emptiness, the house would have been classified a void. All the furnishings were as they should have been, but there was no life. Dr. Holliwell's surgery was the spookiest chamber. Gwen lifted the cloth covering a metal tray. The scalpels, scissor-handled clamps, and other odd-shaped surgical tools laid there seemed sinister under the circumstances.

After they had been through the entire lower story without finding any clue to Mrs. Holliwell's whereabouts, the foursome went to the front room and peered up the stairs.

Jack mounted the steps one by one. He looked down at his companions close behind him. "I'd rather you didn't hold those knives quite so near to my back."

They gathered in the upstairs hallway and stood for nearly a minute, listening. All was silent. They checked Charlotte's bedroom first and then David's. Jack retrieved his saber from the wardrobe where he had left it and strapped it on.

Back out in the hallway, they paused. Mrs. Holliwell's bedroom door was closed. They glanced at one another.

"Mrs. Holliwell?" Gwen called.

"You don't suppose she's dead?" Patrick asked.

"You didn't have to say that!" Jack admonished.

"Open it," Christopher recommended.

"It ought to be you," Jack told Gwen. "In case she's not decent."

The boys stood back but ready. The delicate, aristocratic girl raised her cleaver and turned the doorknob.

Mrs. Holliwell was not there.

Gwen didn't know if she should be relieved or more concerned than ever. "That leaves the attic." She glanced at the door at the end of the hallway.

"Do you think we need to check up there?" Jack asked.

"I'll have a look." Patrick opened the door and hurried up.

The others listened to the movements overhead.

"Not here," Patrick called.

They returned to the parlor.

Jack rubbed his head. "All right..."

Gwen contemplated the front door. She turned the handle and stepped outside.

Jack edged beside her. "Careful."

He needn't have worried. The only danger was that neighbors would see suspicious-looking adolescents brandishing large knives and call the police.

Gwen sighed. Then she turned and saw, wedged in the knocker, an envelope addressed in large script to Colonel Sir Geoffrey. She took the envelope and opened it.

"You shouldn't read other people's mail," Christopher said.

"Under the circumstances..." The space between Gwen's brows furrowed. "'Dear Sir Geoffrey,'" she read, "'The children disappeared into an interstice Sunday ten a.m. We are looking for them. Alfred investigated High Tor and thought he found traces of a skirmish. Otherwise, we are stymied. I prayed through the night and believe the children still alive, but am at wit's end. If you receive this letter, meet us at the bureau.'"

"Who exactly is *we*," Jack wondered, "and what bureau does she mean?"

Patrick shrugged. "Sorry. No idea."

"Where do you suppose Uncle Geoffrey went?" Gwen asked.

"Or what happened to him?" Jack added.

"Demons," Christopher surmised.

"No." Gwen shook her head. "Uncle Geoffrey is anchored to silhouette. Demons can't hurt him." But then she wasn't so sure.

Jack scowled. "Everyone, back inside."

"I'm hungry." Christopher's stomach was empty, breakfast having gone into the airsickness bag.

Jack looked toward the kitchen. "It's after noon. I guess we could eat something. I don't think Mrs. Holliwell would mind if we helped ourselves."

Christopher went with his brother to the pantry.

"I'm going to pray." Gwen dropped into an armchair. She closed her eyes and bowed her head.

Patrick waited for her, shifting his weight from foot to foot. When it became clear she planned an extended meditation, however, he quietly left to join the other boys.

Christopher was rummaging through the icebox.

Seeing that, Patrick had a worry. "Today is Monday. Someone will have to cover my ice deliveries. I need to get word to Mr. Lockland."

Jack shook his head. "Mrs. Holliwell doesn't have a telephone."

"There's one in the chemist's shop down the street," Patrick said.

"We've got a demon problem, and you're worried about ice?"

"I don't want anyone's food to spoil. There's little enough in these times." Patrick went to the back door. "I'll return shortly."

"That's what Uncle Geoff said!" Jack growled, but Patrick had already slipped away. "Ugh!" With nothing else to do, Jack searched for a whetstone to hone Gwen's dagger. Instead, he found a leather strop, out of which he fashioned a crude scabbard. "Mrs. Holliwell will forgive me for taking this, won't she?"

In the parlor, Gwen slumped. She had thought she could keep everyone safe with prayer, as Mrs. Holliwell had done. But she was merely cataloging things she desired: To be home and safe. To be healthy again. To be rid of Miss Harkless. To have good food, clothes, and friends. To have her family close. To be rid of Miss Harkless. For the war to be over. To be rid of Miss Harkless. Her mood changed from wistful to melancholic. When she finally felt the Lord's presence, it was fleeting. Like a tap on the shoulder. But that tap was enough. She was suddenly certain He wanted her and the boys to go to Maham House.

She balked. What would the boys say? Two hours ago, she insisted they come to Buckton! Honestly, she didn't care if Jack and Christopher thought her erratic and unreliable. They were family. But Patrick was… well, she didn't want someone outside her family to think of her that way.

When Patrick let himself back into the kitchen, he found Christopher munching on cheese, sliced cucumbers, and bread. Jack was picking at sardines in a tin.

Gwen came in from the parlor. "Knowing what we do now, we should go home."

Jack stopped picking. "Huh?"

"Something will happen there."

Jack stared at his sister. "Something will happen? Like demons will drag us to Hell and eat our livers?"

Gwen glared.

Jack scowled. "I wanted to go straight home, and you said we had to come here!"

"God wants us in my room," Gwen announced irritably. "I received that guidance while praying."

Under ordinary circumstances, the statement would have sounded arrogant if not deranged. Even as things were, Gwen wanted to scream *I am not a lunatic!*

Jack speared a sardine and twiddled his fork. "I see. We'll go to your room and see if the prism will do something. Beautiful plan." He chomped the sardine. "Lord knows I don't like hanging around here. The devils probably know we're in Buckton. But what's the point of going to Maham House if we're still anchored to Primary? Or is the mirror going to do something?" He sat for a minute. "I wish I could remember what the lieutenant said."

"Colonel Sir Geoffrey said the mirror didn't have anything to do with our anchoring." Patrick looked at his lap. "We know that Mrs. Holliwell will come home sooner or later. Perhaps it would be wiser to stay put."

Jack turned to Christopher. "What do you think?" To himself he muttered, "Now I'm asking a ten-year-old for advice. Some leader I am."

"We should do what Gwen says."

This time, the silence lasted more than a minute.

Gwen was upset—why hadn't God given her explicit instructions, and why had she insisted they come to Buckton?

Jack was sullen—why had they been abandoned and why couldn't he decide what to do?

Patrick was brooding—why had he said something stupid earlier, and why was he opposing Lady Gwendolyn now?

Christopher was uncertain—which would be better on his bread, honey or currant jam?

Gwen murmured, "I said we had a lot to think about. The lieutenant said…"

"No!" Jack's eyes lit up. "You said we had a lot to *reflect* on. The lieutenant said, 'Look in your mirror. What you see will help you.' What if he was being serious?" He swallowed the last chunk of bread and drained his teacup. "You know things, and the lieutenant said to look in your mirror. We'll fly to Maham House."

"Fly? You aren't going to insist we stay on the ground?" Gwen asked.

"Right—and have you and the Irish smirk and point out that

someone put the ocean across the road. Uncle Geoff took Thane, and Ramillies is lame. We can't all ride May. I'm not stupid."

Christopher wrapped the remainder of the cheese and slid it into the bag with Gwen's tin of nuts and the untouched apples he had brought from Maham House.

Fifteen minutes later, Jack boosted Gwen into the F.B.5.

"Switch on," Patrick called. Jack went around back and heaved the propeller.

The takeoff and climb-out were smooth. A farmer in a field waved up at them.

The sky blazed blue, but the interstitial sea between Buckton and western Dartmoor was streaked with whitecaps. Patrick anticipated the wind shear at the shoreline and kept his plane under control. On the far side, above Dartmoor, they flew over the ridge they had vaulted through on horseback going the other way.

Patrick skirted the southern flank of the mountains, flying low, following the country road. But a dense bank of clouds and mist blocked the way to Maham House. He diverted north around the weather, turning parallel to a little-used dirt track that, surprisingly, had new ruts.

A little way on, they came to the remnants of the Whitebarrow tin mine. Except for a brief reopening at the beginning of the century, it had been closed for three decades. The water wheels and machinery were gone, but ruins of the smelting house and wheel pits were visible. Ridges, gullies, and prospecting holes testified to the mining that had gone on there since prehistoric times. As if mimicking what was underground, a tunnel of interstitial space ran alongside the road. Patrick maintained a safe distance.

He dipped the left wing and circled the area. A ribbon of smoke issued from a conical depression that might once have been the top of a mine shaft. He didn't know why smoke would be coming out of an abandoned mine shaft.

Having passed the clouds and fog, he leveled the wings in the direction of Maham house.

It was midafternoon when they crossed the last miles. Gwen studied the medieval towers and ramparts grafted to her house. Home was supposed to represent safety and welcome. But the transmogrified structure she saw was alien and forbidding. She thought she saw a green light flash from a window; it was like a glint from a cat's eye.

Patrick made his best landing yet, touching down on the open field beyond the woods east of the house. They only bounced three times.

CHAPTER 2

Inverse

8-2-6

Gwen gazed at the gray sky. The weather was changing rapidly. The horizon was darkening and the temperature dropping. The wind off the moor whistled hollowly.

With Jack's help, Patrick secured the F.B.5 to stakes they pounded into the ground. The Irish boy stole glances at Gwen. Strands of her hair were streaming in the stiffening breeze. He had been close to Gwendolyn Maham for three days. She was smart, courageous, and resolute despite her illness. *Gallant* wasn't a term usually applied to girls, but it suited her. He walked around his airplane to the port-side tie-down point and attached the rope. Knowing you could never have what you wanted most in the world was torture.

"Let's get going," Jack said.

They took a path through trees into the gardens and skirted a row of azaleas. When they sighted the house, they were near the place where Colonel Sir Geoffrey had first demonstrated the prism.

"Stop!" Jack caught Christopher's coat collar and swung him behind a tall, thick bush. He stared at a limbed shadow on the terrace. "Something's waiting up there."

Patrick peered through the shrubbery. "I don't see it."

Gwen squinted. "I think I do."

Jack addressed the others: "We assumed the battle last night drove the demons out of Devonshire. Maybe it didn't. Maybe the fliers that attacked us this morning weren't random survivors."

Patrick gazed at the terrace. "Do you expect it's seen us?"

"Probably. It knows we're here, at least."

"Why doesn't it attack?"

"It's a sentinel—a lookout."

"It's wary," Gwen guessed.

The boys looked at her.

"The three of you have cut down a lot of them."

"We've been lucky," Patrick said. "It should have gone the other way each time."

"Still, you're not helpless prey. And every demon here was probably called to Buckton when we went there this morning." She looked pointedly at Patrick. "So going there *wasn't* a waste of time."

Patrick was confused. He hadn't said it was.

Jack continued to peek through the bush. "He's waiting for us to come to the terrace. We'll work our way around to the ballroom instead. Pry open one of the French doors." He glanced toward the front of the house. "We're going to be exposed crossing open ground. Can't be helped."

"Do you see Mr. Merrill or Mrs. Nellis?" Gwen didn't bother to mention Greggs.

"No. Anyway, they can't help us."

Christopher said, "Let's use the tunnel."

Gwen brightened. "Good thinking!"

Jack frowned.

Patrick looked from face to face. "What tunnel?"

"You go down a hidden stair in the middle of the hedge maze and end up in the cellar," Christopher said.

"You have a secret passageway?"

"That's right." Christopher shouldered his satchel.

Jack held up a hand. "Wait. Wait. We could be trapped underground. The demons probably know every nook and cranny of our house better than we do."

"If we're going to get to my room without a fight, we have to do it unseen," Gwen said.

Jack stared at the ground, shaking his head. Then he looked at Patrick and Christopher. "Did either of you bring your torch?"

Neither had.

"We're not going back to the airplane for them, and we can't go blundering about in the dark."

Christopher had the solution. "Uncle Geoffrey left his torch by the door in the maze."

Jack continued to hesitate. He stared at the house. He took a deep breath and blew it out through pursed lips. "All right. We'll try the tunnel." He led the others southward until they came to the stretch of open lawn around the maze. "Cross quickly."

Gwen gathered her skirt to keep the hem well above her ankles and reached out to her brother. "Take my hand."

Jack escorted Gwen across the grass, making sure she didn't stumble, and hastened into the maze's boxwood corridors. Christopher and Patrick stayed close behind.

They didn't see a soul. However, after they had made several turns, they heard rustling sounds. Jack stopped.

Gwen grabbed her brother's arm and whispered, "The next two bends will take us toward whatever made that sound."

"Where's the center of the maze?" Patrick asked softly.

Gwen pointed. "That way, but we must ramble up and back to get there."

"Can't we just push through the hedge?"

None of the Mahams had thought of that. They were used to thinking of the maze as a game. Breaking through a wall would have been cheating. Under the circumstances, however, no one could think of a reason they shouldn't.

"Stay with me." Jack got down on all fours and tunneled through the boxwood. A long peal of distant thunder masked the sound. The cold, wet soil dampened his trouser knees. Today, the earthy smell, pleasant on other days, stirred fear of entombment below ground.

Gwen followed on Jack's heels, hitching up her skirt so she could crawl. Boxwood branches caught on her overcoat and scratched her face.

Patrick tried not to look at Lady Gwendolyn's legs. He tapped Christopher on the back. "In you go."

On the other side, Jack checked both directions before forcing his way through the next hedge. One penetration after that, he reached the splashing fountain at the center of the maze. The three marble Nereids paid him no attention. Water fell from their overflowing bowl as steadily as ever.

Jack hurried around the corner. "Where's the secret passage?"

Christopher moved the shrubbery aside, revealing the access panel.

Jack turned the handle and shoved until, hinges squeaking, the door swung inward. "Uncle Geoff's torch?"

Christopher retrieved it and gave it to his brother.

"Follow me." Jack ducked down and stepped through the small opening.

Everyone crowded inside and stood up. Patrick closed the door against the wall of green that had already sprung back into place.

Jack drew Gwen's dagger from his homemade scabbard—his saber was useless in the narrow tunnel—and began to descend. But five steps down the damp stone stairs, he slipped and pitched against the wall. Wildly off-balance, he fumbled the dagger, slicing his palm, and stumbled all the way to the bottom.

He gulped and grimaced but didn't curse, scared to make a sound.

Holding her skirt so its hem was at her knees, Gwen went down the stairs as fast as she could without tripping. "Jack—are you all right?"

"I cut myself." He handed her the flashlight and knife. "Hold these, would you?" He wrapped a handkerchief around his bleeding right hand. Then he took back the things he had given her. "Let's go."

He set off, gripping Gwen's knife in his good left hand. His clothes and hair quickly became glazed with cobwebs. He might as well have been blind—the flashlight held awkwardly in his bandaged right hand was too weak to penetrate more than a few yards into the darkness between the mold-blackened walls ahead. The narrow passage seemed to be squeezing him, and the thick, wet air stuck in his lungs. Every step sapped his strength and will.

Patrick, last in line, couldn't see anything in the lightless tunnel behind him. He kept glancing over his shoulder anyway. He held Mrs. Holliwell's carving knife pointed backward because he was afraid of accidentally stabbing Lady Gwendolyn.

Soon, they came to a cramped room resembling the antechamber of a medieval dungeon. There were two ways out: one straight ahead and one to their left.

Christopher stopped beside Jack. "This room wasn't here before."

"We're in an interstice," Patrick said.

The place had a heavy, oppressive feel. Over centuries, the iron hinges of the room's stout oak doors had rusted away. The fallen doors lay flat on the floor under a thick coat of dust.

Jack asked, "Which way?"

In unison, Gwen and Patrick said, "That way." Gwen pointed left, Patrick straight ahead.

Jack looked from girl to boy and back again.

"We have to turn left," Gwen told Patrick. "You wouldn't know. You haven't been here before."

"But…that tunnel is interstitial."

Jack squinted at the opening. "How do you know?"

"It—can't you tell?"

Jack shined his flashlight beam around the door frame and sighed. "Uncle Geoff's torch doesn't work like the ones we got from the angels. There's no indication of a boundary." He studied Patrick's face. "Are you sure?"

Patrick was at a loss. The space had unusual depth and a subtle extensiveness of color. It was undoubtedly an interstice.

Gwen gnashed her teeth. "We have to go left, or we'll end up under the North Wing. Christopher, tell him."

The little boy hesitated. "When we were going the other way, we made a right turn somewhere." He peered into the passage. "But… this isn't like that tunnel."

Everyone looked at Jack. Jack pointed at the left-hand opening and stared at Patrick. "McCray—you're absolutely certain that's an interstice?"

Patrick glanced guiltily at Gwen and nodded.

Jack said, "Then we'll go straight."

Gwen was flabbergasted. "But…"

Jack set off. "Come on."

Christopher followed.

Gwen scowled at Patrick. She stomped after her brothers.

Not far on, they discovered an intersection with multiple choices. The tunnels joined haphazardly at offset heights as if five brick-lined passages had collided.

Jack stood immobile. "What now?"

Gwen pressed Christopher against the wall to see past him. One look and she said, "This is all wrong."

Everyone crammed into the crossroads. Black shadows pooled wherever the flashlight's weak beam didn't fall.

Patrick studied each alternative. His shoulders sagged. "They're all interstitial."

"I *told* you." Gwen was angrier than ever and about to add something mean, but Patrick looked so much like a scolded puppy that she couldn't. "We have to go back."

Jack aimed his flashlight into a tunnel. "Could the correct passage pick up after an interstitial splice?"

Gwen put her hands on her hips. The space was very tight; one elbow touched a wall, and the other poked Christopher's ribs. "Do you want to explore every passageway? It's only a matter of time before a demon scents us. You're the one afraid of being trapped."

"There's no spectrum to guide us this time," Jack muttered.

Christopher said, "We have the prism. Uncle Geoffrey used it to see how things fit together. Can't we do that?"

"Maybe if we knew how to work it."

"Why don't you try?" Christopher urged.

Jack sheathed his dagger and took out the prism. "It might do something if we lit it with one of the soldiers' torches, but I don't think it will work in this light."

He held the prism in front of himself and pointed the flashlight into it. The glass glowed, but not supernaturally.

Gwen bent closer. "Let me see." She pulled Jack's hand up so that the prism was in line with her left eye.

"Ah! Look through here." Gwen stared into a facet. "You see the silhouette world only. All the Primary bits are filtered out." She turned in different directions, dragging Jack around with her. Her jaw tightened. Only two routes could be seen through the prism—one behind and one ahead. "Hmm. Well. I…" Patrick had been right, and Jack had guessed the situation. They were in an interstice separating the silhouette tunnel behind from the silhouette tunnel ahead.

"We haven't passed the intersection where we go left," Gwen admitted bad-temperedly. "It's ahead." She pointed. "That way." She was even more cross with Patrick than before.

Jack let go of the prism, so Gwen kept it. She slipped it into a pocket in her skirt.

Shortly, at a point demarked by mismatched wall textures, they crossed into silhouette and came upon the T-intersection Gwen remembered. Jack shied away from the tunnel going north. Dread flowed out of it like a cold river.

"Left," Gwen directed, staring at Patrick, daring him to disagree. He didn't.

From then on, the bricks were lighter and less stained, and there were no more interstices. The group continued to the secret door into the cellar. Jack opened it without difficulty and made his way through the storage room. Patrick appropriated a coil of rope from a peg on the wall.

Jack led the way past wine racks and across the cellar to the stairs. He crept up the wooden steps, wincing each time one of them creaked.

Thankfully, the exit to the ground floor wasn't locked. Inside the East Tower, Jack sloughed off his overcoat and tossed it on the floor.

Gwen glared at him.

"What? I need my arms free."

"Go hang that up."

"You've got to be joking."

"M'lady, under the circumstances…" Patrick hesitated. "Shouldn't we go straight to your room?"

Gwen shifted her glare to the Irish boy. She pursed her lips but then shrugged and dropped her own coat on top of Jack's. Christopher and Patrick did likewise.

Jack ascended to the first floor, stopped, and gazed up the stairwell. "We have to find a way to get above that." He meant the wide, empty, interstitial shaft above the second floor. "We can't do it on our own, not even with rope. We need someone anchored in silhouette to take us by the hand."

He led the others out into the East Lobby. "Mrs. Nellis?" There was no answer. He could hear the tick-tock of the pendulum clock in the front hall, but otherwise the house was silent. He opened the door to the first-floor servant's quarters. "Mrs. Nellis?"

Mrs. Nellis was not in her rooms. Jack took everyone back downstairs to check the small kitchen.

The housekeeper was not there.

"Where could she be?" Gwen wondered.

Jack backtracked, and the group made its way to the front hall.

The atmosphere in the normally magnificent space was stale and gloomy. Even though the windows were tall and south facing, their panes were dim because thick black clouds covered the sky.

Everyone paused and listened. The only sounds were those of the clock and the wind outside.

"Mrs. Nellis!" Jack called but immediately clapped his hand over his mouth. His echoing voice sounded thunderous. Was the sentinel still on the terrace? How well could demons hear?

The four humans crept up the grand staircase and got as far as the second-floor gallery. A solid wall of medieval stones and mortar blocked the hallway to the east.

"We're in a trap!" Jack flung his arms wide in exasperation and tipped over a candelabra on a table opposite the balustrade overlooking the front hall. Christopher set the sterling silver piece back in place.

Patrick considered the twelfth-century wall. "Is there a way to get onto the roof from here? We might be able to go around the interstice and back down to Lady Gwendolyn's bedroom."

Jack pointed glumly at the stairs to the third floor. More specifically, he pointed at the rough, interstitial timber planking that, flush with the ceiling, stretched across the stairwell, preventing access to the third floor.

"Oh."

Gwen regarded the unobstructed hallway running westward. "Let's see if the library is intact."

"There isn't a way onto the roof from the library."

"Some of the windows in the skylight can be opened."

"They can?"

"Yes."

"Oh. Didn't know." Jack led the way to the library. Entering it and looking up, he broke into a smile. "It's clear all the way to the roof!"

They circled up the staircase. As they emerged onto the third floor, a timepiece in the room struck three o'clock. Everyone jumped. They jumped a second time when the pendulum clock down in the front hall replied, bonging the hour through the house's empty corridors.

Jack circled up the final spiral staircase to the platform under the skylight. Christopher went next, and Gwen after him.

Once more, Patrick brought up the rear. He had the coil of rope in one hand and Mrs. Holliwell's carving knife in the other. He secured the knife in his belt to have a hand free.

Arriving at the top of the spiral, everyone surveyed the panorama outside the wrought iron and glass dome. The round platform they stood on was flush with the library's ceiling, so they were head and shoulders above the flat roof of the building. They could see north, west, and south. To the east, however, their view was blocked by gray walls; part of the third story of the East Wing was stacked atop Norman-era construction.

Looking up, Jack saw the wing's west-facing bedrooms. But he couldn't see a way to get to them.

"Wait." Gwen lifted the lectern's lid and took out Sir Robert's book of visions. She unwrapped the volume and leafed through its pages until she found *Beset Girl.*

She tapped the last number she had copied. "A lot has happened since then. Where are we now?" She moved her finger to a number at the top right of the oval. "About here, I should think. Someone look up…which book is eighth in Sir Robert's numbering system?"

Patrick took the Bible from the bookshelf and found its table of contents. "Philippians."

"Look up chapter two, verse six."

Patrick located the passage. "'Who, being in the form of God, thought it not robbery to be equal with God.'"

Gwen was silent for a time. "What does that mean?"

"The King James wording is archaic," Patrick said. "When Jesus came to redeem us, he remained limited to his human form even though he was in nature God. He stayed true to his role and mission."

"How does that help us?" Gwen asked no one in particular.

Jack wasn't paying attention. He was leaning over the platform's railing and looking down. "Something's below us."

"What kind of something?" Christopher peered downward.

"I don't hear anything." Gwen kept her voice low.

"Don't you *feel* it?" Jack asked.

Scuffling noises substantiated his claim.

"What do you think it is?" Patrick asked.

"I don't know, and I don't want to find out." Jack looked at the metal-framed, trapezoidal panes of the skylight. He leaned to study one that appeared to be hinged at the top. "Does it swing out?"

"Up and out," Gwen confirmed. "See the latches at the bottom?"

Jack considered the situation. The platform was four feet lower than the windows. Moreover, there was a three-and-a-half-foot gap all around between the ten-foot-wide platform and the seventeen-foot-diameter dome—and there was a long drop through that gap to the floor below.

Jack climbed outside the guardrail. With one foot on the edge of the platform, keeping the fingers of his good hand clamped firmly around the railing, he stretched up to the window.

It took him a minute to unfasten the casement. Even then, the panel didn't move. "Stuck."

Patrick climbed over the railing to help.

Leaning outward and shoving together, the two boys forced the casement open. The hinges were so stiff that the window stayed up by itself. Stormy moist air gusted in.

"Christopher—you're first." Jack had to speak louder than he would have liked in order to be heard above the wind.

Christopher sprang onto the railing.

"All right, McCray—we'll lift him across." Jack put his hand under Christopher's armpit. Patrick, on the other side, did likewise. Acting together, they heaved Christopher to the open window. The little boy scrambled through it.

Jack ignored the pain in his palm. He beckoned to Gwen. "Over you go." He helped her sit side-saddle on the railing.

She looked down. "I don't know about this."

"No choice. McCray—same as before."

Patrick extended his hand toward Lady Gwendolyn's body but balked. "I don't...I mean..."

"Just like Christopher. Under her arm. Here we go. *Now.*"

Patrick had to act. He and Jack lifted Gwen until she was half out the window. She was hardly any heavier than Christopher but taller and less agile. And she was wearing a long skirt. A button at her waist caught on the metal window frame.

She gasped. "I can't—!"

Jack seized one of Gwen's ankles. "McCray! Push!"

Patrick reached blindly and shoved. His heart skipped a beat when he realized his hand was inside Lady Gwendolyn's skirt, on her bare calf. He nearly pulled back, which would have caused them all to lose their balance and fall fifteen feet. He gulped and pushed.

Christopher tugged, and Gwen worked herself outside.

"I'm going." Jack leapt up and clambered through the opening without a hitch.

Patrick tossed his coil of rope and Mrs. Holliwell's knife out onto the roof. Then, with less dexterity but even more adrenaline-pumped strength than Jack, he sprang at the window. His chest made it through, but his stomach landed on the sill, and the weight of his legs dragged him downward.

Jack seized Patrick's collar and hauled.

Patrick twisted, got a knee up, and levered himself onto the roof. He took two very deep breaths, collected his rope and knife, and stood up.

With Patrick safely out, Gwen turned and looked upward. She could see bedrooms, but they were more than thirty feet above her. "What do we do?" The cold wind blew strong and steady.

Jack pointed at a window. "That's our best option. The wall below it can be climbed; the recesses between stones are deep."

He strode east to the Norman-era wall and then northward along it to the balustrade at the edge of the flat roof. He put his fingers experimentally into the gap between rows of stones. The mortar was recessed a good two inches. "It's almost like a ladder."

Gwen looked dubiously at her brother. "You don't expect me to scale that, do you?"

"McCray and I will go first. We'll haul you and Christopher up with the rope." He gripped the top of a block, put his toe on another, and rose up. His bandaged right hand was a problem. He winced and lowered himself back to the roof. "You'll have to take the lead, McCray. Then belay me with the rope while I climb."

Patrick glanced at the window. It was high above him and offset twelve feet to the left of where he stood. He didn't look at the courtyard sixty feet below. "Right."

Gwen gazed up the expanse of wall and nearly lost her balance. Eastward-scudding clouds created the illusion that the house was falling on her.

"Right." Patrick exhaled sharply. He put his left arm and head through the coil of rope so that it hung on his shoulder and draped diagonally across his chest. He looked at the recesses between the stones in the wall and muttered, "It's a ladder…a ladder."

"Go straight up until you're level with the window, then crab left," Jack recommended.

"Aye."

Two rungs up, Patrick's foot slipped, and he fell back to the roof. The point of Mrs. Holliwell's carving knife came dangerously close to carving his leg.

Jack helped him up. "Are you all right?"

"I'm fine." Patrick slid the knife out of his belt, tossed it aside, and started up again.

On impulse, Gwen took the prism from her pocket and peered through a facet. She saw the modern Maham House roof as it would look from where she stood if she were anchored to silhouette. None of the Norman fortress or any other Primary World features were visible. She was standing at the inside corner where the East Wing connected to the main building, and in this view, the third-story windows of the wing to her left were beneath rather than above her.

She was close to the aviary where her grandfather, the sixth Earl of Buckleigh, had kept homing pigeons. After twenty-five years of disuse, the aviary was peeling, decayed, and empty. It was a few steps away in silhouette. In Primary, it sat on top of the house on top of the fortress. Looking at it, Gwen felt she was on the verge of an insight. "Lord God, help us," she whispered, reminding herself to keep praying.

When she lowered the prism and held it out, she noticed it was casting a beam that projected what she had seen in the facet. The only difference was that the projected image was phantasmal—semitransparent silhouette laid on Primary.

Then Jack shouted, "What's wrong?"

Gwen whirled around. Jack was looking up. Gwen looked up, also.

Patrick had stopped several feet below and to the right of the window. He was brushing his fingers searchingly on the wall. "There aren't any gaps here," he called down. "There's nothing to hold onto."

Gwen saw the problem. In that place, the mortar was flush with the stones.

"Work your way left," Jack called. "Then go up again."

Patrick inched his way sideways, sliding one hand or foot at a time. He was headed for a section of wall that appeared to have deep recesses between the stones—perfect hand and toeholds.

Gwen went rigid. They weren't recesses, after all. They were lines of dark, slippery lichen. "Be careful!" she shouted.

A fat raindrop splattered slantwise on the roof, followed by three more rat-tat-tat, and the wind shifted. The storm was about to arrive.

Patrick was no longer over the flat roof—and it was a long, long way to the ground. He stepped on the edge of a block; the stone broke, and his foot slipped. He managed to hold onto the wall, but it was a close thing.

"Don't fall!" Gwen yelled.

"I'm fine. I'm fine!"

He wasn't. All around him, the masonry was entirely smooth. There were no hand or footholds in any direction.

"Actually, I'm stuck."

He gazed up at the window—specifically, its shutters. He let go his right hand and fumbled with the coil of rope slung over his shoulder. One by one, he worked four loops over his head so that he had paid out several feet of rope.

"What are you *doing*!" Gwen screamed.

"I'm going to lasso the shutter."

"*What?*" He was going to fall at any moment.

"Demons are coming…" Jack whispered hoarsely.

Patrick looked down. The dangling rope slithered erratically in the wind. His arms and legs trembled badly.

"He's going to swing it over the shutter," Jack guessed. "Or die trying."

"Dear God—help us!" Gwen prayed again.

A raindrop splashed on her head. When she flinched, she caught a tiny movement out of the corner of her eye: a dove poking its head out of the derelict aviary. She saw it in the spectral image still projected by the prism in her hand. In that instant, she knew how to save Patrick. The boys had used mice to bypass interstices. If she held the dove, she could walk across the continuous silhouette roof to the door in the East Tower. She could go to the bedroom and help Patrick from the inside.

It did not occur to her that the aviary was on the other side of the interstice—anchored to Primary, she couldn't get to it.

She felt God's presence. It was as if He were holding her up. She leaned on Him. She leaned wholly on Him. His will, not hers. She stepped forward. It felt like turning sideways to slip through a narrow opening.

She rushed to the aviary. When she got there, however, the pigeon flew off, unreachable. Her heart sank. As she stood despairing, the drizzle became a steady rain.

And then she realized with a jolt that she was already past the Primary World wall that had blocked her way: she had temporarily anchored to silhouette, crossed the interstice, and re-anchored to Primary. She didn't stop to wonder what had happened. Stuffing the prism into her pocket, she raced to the East Tower. She wrenched open the door and rushed pell-mell down the stairs, nearly tripping on the hem of her wet skirt.

Reaching the third floor, she exited the tower, turned, and ran up the interstitial Norman corridor, which still seemed alien but no longer exotic. She dashed into the bedroom above Patrick and dodged around the bed to get to the window. She released the catch, yanked up the restraining bolt, and pulled open the casements.

A torrent of rain blew in.

Below, Jack and Christopher were staring at Patrick in horrified fascination. Their fascination changed to utter surprise when they saw Gwen in the window.

Christopher pointed. "Look!"

Jack's jaw dropped. *"Gwen!"*

"Patrick!" she called down.

He raised his dripping face. There was fear there, but suddenly, also, a good measure of wonder.

Lightning lit the sky.

"Throw me the rope!" Gwen yelled.

Patrick looked at her, calculating, then swung his arm so powerfully he nearly lost his grip on the wall. But it was no good. He had paid out too much rope. He couldn't get the end of it much higher than his head.

"Stop! Wait!" Heart thumping, Gwen looked around the unused bedroom. Thankfully, there was a sheet on the bed. She yanked it off, twisted it, and cast three-quarters of it out the window. At first it streamed sideways in the wind, out of Patrick's reach. Fortunately, it became waterlogged and dipped downward.

She closed one of the windows on the sheet, pinching the fabric between casement and sill to anchor it; she wasn't strong enough to hold Patrick's weight by herself.

He caught the fluttering linen.

Gwen leaned her head out the open half of the window. "Climb!" she ordered.

Patrick pulled himself upward using the sheet. That caused him to lose his hold on the wall. He dangled.

Gwen's hair was soaked. Rain ran down her cheeks and off her chin. *Dear God, bring him inside!*

The bedsheet began to tear where it was pinched.

Patrick hauled himself upward hand over hand. He tried to use his feet, but they scraped uselessly on the wall. When his head was a few inches below the window, he reached and got his fingers on the outer sill.

The sheet tore in two. Patrick let go of it.

"Take my hand!" Gwen commanded.

He looked up at her. "I'd pull you out, and we'd both fall."

Gwen ignored that. She grabbed his lapels and attempted to lift him. Her feet slid backward on the wet floor, and sure enough, she toppled forward, half out the window.

Patrick kept his one-handed grip on the sill. Now it was he who was supporting her, pushing her upward. He shoved her shoulder until she was back inside.

Gwen changed strategies. She pressed on Patrick's fingers to help him hold onto the sill.

Lunging, he got an elbow inside. Then, fighting against the encumbering coils of rope still around his chest, he heaved his body over the sill and fell into the room.

Panting, he extricated himself from the tangled cords and struggled to his feet. "Lady Gwendolyn! You saved me!"

Gwen didn't speak. Instead, her drenched hair flat against her head and strands plastered across her face, she went up on her toes, threw her arms around Patrick's neck, and kissed him hard on the mouth.

Jack struggled to see. "What's happening?"

Christopher couldn't tell, either. "I think they made out all right."

The rope came down, uncoiling as it dropped.

Jack looped the wet cord around his brother's thighs and waist. He put two fingers in his mouth and whistled.

"McCray! Haul Christopher up. Haul him up!"

Patrick pulled furiously, his face a mask of shock and confusion.

Christopher was in the bedroom in less than thirty seconds.

Gwen stood out of the way as her little brother came through the window. Stupid! What had she done? What had she been thinking?

"Gwen!" Christopher hugged his sister as warmly and joyfully as Patrick had gone cold and stiff. "That was brilliant! How did you do it?"

"Hold still." Patrick untied the improvised climbing harness. Why had it happened? Sudden relief of terrible strain? Still, what kind of girl would do that? Kiss a boy who was neither her fiancé nor even a potential suitor? Was it somehow his fault? He felt low and verminous. He dismissed again and again the other thought: Something was seriously wrong with Lady Gwendolyn Maham.

He gathered the rope and, holding one end tightly, tossed the rest out the window.

In no time, Jack had fashioned himself a harness and started up the wall. With Patrick pulling, Jack made quick progress despite his injured hand. He climbed in lunges and jerks as if prodded by something terrible below. Then he got to the place where Patrick had been stuck.

"I can't go any farther," he called.

"I've got you," Patrick said.

Jack let go of the wall and swung like a pendulum under the window. Christopher and Gwen took hold of the rope behind Patrick. All working together, they pulled Jack almost to the window. Then the taut rope splintered the wooden windowsill and snagged in the jagged cleft.

Jack looked up to see why he had stopped rising. And he froze. On the North Wing's roof, a lithe, liquid gray, mantis-like thing was creeping toward him.

Patrick leaned out. Seeing Jack's fixed gaze, he looked over his shoulder. He saw the crawling thing and stiffened. He turned to Jack. "M'lord, take my hand."

Jack was mesmerized.

Patrick straddled the windowsill and reached down. "Take my hand!"

The demonic creature moved like a feral cat. Jack stared in horrified fascination, not even blinking the rain from his eyes.

Patrick clamped his hand on the rope at Jack's chest and yanked. "*Mayfield*! Snap out of it! Get in the house!"

Jack shuddered. Released from his enchantment, he scrambled madly inside.

Patrick flung the casements shut and drove home the restraining bolt.

Jack shoved the rope harness down his legs and stepped out of the snarled loops. "Go! Go! Go!" he shrieked.

Everyone sprinted into the hallway and ran to Gwen's room. Patrick, the last one inside the bedroom, slammed the door.

Jack stared dumbly into the mirror. Gwen took the prism from her pocket and thrust it into her brother's palm. He made no move to take it, so she held it there.

Gwen said: "What did the lieutenant mean? 'Look in your mirror. What you see will help you'?"

Jack just shook his head.

What Gwen saw in the mirror was herself: a powerless child. If she was made in the image of God, then she was a tiny, counterfeit image. She might have the ability to affect His creation, but she had never done anything worthwhile for His kingdom. On Saturday, she had attempted to stop Jack from attacking Patrick. She did her best to take control. But nothing good had resulted from her taking control.

"They're almost here," Jack said. The wind outside howled like rampaging ghosts. "A lot of them."

Gwen looked at her brother. He was still staring into the mirror, but his eyes weren't focused.

Patrick dragged the bed across the room to barricade the door.

Christopher said, "Jack, do something!"

Gwen looked again into the mirror and saw, very faintly, on her arm and buckled at her side, the shield and the sword. However, they were gifts, not things she had made herself or earned. And she didn't know how to use them. *What is it you want us to do, Lord?* On earth, Jesus had remained obedient and stayed fixed to the limitations of his earthly body. But he had performed miracles and given his disciples the authority to perform miracles.

Outside, the sky lightened. Somewhere, the sun broke through the storm clouds. The prism reacted to the light, diffuse as it was, by glimmering. Gwen looked again at the mirror. What did a mirror do? It reflected.

Jack reached for his saber with his free hand, wanting it rather than the prism.

Gwen told the Lord impulsively, *I'll do what you ask. I'll reflect you.*

The next moment she felt sideways again, as she had on the roof, slipping through the world at an angle. This time the feeling ended with a sensation she could only describe as arriving. What had Jack done?

The bedroom door swung violently inward. The bed was no barrier; it slid across the floor.

"They're here!" Jack screamed.

Mrs. Holliwell's carving knife—the one Patrick had left on the roof—shot like a missile at Gwen's chest. Jack, by pure reflex, snatched it out of the air.

"What's attacking us?" Patrick cried.

The rope flew through the door, jerking and swinging in midair as if in the hands of an invisible maniac. The end, knotted in a noose, dropped around Gwen's neck and pulled tight.

She clutched at the rope. It had gone limp as soon as it touched her skin, but the knot held.

Jack sprang to his sister and tugged on the noose. He couldn't loosen it.

Her face turned purple.

"Hold still." Jack yanked Gwen's dagger from his makeshift scabbard and sawed through the knot. He came dangerously close to slashing her throat.

The rope fell away, and Gwen gasped for air.

Jack dropped the dagger and drew his saber. But there were no demons in the room. He ran out into the hallway, trembling but ready to fight. He saw no movement north or south. All was quiet. He walked a few yards so that he could see into the East Tower.

Patrick joined him. "What do you suppose…"

Both boys waited tensely. The next attack didn't come.

Their eyes went wide almost simultaneously.

Patrick put his realization into words. "The interstice is gone."

Jack turned around and around. "Our house has changed again."

Patrick went back into Gwen's room and gazed out the windows. "No more mountains."

"We're back the way we should be!" Christopher exclaimed. "We're anchored to silhouette!"

Hi Paige, Lara,

Yes, Gwen's scribbled diary entry was weird, but you have to understand her circumstances. "What mad monkeys were whisking my brain?" In the early twentieth century, no respectable unmarried girl would have kissed a boy on the mouth. Even holding hands in public caused unease. Of course, there were individuals who broke the rules, but they were considered bad people.

Also, a romantic relationship between an aristocratic girl and a commoner boy would have caused dismay. It isn't possible for someone living in the United States in the twenty-first century to fully understand because we have nothing like the class system they had then.

There was one additional problem with a romance between Lady Gwendolyn Maham and Patrick McCray. She was English, and he had been born in Ireland. It is only in the last hundred years or so that conquering and repressing have been generally acknowledged to be bad things. Before, it was pretty much a routine practice of every empire, kingdom, nation, and tribe. It was just a matter of who got the upper hand. In the case of England and Ireland, it was the English. For good reasons, Irish nationals hated their overlords, and some of them caused problems during World War I. Consequently, many Englishmen suspected that his majesty's Irish subjects were traitors.

After the war, the British granted independence to the southern part of Ireland. But that history is not part of this story.

Kirk

CHAPTER 3

On Edge

45-7-25

"Touch everything we've anchored to Primary!" Patrick yelled. He yanked open Christopher's knapsack, thrust in his arm, and stirred the contents: shirts, pants, tin of nuts, apple, and cheese.

Jack stared at the sack. "What in blazes?"

Patrick ran out the door.

Jack turned to Gwen. "Are you all right?"

She nodded.

The brothers sprinted after Patrick. They caught up with him in the west-facing bedroom they had come through earlier. Patrick was rubbing the bedsheet.

"McCray! What are you doing?"

Patrick touched the window latch and bolt. "What's the quickest way to the library from here?"

"Go to the end of the hallway and turn right." Jack dodged out of the way as Patrick barreled past him.

"What's going on?!" Jack demanded, chasing the Irish boy down the corridor, leaving Christopher behind.

"Demons can handle anything we touched!"

"What do you mean?"

But Patrick had already turned the corner. Jack kept pace with him until, racing past the Grand Hall stairwell, he felt enveloped in malevolence. It was as if his skin were crusted with angry insects. He stopped and spun around.

There wasn't anything there. His heart raced.

It was not some *thing,* Jack intuited, but some *one.* His heart beat even faster. Then he was overwhelmed by astonishment…except that the astonishment was not his own. He was feeling someone else's surprise.

As abruptly as the sensations had come over him, they were gone. He ran on.

When Jack reached the library, Patrick was leaping up the spiral stairs to the platform under the skylight. Jack was certain that the malevolent entity he sensed had been jolted by a momentous realization and was tearing after Patrick.

Christopher, huffing, came in. He was thoroughly confused.

Rain drummed hard on the glass dome. Water streamed from the edges of the open window and would have blown into the room if the casement hadn't been on the lee side of the skylight. A brilliant lightning arc lit up the sky, momentarily blanching the interior of the library stark white. The thunderclap arrived two seconds later.

Patrick reached the platform, but an instant before he got to the lectern, its lid flew open of its own accord. Sir Robert's book of visions shot out. Patrick lunged and managed to bat the book out of the air. It fell to the platform's floorboards.

Patrick picked up the volume, rubbed it, and set it back in its compartment in the lectern. Glancing around, he brushed his fingers across the spine of every book on the shelf. "Anything we've anchored to Primary can be used against us," he called to the Maham brothers. He corkscrewed down the spiral stairs. "We've got to fasten it all back to silhouette."

Jack looked around. "So…everything we've touched since Saturday?"

"Exactly!"

"There's a demon here now." Jack felt the spirit strongly. In its presence, he had an almost overpowering urge to curse, strike, and destroy.

Christopher put his hands together in prayer. "God, keep us safe. Drive away all evil things."

The demon was furious. It had not known that the book of visions had been anchored to Primary. It should have known! Gathering information was its job. It was an apok—a spy. But apoks remain hidden except when guiding troops. Like pseustees, they are ill-adapted to fighting. The apok had held back; it had feared the prism. It had not discovered until too late that the children had virtually no understanding of what they possessed. Because of that, the book had been slapped from its hand and re-anchored to silhouette. The apok's rage was all the more ferocious because it was afraid. It had failed. There would be hell to pay. As it scurried off to report to its master, another question was on its mind: Had the Maham boy really sensed its presence? How could that be?

The three boys swarmed down to the first floor.

"We've only touched a few things," Jack said. "How bad can it be?"

"They have a fighter plane," Christopher said.

The boys ran to the bottom of the East Tower and re-anchored the pile of overcoats. From there they descended to the cellar.

Jack paused in front of a wine rack. "If someone touched the frame, would individual bottles be dangerous?"

"No. Well…probably not." Patrick halted. "Actually, I don't know. Are any gone?"

"Ah yes, a '98 Bordeaux is missing."

Patrick considered the rack. "Really?"

Jack rolled his eyes. "No, not really! I don't keep a personal inventory of our wine stock."

The three boys pondered the racks. Finally, Jack shrugged. "Let's go."

They went into the utility closet and touched everything they might have brushed against. Colonel Sir Geoffrey's flashlight rested on the shelf where Jack had left it.

He opened the doorway to the secret passageway. He felt uneasy traveling through the tunnel—especially when he passed the branch that ran north. Happily, the trek was shorter without the interstices, and the route had already been swept of cobwebs.

Emerging into the hedge maze, they hurried through the soggy boxwood corridors. The Mahams knew the pattern by heart.

From the maze, they jogged out of the gardens, scarcely conscious of the cold rain. They all dreaded that the machine gun, if not the whole F.B.5, would be gone.

But they found the airplane swaying, shuddering, and straining at its tie-downs in the gusting wind. The Lewis gun was still attached. A squirrel poked its head out of the cockpit, where it had sheltered from the storm.

"Thank you for anchoring my machine to silhouette, Mr. Squirrel!" Patrick yelled joyfully as the animal ran across the waterlogged grass and up a tree.

Jack stared at the airplane. "So…anything we anchored to Primary will be anchored back to silhouette if it is touched by any kind of mortal creature?"

"That's right."

Patrick climbed onto the rocking aircraft's lower wing and checked both cockpits to verify that nothing was missing.

Jack watched. "Do you suppose anything we touched in Buckton will be a problem?"

"By now Mrs. Holliwell will have discovered we were back in her house. She'd know the danger and neutralize anything we might have handled, don't you think? Do you remember—she insisted on doing the dishes by herself? I think she had ulterior motives."

Christopher wiped water from his face. "What about the pebble Jack threw at Gideon Moran?"

"Well…the world is full of animals," Patrick said. "Something will eventually step or crawl on that pebble."

Jack wasn't convinced.

After Patrick finished his inventory, the three boys slogged back to the house. They touched everything in the small kitchen, including the contents of drawers and cupboards they might have opened on

Saturday. Then they hurried upstairs and made a thorough job of Jack and Christopher's room.

Gwen met them in the hallway. "What on earth were you three racing around for?" She looked at their sopping wet clothes. "You went back outside?"

"A moment." Jack went into Gwen's bedroom and headed for her dresser. Christopher went into the bathroom. Patrick waited self-consciously in the hallway, dripping water.

Jack riffled through Gwen's drawers.

"Just what do you think you're doing!" she demanded.

"Everything in here could be dangerous."

"Just how could my underthings be dangerous?"

"Whatever we touched while anchored to Primary is still anchored there. Those things—demons can pick them up and use them. We have to re-anchor them back to silhouette."

Carefully, as if she might be dealing with a sleeping snake, Gwen nudged the tangled heap of rope with her shoe. "So that's why…"

Jack handled everything on and in the desk. "I anchored Mrs. Holliwell's carving knife back to silhouette when I grabbed it. You took care of that rope with your neck."

"It almost took care of me."

Christopher came out of the bathroom. "Done in there."

Jack looked around. "Is that everything?"

The storm produced a low, diminishing rumble and grudgingly paused to catch its breath. The wind slackened. Water gurgled in gutters and dripped past windows. With nothing to drive it, the rain fell straight down.

Everyone stood stock-still but tense, like sprinters on their marks, ready for the gunshot that would start the next race. But there was apparently no next race. No urgent, life-or-death task to complete.

Gwen looked at Jack's bandaged hand and then at his good hand—the one she had put the prism into. After a furtive sideways glance at Patrick, she leaned forward and touched her lips to Jack's cheek as if kissing were a normal thing she frequently did with everyone. "You saved us, Jack. You re-anchored us. Demons can claw our shadows all they want." She handed him the prism.

Jack stared at the lump of glass with an odd, distant look in his eyes and then at his sister with an even more peculiar expression. He set it on her desk.

She waited awkwardly. "Well…" She glanced around. "You touched everything?"

Jack nodded.

"What about the walls and floors?"

No one had thought of that. Jack and Christopher looked at Patrick.

The Irish boy glanced around nervously. "I don't think it works that way. Doors and windows, possibly, but not fixed structure. No…"

Christopher clapped his head. "The candlestick!"

Jack gasped. "Oh!"

Christopher darted off. Jack and Patrick caught up with him in the second-floor gallery above the Grand Hall.

Sure enough, the candelabra Jack had knocked over was missing.

The three boys stared at the bare table.

Jack groaned. "We have to search the house."

"You had better change first." Gwen panted as she labored down the flight of steps from the third floor. She leaned heavily against the banister. "You're leaving puddles everywhere. You'll catch pneumonia."

Patrick looked down at his sodden clothes. "You have a point. Pneumonia is a leading cause of death these days."

"Yeah," Jack said. "After bullets, shrapnel, and poison gas."

Everyone went back upstairs to Jack and Christopher's bedroom. Gwen waited outside while the boys changed.

Jack gave Patrick a fresh shirt and pair of pants. "We finally detach ourselves from the blasted Primary World, and now we're in danger of being brained with a candlestick out of nowhere." He buttoned his pants and put on a dry pair of shoes. "I guess it can only get one of us. It will reattach to silhouette after bashing somebody, won't it?"

Patrick nodded.

Gwen came in when they had finished dressing.

Jack had a steel combat helmet in his closet. Freddie had given it to him. He put it on his sister. "The rest of us will have to take our chances." He touched her damp blouse. "You'd best change, too."

"I haven't anything to change into."

"Borrow something of Mother's."

So Gwen went to her mother's dressing room in the master bedroom suite on the second floor.

The boys stayed in the hallway.

Gwen was uncomfortable taking clothes without permission, but she got over it. She borrowed one of Lady Buckleigh's gardening outfits. The dress hung loose on her willowy frame. She cinched it at the waist with a leather belt and regarded herself in a mirror. "What a hideous sight."

"At least you're dry," Jack said when she came out.

She adjusted the steel helmet so that it hid her eyes. She hated Patrick seeing her in the ugly ensemble. Couldn't he be sent home?

The hunt for the candelabra began. The quartet went down every corridor and into every open room in the house, on the lookout for flying objects hurled by invisible demons. Gwen lagged behind, wishing she were invisible. She and Patrick kept their distance by unspoken consent.

The candelabra wasn't in Lord Buckleigh's study or Lady Buckleigh's day room. Nor was it in any of the second-floor guest bedrooms, bathrooms, sitting rooms, service areas, or the card room. Nothing was out of place.

Miss Harkless's chambers were locked and inaccessible; Gwen was relieved.

They went upstairs, looked everywhere, and made their way back downstairs through the library. They searched the ballroom, drawing rooms, powder rooms, formal dining room, billiards room, solarium, morning room, and breakfast room without result. They double-checked each of the sterling silver candle holders stored in the butler's pantry to be sure the missing candelabra hadn't been hidden among them.

An inspection of Mrs. Nellis's quarters turned up neither the stolen object nor any clue as to the woman's whereabouts.

Nor did they find the missing article in the kitchens, laundry room, or scullery. They went through empty servants' rooms and found nothing of interest except a love letter sent by a soldier to a Maham House maid before she departed to serve in a hospital. The letter had fallen behind an empty wardrobe. Gwen read it twice, her heart stirred by the young man's candidly expressed fears and simple wishes. She fervently hoped he would survive the war and have a long, happy life together with his sweetheart.

They ran out of places to look. No one had any desire to break into the North Wing or brave the storm to visit Merrill's apartment above the garage. Greggs lived alone in a small cottage on the grounds. That was right out.

"A demon probably took it into an interstice," Jack said.

So they gave up. If an evil spirit intended to use the candelabra to commit murder, it would have done so already, wouldn't it have? But the missing metal object remained a concern at the back of everyone's mind.

As did the empty house.

"Why is no one home?" Christopher asked. He and the others had settled into chairs in the breakfast room.

Gwen slumped with her elbows on the table, palms under her chin—horrible manners, but she didn't care. She coughed: a husky bark. "Mama and Papa must have been delayed. Mr. Merrill probably stayed in Plymouth to wait for them. He has family there." She avoided looking anywhere near Patrick. She didn't know how to act around him. Did her movements and words seem natural? Could she recognize natural behavior? You did things by habit. When you were self-conscious, you couldn't remember how you ordinarily did them.

Patrick sat stiffly at the table.

Jack cupped his hands against a window to see outside. Water was pooling in the gardens. "Where do you suppose Mrs. Nellis has gotten to?"

"Buckton, I'll wager." Gwen rubbed her nose tiredly. "Poor thing must have been mortified by Uncle Geoffrey's note. I'm sure she went to look for us when we didn't come home yesterday."

"In that case, she won't be back before tomorrow." Jack stared out the window. In the darkness, nothing could be seen of the terrace, let alone the moor. "The road is impassible, surely."

The wind was rising again. It moaned softly. Patrick asked, "May I use the telephone in the butler's office? I'll try to reach someone in Buckton."

Jack waved approval.

But when Patrick returned to the breakfast room, he said, "The phones are dead. The lines must be down."

Gwen sent Christopher to her bedroom with instructions to get her Bible and sketch of Sir Robert's *Beset Girl.* When he came back, she said, "While you three were gallivanting outside, I went to the library and copied the references we didn't have before." She set her Bible on the dining table. "Someone look them up. First is forty-nine, four, nineteen."

"That's Lamentations 4:19." Patrick took the Bible and turned pages until he found it. "'Our persecutors are swifter than the eagles of the heaven: they pursued us upon the mountains, they laid wait for us in the wilderness.'"

Jack munched a walnut from the box Colonel Sir Geoffrey had given Gwen. "That's about the pseustee."

The following two, Jerimiah 50:5 and John 8:44, foretold their time lost and confused and the pseustee's treachery.

Gwen put her finger on the next number. "One, three, sixteen."

"John 3:16. 'For God so loved the world, that he gave his only begotten Son, that whosoever believeth in him should not perish, but have everlasting life.'"

After a short silence, Gwen said, "That was for me." She did not elaborate. "Twelve, six, twelve."

Patrick turned pages. "First Timothy 6:12. 'Fight the good fight of faith, lay hold on eternal life, whereunto thou art also called, and hast professed a good profession before many witnesses.'"

Gwen looked at the sword and shield on the vision drawing. "I think that also was meant for me." And she still wasn't sure why.

The next verse, from Revelation, clearly related to the battle with the demons in the fortress above the Defile of Ash.

Gwen slid her finger toward the top of the mirror's oval frame. "Forty-three, thirty-four, four."

"Psalms. 'I sought the Lord, and he heard me, and delivered me from all my fears.'"

"I was terrified of the taraph," Jack blurted, then shuddered so violently he accidentally flung a nut across the table. He reddened. "Well, it's not like I lost my nerve."

"No, you didn't," Patrick affirmed solemnly. "You beat him."

"Yes, well…" Jack felt an instant of pride but then sank back into dejection. It was all the Lord's doing, wasn't it? Just as the verse said.

The reference after that told of the comfort they received from the soldiers.

Gwen continued the accounting: "Four, one, ten."

"First Corinthians," Patrick announced. "'Now I beseech you, brethren, by the name of our Lord Jesus Christ, that ye all speak the same thing, and that there be no divisions among you; but that ye be perfectly joined together in the same mind and in the same judgment.'"

"Hmm." Jack stared at nothing. "I guess that's more an admonition than an event."

Gwen looked down at her hands. She and Patrick had not been of the same mind. She looked at the drawing. "We've come to the verse we read in the library. Jesus limiting himself while he was on earth."

"How do we use that?" Jack wondered.

Gwen smiled at her brother. "You already did. We're back in our normal state…not an elevated position."

Jack didn't smile or even look at his sister. He stared at the table.

There was a long silence. Jack ate a nut.

Watching his brother munch, Christopher asked, "What are we going to do about supper?"

They were all hungry. Their odd luncheon had not provided anywhere near enough calories for a day of running, climbing, and demon fighting.

"I'll make dinner." Gwen felt left out and wanted to prove that she was useful.

They went down to the small kitchen.

Gwen browsed pantry shelves and foraged through cupboards. She found stewing beef in the icebox. When finished scrounging, she had arrayed an eclectic selection of foodstuffs and utensils on the kitchen counter. She set a pot on the stove and stood there deliberating. She had never in her life prepared anything other than tea.

Patrick watched anxiously out of the corner of his eye.

Gwen loaded potatoes and onions into the pot. She unwrapped the meat and tipped it in.

When she went to light the stove, Patrick stepped to her side. "Shall I help?"

She pushed up the brim of her steel hat. "I'll manage, thank you."

Nevertheless, Patrick proceeded to take everything out of the pot. He chopped the potatoes and onions. He also chopped carrots, celery, parsnips, parsley, and garlic. He cut the meat into cubes. Gwen watched for a while, then slunk away to let him work.

He browned the beef and put it aside. He sautéed the onions, garlic, and vegetables. He stirred in flour, cooking wine, beef stock, and tomato paste. Finally, he added the beef and potatoes, seasoned with salt, pepper, and thyme, and covered the pot.

Seeing Jack's dubious expression, Patrick said, "Living alone, you learn to manage."

While the stew simmered, they sat at the kitchen table and looked up the remaining vision verses. Patrick called out references, and Jack read them. Some seemed to be warnings of things yet to happen. Others were encouragements or spiritual guidance. A few were cryptic. Gwen sat up when Jack read Daniel 3:23. "And these three men, Shadrach, Meshach, and Abednego, fell down bound into the midst of the burning fiery furnace.'"

"Whitebarrow!" Gwen exclaimed.

Patrick understood. "When we flew over the old mine, I saw smoke coming from a shaft."

"It's about what's happened to Uncle Geoffrey," Gwen said with certainty.

Jack was not so sure. "Imagination can invent details that lead to false conclusions."

"That site has been abandoned for years, but somebody's been up there recently," Patrick said. "There were fresh tire tracks running from the road to the mine."

Christopher was ready to go to the police that very instant.

"Calm down," Jack ordered. "They'll lock us up in an asylum if we tell them what we suspect and why. Patrick and I will go to Whitebarrow tomorrow and see what's what."

"Lucky we're on holiday," Patrick said.

Jack looked at the other boy questioningly.

"So we don't miss school."

"Oh. Yeah. Hurray."

When the stew was ready, they took it up to the breakfast room.

Gwen laid out napkins and silverware. She set four places. Then she took off the combat helmet and plunked it down on the sideboard. "I've had enough of that. I'm not wearing it anymore."

Jack opened his mouth to argue but shrugged instead. He sat down at the head of the table.

Patrick served the food. He looked hesitantly at the extra place setting. Now that some semblance of normalcy was returning, the dictates of class structure should also return. He should eat below stairs.

Jack waved at the empty seat. "Just sit there."

Patrick found himself across from Gwen.

Jack contemplated the stew. "I'll say grace." He closed his eyes and bowed his head. "Thank you, Lord, for this food. Please bless it so it nourishes our bodies." He opened one eye to peek at his plate. "And doesn't poison us. Amen."

As much as Gwen wanted to distance herself from Patrick, she shot her brother a scathing look. "That was uncalled for!"

But Patrick snickered, and then they all laughed.

The food was fine—nearly as good as Mrs. Nellis could have made. The boys finished everything on their plates. Gwen began well, but her stomach hurt and she ate less than half her helping.

There was little conversation. Gwen and Patrick avoided each other's eyes, which was difficult since they were facing each other.

After dinner was finished and the china and silverware taken to the scullery, everyone went upstairs. Patrick had to stay the night. He and Jack intended to leave for Whitebarrow first thing in the morning, and anyway, the weather made it impossible for him to go home. Jack seemed ready to let the Irish boy stay in a guest bedroom, but Gwen sent him with sheets and blankets to a dusty maid's room beyond a door at the end of the third-floor East Wing hallway. The small bed needed new springs, the mattress was lumpy, and wind whistled through a gap between the window and its sill, but Patrick was glad to be dry.

Gwen wrote a diary entry but put down her pen after describing the breakfast the angels had served them. It was a good place to stop, and she had come to the last page in the diary. She would have to start a new book.

She lay down and listened to the patter of rain. That kiss...*stupid!*

Curled up on her side, she worried about what might be stirring in the dark. It is one thing to wonder if there are monsters concealed in your closet and quite another to know there are monsters concealed everywhere. And to hope that dreams are not doorways. Earlier, fearful of what might appear in her mirror, she had draped a blanket over it.

When her body finally went lax and her thoughts drifted, she was standing in the middle of the floor in front of the uncovered mirror, nightgown fluttering in cold air currents. Things with smoldering eyes beckoned from the depths of the cheval glass and, try as she might to resist, she crept toward them.

Patrick was already in the mirror. He took her hand and pulled. "I'm only doing what you asked."

She had the same dream twice. Both times, she woke on her back, bathed in sweat, feeling as if something heavy were pressing down on her chest, and she was hardly able to breathe. She began praying. After that, when she dreamed, she saw the Lord standing guard beside her bed. Only then, in the small hours of the morning, watched over, did she slip into a peaceful, restful slumber.

Jack had a similar night. Patrick had told everyone that the candelabra wasn't a threat so long as doors were closed, so Jack stopped obsessing about that particular danger. But he sensed more than one evil spirit prowling the estate. Gwen had forced him to take the prism; however, he did nothing with it.

Like her, he prayed and eventually fell asleep.

Jack's alarm clock rang at six a.m. There was little light; a thick, drizzling overcast blanketed the moor, smothering it in dismal gray gloom.

Patrick volunteered to make breakfast. This time, however, Gwen could not be deterred. She fried eggs to hard brown pucks and turned toast into charcoal.

"Congratulations, Gwen." Christopher impaled an egg on his fork and held it up. "You've invented a new kind of rubber."

Patrick ate, but Jack only picked at his food.

After the meal, Jack went to his father's study and took the Webley revolver and a box of bullets Lord Buckleigh kept in a cabinet. Then he joined the others in the small kitchen.

Christopher pouted when told in no uncertain terms that he could not go to the mine.

"We don't know what we're going to find." Jack put the Webley and box of ammunition into his pack. "There could be a fight; frankly, you'd be in the way."

Christopher disappeared and did not return.

Gwen had never expected to go along but felt abandoned anyway. There was now a great distance between her and Patrick. They spoke, but their conversations were awkward. He complimented her appearance, which was irritating because she knew she looked awful. He was effusively grateful when she suggested that he and Jack take a kerosene lantern to the mine, repeating twice what an excellent idea it was and how useful the lantern would be if they had to go underground. She smiled politely but fumed inside, hating his condescension.

The three teenagers went outside. Patrick's truck was still parked in the kitchen yard where he had left it on Saturday. He opened the door, pumped the primer, switched on the ignition, and walked to the front to crank the engine.

Jack grabbed Gwen's wrist. "Keep this." He shoved the prism into her palm.

"Why? You have to give it to Uncle Geoffrey. Or you might have to use it yourself."

He looked at the ground. "I don't want it to get lost."

"That's—"

"You keep it," he said flatly.

"All right. I'll put it away."

"No. Keep it with you."

Patrick got the engine started.

Gwen slipped the prism into a pocket.

Jack joined Patrick in the truck, and they drove away.

Gwen made her way through the drizzle back to the house. Inside the kitchen, she toweled her feet and calves. The bottom of her mother's gardening dress was soaked, but she didn't want to take it off. The clothes Mrs. Holliwell had lent her were not completely dry, and she hated to limit herself to a nightgown.

She had assumed everything would be resolved when she and the boys escaped the Primary World, but she had more worries than ever. The world was disordered and disorienting. All around her, powerful beings, good and evil, were going about their inscrutable business out of touch in spaces she could not see. She was an alien in her own home.

She wandered slowly up to the breakfast room. One minute she was angry, the next ashamed, and the next longing hopelessly for she knew not what. What part had Patrick in it? She shouldn't care at all what a common Irish servant boy did or thought of her. Well, he wasn't exactly a servant, and his father was a respected engineer and officer in the Royal Flying Corps *and* a hero, but Patrick was as common as they came. Yes, some girls might consider him handsome…no, *presentable* was a better word, not *handsome*. Well, perhaps he might be handsome, but he would never be dashing or suave. He was no one to be concerned about.

She stopped inside the breakfast room door. Why had she kissed him? It was only the excitement of the moment. *Surely* he understood that? She had to talk with him. Explain matters so he didn't get any ideas.

She plopped down into a chair at the table.

Why hadn't she explained before he left?

"Oh!" she cried and slammed her fist on the table.

An instant later she was rigid, alert, listening, the tang of adrenaline flooding into her veins. What was the noise she heard? A door? Which one? She rose. Hesitated. She padded softly across the East Lobby.

Now she heard footsteps but couldn't tell where they were coming from because they echoed in the otherwise tomb-like building. The hair on the back of her neck went up. Could it be her mother and father? She tiptoed to the Grand Hall but stopped in the archway, close to the wall, looking at the staircase. The footsteps started and stopped again. These were bold steps, not like Mrs. Nellis's soft tread. Not her parents'. Not Christopher's.

Christopher! Where was he? She was suddenly afraid.

She crept back to the East Lobby. Then from behind her came the voice she dreaded: "Just what do you think you are doing?"

CHAPTER 4

Harkless

2-8-9

One cold night in the bleak January of 1916, Gwen dreamed she came upon a mausoleum in a gloomy forest cemetery. She ran her fingers along its cold, mold-stained surface. Magic words were spoken; she did not know if they came from her own lips, someone else's, or the atmosphere itself, but the air darkened and thickened, and then she was inside the tomb.

On a low dais in the center of the room was a sarcophagus carved with a crowd of tortured faces. The lid was open, ready to receive new dead. Sensing a presence, Gwen turned around and found herself face-to-face with a granite statue of a beautiful woman in a ball gown. The woman's eyes locked on her. Gwen went as rigid as the statue. Woman and girl stared at one another.

Suddenly, the stone visage split wide, and fleshy streamers extended from the cleft, groping and gripping Gwen in a twining embrace. The maw expanded, revealing teeth and rotten green goo. The gruesome streamers pulled with overwhelming force until, resist as she might, Gwen's arms entered the mouth. She woke wet and shaking.

Three days later, the woman arrived.

Miss Harkless had the hourglass shape of a woman who had worn a tightly laced corset all her life, and she walked with grace, but little movements of her head and hands could be abrupt, like a bird's. The indigo irises of her eyes were so large that, when she looked straight on, almost no white was visible. Some men found those eyes intoxicating. Her mouth was small and feminine, her smile that of the Mona Lisa: cryptic and fey, lips always pursed.

There was a reason Miss Harkless did not show her teeth. She had two rows of them. In childhood, eighteen had erupted from each jaw—a total of four more than normal—so alternating incisors and cuspids leaned backward and forward to fit. The only time she displayed the interior of her mouth was when crossed by subordinates or children. Her disquieting dental arrangement was not her fault, but her cruel, devious behavior was.

Her day-to-day wardrobe consisted of four stiff black dresses she believed made her presence commanding. Intimidating would be more accurate. She had a habit of clicking her tongue when challenged and would punish the children by digging her chemical-stained fingernails into their arms. She spent long nights in her locked room reading arcane books of the occult. Lord and Lady Buckleigh didn't know that. Gwen did.

Miss Harkless was born in Switzerland, but Jack called her "The Prussian" because she was a rigid disciplinarian. Gwen was forced to study English grammar, mathematics, and Latin when she wasn't bedridden. Rules, formulas, and vocabulary were drilled into her. To be fair, Gwen was well taught in those subjects. Harkless's instruction in literature and history, by contrast, was peculiar. The woman chose books based on what she claimed was personal insight and wisdom acquired through years of study, meditation, and reflection. Miss Harkless taught that the weak should stay out of the way of superior individuals. One day, those superior men and women would merge all the world's nations into one great empire and benevolently rule the needy masses, establishing never-ending peace and prosperity.

When home from boarding school, Jack was educated in the writings of Hegel and Nietzsche. Harkless said that philosophy was the true religion of man. Yet she also practiced spiritualism, seeing no contradiction. After a suitable period of "getting used to," she had begun carefully introducing her beliefs to Lady Buckleigh. Miss Harkless was smart enough to keep her "special" knowledge to herself. The nurse-cum-tutor was a model of courtesy and good cheer in the countess's presence. Lady Buckleigh considered her an invaluable advisor. That was why Miss Harkless had been installed in a bedroom on the second floor instead of in the servants' quarters. Lord Buckleigh held the woman in distaste but accepted her. He relied upon the order she brought to his house.

Her behavior with the children was quite different.

Gwen literally jumped when she heard the cold, contemptuous voice. She spun around.

Miss Harkless stood in the solarium doorway. "Why are you out of your room?" It was an accusation, not a question.

"I'm healed!" Gwen cried shrilly.

Harkless nodded.

For an instant, Gwen thought her announcement had been accepted. A moment later, she realized the woman's nod was meant for someone behind her. She twirled and collided with a barricade. Actually, it was a man, but he could have been a barricade. He was thickset, with a broad neck and powerful arms. She gasped. He took hold of her shoulders and rotated her to face Harkless.

"What do you mean, *healed*?" This time it actually was a question.

"Let go of me!" Gwen shrieked at the barricade.

A second stranger appeared, drifting silently toward them from the East Tower—a thin, sallow fellow with long fingers.

Miss Harkless put down the black doctor's bag she had been carrying. She pinched Gwen's chin between thumb and forefinger and pushed it side to side, examining eyes and skin. Displeased with what she saw, she picked up her black bag and nodded toward the barricade man. "Mr. Killen will assist you to your room."

Killen pulled Gwen toward the entrance to the East Tower. She stumbled, but he walked on as if she weighed nothing. Seconds later, however, he stopped abruptly.

Mrs. Nellis stood in the tower doorway.

"What's going on here?" The housekeeper's eyes flitted between Gwen, Killen, Harkless, and the thin man.

Miss Harkless inspected Mrs. Nellis up and down, her gaze lingering on the housekeeper's wet overcoat and hat. "Where have you been, Mrs. Nellis? Lord and Lady Buckleigh trusted you to care for their daughter."

Mrs. Nellis's expression of surprise and outrage became one of uncertainty and apprehension. She seemed to shrink. The thin man looked at her the way a cat looks at a grounded sparrow with a broken wing.

"Leave her alone," Gwen yelled. "Mrs. Nellis took very good care of us the *entire* time you were gone." She looked pleadingly at the housekeeper, silently imploring her to go along. "I've gotten better precisely because of her excellent care."

Mrs. Nellis looked uncomfortable.

"She also took good care of Christopher and Jack," Gwen continued before the housekeeper could speak. "She's just come from outside, seeing Jack off safe and sound to Buckton where he and Patrick—Mr. McCray, who is Jack's school chum—where they went to report to their…er…flying club…about their airplane."

Everyone stared at Gwen.

"Airplane?" Harkless squinted.

"Yes. Mr. McCray flew it here yesterday, but it broke in the rain. So they've gone to go get a spare…er, confabulator. So the airplane can be flown back to its barn in Buckton."

This report was met with silence.

"They'll probably return tomorrow. Isn't that what Jack said, Mrs. Nellis?"

The housekeeper hesitated.

"So, you see," Gwen said, "everything has been quite normal here with all of us in the house and Mrs. Nellis at our side while you were gone. Absolutely normal. And I'm fine."

Miss Harkless glared at Gwen. Her lips pulled back in a snarl.

Mrs. Nellis straightened her back and advanced a few steps. "Who are these men?"

Harkless took a slow breath. "This is Mr. Killen and Mr. Wye. I have retained their services for the party."

"I see."

Gwen suspected that Mrs. Nellis didn't see at all. That what the housekeeper really wanted to say was, *These suspicious blokes? You must be joking!*

Harkless retook control. "Lady Buckleigh informed me of the out-of-doors incident engineered by Colonel Sir Geoffrey on Saturday morning. Do not mistake Gwendolyn's willfulness for vigor. Her underlying health is much damaged."

Gwen was, in point of fact, drawn and pale. Of course, it was due to Miss Harkless's aggression and Mr. Killen's tight grip.

Miss Harkless addressed the thin man: "Mr. Wye, you should become acquainted with Mrs. Nellis. Perhaps she could make you a cup of tea down in the kitchen while Mr. Killen and I help Lady Gwendolyn to her room."

He smiled pleasantly. "Certainly."

The man's soft, melodious voice made Gwen shiver. "I want to go to the kitchen," she squeaked.

Killen tightened his grip.

"I'll be back down presently," Miss Harkless told Mrs. Nellis. She motioned for Killen to follow her.

Killen lifted Gwen and cradled her in his rock-hard arms. The contact with his body repulsed her. He wore cologne that otherwise might have been nice, but she hated its fragrance from that moment on. He carried her to the East Tower.

Mr. Wye stood in Mrs. Nellis's way.

Gwen was horrified when Mr. Killen entered her bedroom. It was her private place, but she couldn't prevent the stranger from walking right in.

Miss Harkless paused when she saw the blanket draped over the mirror but didn't ask about it. Killen set Gwen on her feet beside the bed. The nurse put her bag on the floor, took hold of Gwen's dress, and began unfastening buttons.

"What are you doing!" Gwen shouted.

"Putting you to bed."

Gwen pointed at Killen. "Get him out of here!"

Harkless glanced at her servant.

Gwen said, "Do you think my mother wants me stripped in front of a man?"

The nurse's face went blank. She flipped a hand to command Killen to wait outside. He went into the hallway but left the door ajar.

Miss Harkless slid Gwen's dress down and pushed her backward onto the bed.

"My mother and father—"

"Will be alarmed to hear that you have been wandering far and wide." Miss Harkless glanced out the window, a distant look in her eyes. "You said your brother flew over the moor yesterday afternoon?"

"That's right." Gwen realized too late that she hadn't said Jack had flown over the moor—only Patrick. Miss Harkless had made an inference. And the woman was unhappy about something.

"I see." Harkless regarded the landscape for several more seconds before returning her attention to Gwen. "You need to rest, dear." She drew a bottle from her doctor's bag and extracted its cork. She poured an ounce of amber liquid into a glass and handed it to Gwen. "To calm your nerves. You are overly excited. You must admit that."

Gwen covered herself with bedclothes but remained sitting up. "I don't need a sedative."

Killen returned without being called.

"Don't you think it would be better if you were able to drink it by yourself, dear?" Miss Harkless smiled kindly. "But Mr. Killen can assist you if you'd like?"

Gwen took a look at Mr. Killen and drank the bitter mixture.

Jack watched the fast-running stream in the ditch alongside the road. To his eye, the road climbed as much as it dropped, but all he could feel was descent. The green grass, purple heather, yellow gorse, and occasional stand of semileafless, washed-out gray trees all melted into the mist. Rainwater collecting in marshy spots seemed destined for basins without drains. At times, sunlight broke through the clouds to glint in silver traces off wet rocks and hills, but that happened only infrequently.

The truck lurched, and Jack grabbed his seat to keep from sliding. His wounded palm stung, and he nearly lost his grip. "Why in blazes do you suppose Uncle Geoff went to Whitebarrow?"

"Shadrach, Meshach, and Abednego didn't go into the furnace of their own accord." Patrick kept to the hard-packed ruts, but they were filled with water, and the wheels kept slipping.

Jack reached into his bundle and closed his fingers around the handle of the loaded Webley. The pistol reassured him.

Patrick was glad for the difficult driving conditions. It forced him to focus on something other than Lady Gwendolyn. "Perhaps we've got it wrong. There was smoke, but you said yourself that the vision might not have anything to do with Colonel Sir Geoffrey."

"Gwen was pretty sure it did."

Patrick couldn't escape reminders of her.

The meager output of the heater failed to counter the bitter, wet air coming through tatty seams and holes in the cab. Jack was miserable. He needed his great-uncle. Returning home had not resolved matters or solved the mysteries. What was the rest of Sir Robert's vision about? The future was as obscure and frightening as ever. He wanted to turn his responsibilities over to someone else. He wanted to be carefree, as he had been as a child. But at the same time, paradoxically, he wanted to prove himself. He wanted to be a hero.

And what of Gwen? When he thought of her and the prism, he was increasingly bitter. The truck bounced and swayed. Jack peeled back his glove to verify that the cut in his palm wasn't bleeding.

Patrick shifted gears to climb a hill. "What do you think we'll find when we get to Whitebarrow, m'lord?"

"Drop the 'lord,' will you?" Jack snapped. "Are you mocking me?

It sounds pompous."

"I'm sorry! As you wish, sir."

Jack grimaced. "No 'sir,' either! Mayfield is fine. Or call me Mayhem. Everyone else does, behind my back. I'm thinking of pretending I like it so they don't get any satisfaction."

"I…that is…is Mayfield all right?"

"Fine." Jack couldn't see anything through the fog at the top of the hill. "Half the vision is yet to come. We need Uncle Geoff." He hadn't intended to say it out loud.

Patrick nodded.

Jack changed the subject. "Did Gwen seem out of sorts to you?" He clutched at his seat to keep from being thrown against the dash as the truck splashed and heaved through a dip at the bottom of the hill.

"Oh, well…" Patrick began. "I suppose after what's happened, we're all a bit out of sorts." It seemed a safe thing to say, even if it wasn't what he was thinking.

They pressed on through banks of vapor and drizzle. The odd shapes of the rugged, rolling moor appeared and disappeared. Patrick's imagination superimposed the interstitial mountains he knew were there, their outlines intermingled with wreaths of cloud scraping the tops of the silhouette hills. He periodically pumped the handle of a wiper that swept water and accumulated mud off a wedge of the windscreen.

Jack sensed more than he saw. He felt demonic presences, though he couldn't tell where they were or if they had any interest in the truck.

Both boys had been silent for a while when they came upon a roadblock. Three soldiers—the human kind—stood casually but ready with Enfield rifles in their arms. A fourth soldier, an older man with sergeant's stripes and a pronounced limp, came to the driver's side window.

"Who might you lads be?"

Patrick handed the sergeant his license paper. "I'm Patrick McCray, and this is—"

"John Maham." Jack did not think using his title would be helpful.

"Where are you headed?"

Both boys hesitated. Patrick said, "To the old Whitebarrow site, Sergeant."

"Oh? And what's your business there? Not treasure hunting, are you?"

"No, sir. Mr. Maham's uncle is missing. We think he might have gone there."

One of the soldiers circled the truck.

The sergeant said, "My men will have a look in the back if you don't mind."

"Not at all."

"What's going on?" Jack asked.

The sergeant waited while his men opened the back doors.

"No one there, Sergeant."

"There's been an escape from Princeton," the sergeant said. "Three German prisoners of war. Two have been picked up, but the third is at large."

Patrick looked at Jack for guidance.

"We'll keep a watch out," Jack said.

"You live hereabouts?"

"Yes, sir. Buckton and…" Patrick glanced at Jack. "And vicinity."

The sergeant looked thoughtfully at each of the boys. "The fellow will be wearing his uniform if he doesn't want to be shot as a spy. But he might have stolen other clothes from one of the farmhouses hereabouts. Come straight back to us to report strangers."

"Yes, sir. We will."

The sergeant returned Patrick's license. "That mine's on private property. You might be trespassing. And the ground is full of holes."

"We'll be careful."

"All right. I'm not your father; I won't stop you. But don't be caught on the moor after dark. Good luck." The sergeant waved them on.

Soon after that, they came to the turnoff to Whitebarrow. From there, the going was increasingly difficult. The fresh ruts running north were indistinct and soft. Patrick adjusted the throttle and endeavored to maintain forward momentum, but his truck became mired in the mud.

Fortunately, he kept spades and planks in the back. He and Jack got out, shoveled in front of the wheels, and slipped a board under each tire. Jack stayed outside to push and recover the wood. The truck broke free, Jack tossed the wood in the back, and they continued on. But it wasn't long before they were stuck again.

Patrick scanned the ground ahead. Getting his truck to the mine was going to be a lot of work.

Jack had the same thought. "It would be quicker to walk."

"I'm afraid you're right."

"Blast it all! Get your kit and we'll go."

"Yes…Mayfield."

They trudged through the mud. After they stopped for a minute to rest, Jack struggled to pull one boot from the muck, only to have the other one sucked down. As they crested the next hill, the weather began to deteriorate.

Gwen stared at a wall for ten minutes before she was able to form the thought, *I'm awake.* She had curled into a ball. The pounding in her head dissuaded her from straightening out. She wondered if recent memories were more than episodic nightmares: Uncle Geoffrey's arrival, the prism, the Primary World, the demons…

She moved experimentally, discovered she was wearing nothing but undergarments, and decided her recollections were genuine. Dim gray light came through the windows. Was it afternoon or morning? What day was it? How many times had Miss Harkless drugged her—once or several? How long had it been since she had seen her parents?

Her parents!

They should have returned. Were they home? Or had something else gone wrong? Perhaps they had been killed in a railway accident. Perhaps Miss Harkless was now her legal guardian!

She sat up and swung her feet over the side of her bed. Almost as quickly, she lay back down, dizzy and nauseated. *Lord,* she begged in silent petition, *help me. Give me strength. Or at least settle my stomach and stop the throbbing in my head!*

Her parents were not dead. They couldn't be. They must be home. She sat up again, slowly this time, and stepped onto the cold floor. Hugging herself, she lurched to the bathroom and pulled on her robe.

The medicine bottle was at her bedside. She emptied it out the window, taking the opportunity to get fresh air. Miss Harkless would be furious; Gwen didn't care. She wobbled dizzily when she leaned into the cold, wet air. She pushed back from the windowsill—it wouldn't do to fall out.

While fastening the casements, she heard murmurs. She crossed to the door and leaned against it to keep her balance, wondering if demon talk was bleeding over from the Primary World. Head swimming, she put her ear to the wood.

"...better to let her rest. Frankly, I'm amazed her condition isn't worse."

"Do you think it would hurt to look in on her?"

"I don't advise it. I'll call you the minute she's awake."

"Very well. I'll rely on your judgment."

"Mama!" Gwen yanked open the door. "I'm healed! I'm healed!"

Gwen had the satisfaction of seeing Miss Harkless shocked speechless. The woman had underestimated the tranquilizer dosage, no doubt believing her patient still weak from malnutrition and months of medication.

Unfortunately, Gwen wasn't fully recovered. Her legs gave out, and she dropped to the floor.

"Gwendolyn!" The countess rushed to help her daughter.

Miss Harkless got to Gwen first. "My darling—what were you *thinking,* child?"

The woman seemed sincerely concerned; Gwen hesitated for a split second before thrusting her away. "Leave me alone, you witch!"

Lady Buckleigh gasped. "Gwendolyn!"

"She's poisoning me!"

"Oh, darling!" Lady Buckleigh's face went dark.

"It's not her fault, m'lady. Don't scold her. She's delusional. What Colonel Sir Geoffrey did was unconscionable." Harkless stroked Gwen's head soothingly.

Gwen was in tears. "Uncle Geoffrey *helped* me."

Harkless put an arm around Gwen's back and lifted her to her feet.

"M'lady," the nurse said to the countess, "I'm sorry, but your presence is doing more harm than good right now. It would be best if you left. I'll give my little mistress something to calm her."

"Knock me out, you mean!" Gwen wondered what would transpire when Miss Harkless discovered the bottle was empty. "Mother, *please,* she—"

"Gwen…" Lady Buckleigh shook her head. "Miss Harkless is right about this. I'm sorry. I'll look in when you're better." And she left.

Gwen could not think what to say.

Miss Harkless marched Gwen to her bed, bent close, and whispered, "I'll teach you to be smart." She smiled, showing all her teeth. But her expression changed when she saw the empty bottle on the butler's table.

Gwen shrank back. She braced herself to be hit hard. It was a close thing. Fortunately, Miss Harkless knew better than to leave bruises. But the woman's face was an unearthly mask of rage. She stomped out of the room and pulled the door shut.

Gwen heard metal-on-metal scraping followed by two loud clicks. It took her a minute to work up the courage to creep across the floor. Turning the knob confirmed her guess. The door was locked. She went to the window and stood there looking down, wondering what to do. She saw her nurse traverse the kitchen yard and storm northward with Mr. Wye in tow.

Not knowing what she hoped to achieve, Gwen threw on the skirt and blouse Mrs. Holliwell had loaned her. Someone—probably Christopher, certainly not Miss Harkless—had brought the clothes up from the laundry room. Next, she donned her overcoat and, thinking ahead, stuffed a handkerchief and scarf into a pocket. Then she dove into the back of her closet, swept aside hat boxes, and pried open the secret access panel to get to the space behind the wall where the boys had nailed rungs. She climbed up into the attic.

Fifty paces north, she descended another makeshift ladder to reach a third-floor room beyond the partition that separated the new and old wings of the house. She took care to avoid spots where the floorboards were weak. A dusty hallway took her to the Beacon Tower, which was the farthest the children had explored. Freddie said the rest of the wing wasn't safe.

The Beacon Tower's third-floor, north-facing window was coated with grime. Rubbing it smeared the glass without improving visibility. But a corner of one of the panes was cracked, and it popped out when Gwen pressed it. That gave her an excellent spy hole.

Miss Harkless was speaking with Mr. Wye at the far end of the North Wing. The woman pointed north and dismissed the man. Then she inserted a key into a door and went inside.

More than ever, Gwen disliked the abandoned old wing. But she was going to go into it anyway.

Paige,

Sorry, I don't have a layout of the North Wing. Nothing better than the guesses on the floorplan I sent a few weeks ago. But Gwen's next diary entries give you an idea of the interior as it was in 1918.

Oh—I got a girlfriend. For a few days. She was all over me at a party last Saturday, but she walked out on Tuesday when I said there were things I wasn't ready for. She acted as if I had insulted her. Now she's blocked me.

Kirk

CHAPTER 5

The North End of the House

7-6-11

The reason Freddie never let his siblings go farther than the Beacon Tower was evident. The top floor of the North Wing was sealed off, and the winding tower staircase had decayed treads. Hugging the wall, testing every step, Gwen inched her way down one story. But below that, the stairs were entirely missing. She proceeded northward on the second floor.

It was like one of her dreams. The suites of rooms filled with strange assortments of objects led one to another. Several times, the afterimage of a bolting rat registered on the periphery of her vision and she stifled a shriek. Also like a dream, Gwen felt she knew the rooms even though she had never been in them before.

She passed through bedrooms and sitting rooms cluttered with furniture stored and forgotten. Jacobean, Georgian, and Rococo tables, sofas, and chairs lay under dusty covers. There were cedar-lined wardrobes packed with clothes thirty years out of fashion. Perhaps she would come back one day for some of the better-preserved gowns, though determining their true condition was difficult. The day was so gloomy that the tall windows were little more than gray panels. Things around her, Gwen thought wryly, appeared in silhouette. Their murky exteriors didn't reveal much of their actual condition or history.

All at once, she yearned to return to the great city of the Lord, where everyone and everything was vibrantly alive and real. But she had agreed to do what the Lord wanted, and for whatever reason, He wanted her in the derelict North Wing of her house. She knew that because Ecclesiastes 2:6, the seventeenth vision verse, said *I applied mine heart to know, and to search, and to seek out wisdom, and the reason of things, and to know the wickedness of folly, even of foolishness and madness.* The following reference, Acts 8:9, provided context: *But there was a certain man, called Simon, which beforetime in the same city used sorcery, and bewitched the people of Samaria, giving out that himself was some great one.* That was clearly about Miss Harkless. What sorcery was she planning, and who was she going to bewitch?

Ephesians 6:11 told Gwen *Put on the whole armor of God, that ye may be able to stand against the wiles of the devil.*

So she was on her way to her father's decommissioned home laboratory. She assumed she could get into the lab from inside the house. Her father had always used the outside door—the one Gwen had seen Miss Harkless enter. It wasn't difficult to guess what the woman was doing there. Gwen planned to learn the names of the drugs she was being given and use that knowledge to her advantage.

But where had God gone? When Gwen was a little girl, He was ever present. Even when she was pushing Him away, He had waited nearby. Now, He was entirely gone. He had given instructions and left.

She draped her scarf over her hair and knotted it under her chin. Jaw clenched, she used a discarded fireplace poker to sweep aside walls of cobwebs. The poker soon became wrapped in grubby, sticky webbing. Gwen scraped it on a decaying sofa. She screamed and jumped backward when a rat darted across the seat. The wriggling cushion was home to a colony of rodents. She stared. Would they bite? They had small mouths, but their teeth were razors. And they carried diseases, didn't they? What if they scooted under her skirt and ran up her legs?

Praying for courage, she hurried on. The rats didn't follow. She found the main staircase but couldn't use it because a huge crystal chandelier, grimy and dull as dirt, lay fallen across its steps. So she stayed on the second floor. Stopping momentarily to look out of an east-facing window, she saw crates, lumber, and sawhorses under a big tent set up in the shabby courtyard below. She pondered. Something whizzed past her face. She shooed it away, thinking it was a fly.

It was not a fly. The insect had a tiny waist, long legs, and yellow bands on its bulbous abdomen. And it was not alone. There were several buzzing around. A wrinkled brown hornet's nest twice the size of a human head hung from the top of the doorway to the next room.

Gwen stood very still. When hornets attacked en masse, their stings could be lethal. One of the Maham House gardeners had nearly died when he accidentally set a ladder against a hive.

"I'm not a threat to you," Gwen murmured to the insects. "I'm not a threat." She remained perfectly motionless. The way into the lab—if there was a way—was past the hornets' nest. "It's too much, Lord. You shouldn't have put that in my way. I'm stuck." She stared at the wood-paste nest hanging by a thin stalk like a grotesque uvula. "Is this expedition your will, Lord? Or is it only my idea?"

She stood thinking for a minute.

"Lord, I vowed to do what you asked. The verse said to search and seek out the reason of things. What do you want me to do?"

The room beyond the doorway was full of boxes. A suit of armor stood against the far wall. She did not think it was a sign—more of a joke. "Put on the armor? It's out of reach." She became a little angry. It was one thing to deal with a few spiders in webs, creepy as they were, and quite another to challenge an army of hornets. She was so close to her objective! *Now* was the time to see what was in Harkless's potions!

Ever so slowly, she knelt down. Pulling her skirt up out of the way of her knees, she crawled toward the doorway. Several hornets came to investigate.

"I'm not a threat," Gwen told the hornets once again. It was a false statement, but she didn't know that yet. She kept her head down. She prayed with a focus equal to when she had faced the pseustee on High Tor.

A few more hornets emerged from the mouth at the bottom of the nest. Hundreds might be inside the dirty brown blob. Gwen crawled beneath it. And got past.

Once she was in the next room, The hornets lost interest. Pulse high, weak with relief and flushed with joy, Gwen scrambled to her feet and laughed. "Did it!"

A crate beside her contained mosquito netting, pith helmets, and tent canvas, among other odd things. They were of no interest to her. She went into the hallway beyond the final door.

And came to an abrupt halt.

"Fiddlesticks!"

It was a dead end. The crew that constructed Lord Buckleigh's home laboratory had built a firewall to separate a Restoration-era kitchen from the rest of the house. Gwen stared at the bricks in dismay. God had given her an impossible assignment after all.

She stood unmoving for more than a minute. She had never been in this part of the house. If there was a way into the lab from where she was, she didn't know it.

The light coming in the windows brightened, making the firewall bricks appear very red and the mortar especially rough. Could there be an opening somewhere? She had no way of knowing.

Why must she be blocked by walls? Like yesterday—the wall across the roof. Like that. Yes, like *that*.

Well…the prism was in her coat pocket. She took it out and peered into one of the facets. Sure enough, looking through the prism, she could see the Primary World, which allowed her to see beyond the wall. An interstice—a parapet of the Norman fortress—cut diagonally through the modern masonry. If Gwen were able to step into the interstice, she would have a clear view down into the laboratory.

She chewed her lip. She positioned the prism so that it caught the light and cast a faint image like a projector, as it had on the roof, except this time she was in silhouette and the image was of the Primary World.

"Lord…if this is what you want me to do…then…"

She thought of Jesus living as a man on earth. His faithfulness.

The interstice clarified and intensified. She stepped and, mindful of the peculiar sensation she had felt on the roof, turned her body sideways. That wasn't necessary, she believed, but it helped her replicate what had happened before.

It worked. She was on the Primary World parapet.

"By the way, Lord," Gwen whispered, glancing around the medieval place, "this time I'd prefer only a short stay in the Primary World, please."

She crept along the interstitial rampart. Lord Buckleigh had not used the laboratory for some years. Most of the counters below were cluttered with dusty, haphazardly placed apparatuses: scales, burners, a centrifuge, and a lot of glassware, including complicated assemblies of tubes. Only one table had clear working space. That was where Harkless was standing. Gwen knew it was Miss Harkless even though the woman was wearing a hood to keep dust out of her hair. Gwen watched her use a mortar and pestle to grind leaves into powder.

Despite the weather, Harkless had opened a window for ventilation. The sound of the rain was musical static behind her percussive clinking and scraping.

"Witch!" Gwen muttered.

Harkless looked up.

Gwen ducked out of sight. She couldn't be detected, could she? She was in an interstice. Wasn't that the way interstices worked? She peeked over the parapet. Harkless had returned to her grinding.

Now that she was in the lab, Gwen realized there wasn't much she could actually do. She was too far from the tins and bottles on the table to read their labels. Her notion of naming ingredients to convince her father she was being poisoned had been naive. A flight of stone steps descended to the ground floor, but she couldn't get close to the table without leaving the interstice, and if she did that, she would be seen. She would have to go back to her room and drink Harkless's noxious concoction even though she had won her way past the hornets.

Hornets.

Gwen watched Harkless pour amber liquid through a funnel into a brown glass bottle.

Hornets.

Could it work? Her notion became a full and mature plan in seconds. Trembling with nervous excitement, she scrambled back to the last room and hunted through the crates. She donned a pith helmet. Over that she draped mosquito netting. Next, she worked herself into a man's vest so that the netting form-fit her overcoat. Then she put on the gauntlets from the suit of armor. It was not easy—she had to wiggle her mesh-wrapped fingers into the sockets. She managed it because the gauntlets had been made for someone with large hands. When finished, she was fully encased in netting, with the vest and gauntlets holding everything in shape. She bent her fingers to confirm she could curl them individually, then swung her arms out and over her head. Her range of motion was limited but satisfactory, as was visibility through the mosquito netting.

She took a lady's purse from a box, hung its strap around her neck, and put the prism into it so she had both hands free.

"Lord, shield me." She strode resolutely to the hive.

When she was within six feet of their nest, every hornet in the room streaked at her. They smacked into the mosquito netting and clung. She couldn't feel them through her heavy clothes, but they poked their stingers through the mesh around her head.

Trembling but keeping her nerve, she reached up, took hold of the thin stalk that attached the nest to the door frame, and plucked the thing from its mounting. Hornets spewed out of the hive's mouth, enveloping her in a deadly, furiously droning, black and yellow cloud. They zoomed in tight orbits around her head, and their wriggling bodies caked her protective gear. The brim of her pith helmet prevented the netting from touching her face, but the hornets jabbed their stingers to within a hair's breadth of her nose.

Encased in the seething swarm, she rushed to the interstice, carrying the hive by its stalk. But she stopped short of the threshold, sensing that something was off. She extended her hand. She could see into the interstice, but its boundary was as solid as the lab's brick wall. She tapped the boundary with a gauntlet. It *was* the lab's brick wall.

"Oh." The hornets were anchoring her to silhouette. And anchored to silhouette, she couldn't get into the interstice.

Gwen thought back to Saturday afternoon. When enveloped in the prism's light, she and the boys became anchored to the Primary World. She reached her free hand into the purse hanging from her neck, took out the prism, and cast a beam all around. The hornets shined. She saw them with terrible but beautiful clarity.

"Lord, anchor them to Primary. Let us all go together."

It worked. Her hand passed without resistance into the interstice. She stepped onto the medieval rampart.

Miss Harkless was filling a second medicine bottle. Gwen didn't hesitate. She flung the hive down into the lab. It smashed on the floor by the open window. The hornets clinging to Gwen's clothes rushed after their shattered home. They dove and formed a living tornado around the broken nest.

Miss Harkless's eyes went so wide the whites were fully visible. Her mouth formed a gaping *O*, and she ran for the door. She was outside in seconds, every hornet in the room chasing her.

Gwen hurried down the stairs. She retrieved the crumpled hive and dropped it out the open window. With luck, Miss Harkless would think the nest had fallen from the eaves, and the hornets had swarmed into the lab from outside.

Hurrying to the table where the woman had been working, Gwen sloughed off her gauntlets and vest. Reaching trembling hands from underneath the mosquito netting, she plucked the corks from Harkless's two medicine bottles, poured their contents into the steel sink in the counter, and rinsed the residue down the drain.

Using a funnel, she refilled the bottles with tap water, grimacing at its reddish-brown color. The color was only rust from the old pipes, but it was going to be nasty to drink. Perhaps she was lucky the liquid was dusky—otherwise, Harkless might realize that her so-called medicine had been replaced.

Gwen spotted a bottle of brandy nestled among the others. She added a small measure to the water to give the "medicine" the right smell.

"Insufferable!" Harkless cried. "Insufferable!"

Gwen jumped. Her enemy was just outside, only seconds from returning. She jammed the corks back in the bottles and positioned them on the counter. Where exactly had they been? She guessed. She grabbed her discarded gauntlets and vest, dashed for the interstitial stairs, and got to them just in time: Harkless came through the door pumping a fog of insecticide from a large atomizer. Hornets milling by the window fell and lay twitching.

Miss Harkless went to investigate the source of the swarm. She scowled at the hive on the ground outside and slammed the window. Then she stomped to the work table. Her eyes narrowed. She set the sprayer on the counter.

Peeking over the parapet at the top of the stairs, Gwen held her breath.

Satisfied that nothing was amiss, Harkless put her black bag on the counter and slipped the medicine bottles into it. "She'll not pour these out."

Gwen retreated past the brick wall into the room with the crates and whispered, "I already have, you evil hag." When she held out the prism, the glass sparkled even though there was scant light in the room.

"Oh, Lord, please get me out of here!"

With that, the interstice was gone and the brick wall back in its proper place; Gwen was re-anchored to silhouette.

She tossed away the gauntlets, vest, netting, and helmet. She grinned as she hurried toward the Beacon Tower. Patrick would be impressed with what she had done. He was always able to figure things out, but this time she had done it without him. She was so preoccupied congratulating herself that, halfway back, she became lost in the increasingly dim rooms.

Walls of furniture hemmed her in, and it was not until she went to look out a window that she realized she had gotten turned around and gone back north. And it was nearly dark outside.

She panicked. What if she didn't get to her room before Miss Harkless? What would the woman do when she discovered Gwen was missing?

Gwen stepped on something squishy, and a rat squealed. She ran, only to slam into a dresser. Pain shot up her leg and she stumbled, careened sideways, and plunged through a huge spider web. Pulled from its anchors, the web stuck to her overcoat, pinning the writhing spider to her chest. Gwen screamed and brushed frantically at the arachnid, smearing web and half-smashed spider on her hands and overcoat. She stumbled into a short corridor and ran blindly, sucking in dust, coughing and hacking violently.

She finally reached the Beacon Tower and bounded up its stairs. However, before she got to the third floor, a rotted step splintered under her foot. She grabbed wildly but couldn't catch the banister and went down hard, hitting her forehead. Her vision went red, then stark white. The entire staircase swayed drunkenly and pulled away from the wall. Somehow, it held together long enough for her to gain the third-floor landing. But no one would ever use those stairs again. Her heart thumped so hard that her whole body quaked.

She scurried recklessly through the hallway, up into the attic, over to the other ladder, and down into her closet. She tossed her coat aside and whipped away the filthy head scarf. Running out into her room, she caught sight of herself in the mirror. She would have gasped if she had not already been panting. Her face was caked with grime.

She unfastened her skirt and blouse, slipped out of them, and threw them in the closet. After scrubbing her hands and splashing her face in the bathroom, she used a damp washcloth to wipe dirt from her chemise. She could do nothing about the sweat stains.

"Oh!" She pulled all the pins from her hair and brushed out clinging dust.

She jumped into bed. She had just pulled the covers up to her chin when Miss Harkless stormed in. The woman said nothing. She drew one of the bottles from her bag, uncorked it, and tipped it into a glass, not bothering to measure the dose.

Gwen sat up slowly, pulse pounding in her ears. "Give me your medicine, then."

Harkless thrust the glass at her.

Gwen drank it in six gulps, took a breath, then sputtered and coughed. She wasn't acting. The rusty sediment was gritty. But she rejoiced when Miss Harkless corked the bottle and put it back in her bag.

The nurse paused when she reached the door. She didn't look back. "You'll do well to follow orders. The dosage might be reduced."

Gwen felt she ought to reply submissively that yes, she would obey. But she couldn't bring herself to do it. She doubted Harkless would believe her, anyway.

The door shut, and its latch clicked. Utterly exhausted, Gwen closed her eyes and, even though she had taken no narcotic, was asleep in minutes.

CHAPTER 6

Prisoner on the Moor

51-3-23

Jack loved the open spaces of Dartmoor. When he was small and the weather fair, his eyes would follow the creases and slopes of the grassy expanse out to the line of the horizon. He would yearn to run and climb the stony hills and see what lay beyond the edge of the world. The feeling of volume was emancipating—he could escape in any direction. Since the war started, and especially since he became heir to the earldom when Freddy died, Jack was always looking for a way to escape.

But today, the moor was a breathing, maneuvering prison, checking him and Patrick at every turn. Fog advanced in thick banks and tendrils that reached and rolled and abruptly enveloped them. The mist muted sounds and filled the boys' noses with its humid organic smell. And Jack sensed in the vapors a presence that sent chills rippling up and down his spine. Today, the moor was a toadstool pâté.

"Not a good day for a ramble," Patrick observed.

Jack was about to say something about the malignant presence he felt, but the fog to the west cleared momentarily, and he saw, crouching in a ravine no more than two hundred yards away, a figure in gray.

He pointed, arm rigid. "It's the German!"

Then the weather closed in again.

Patrick stared, tilting his head first to one side and then the other as if that would allow him to see through the mist. "What do we do?"

Jack was silent.

"Turn back?"

"No." Jack shrugged off his pack and took out the revolver.

"Are we going to try to capture him?"

"Of course not. We have to find Uncle Geoff. Get a move on!"

The road was so little used it had nearly vanished. The boys followed traces. Neither was certain of direction. The wind shifted from one bearing to another, making it seem they had changed course when they had not.

The fog became so dense that Patrick had the impression he was breathing sticky liquid. Soon he could barely see the ground at his feet. He prayed over and over for clear sight.

Another hole opened in the mist, and the man in gray appeared again, this time not far from their path. But the hole closed a moment later.

Jack gripped his pistol. "The blackguard is trying to intercept us!"

"The road curves. Isn't it possible we turned toward him?"

Jack didn't answer.

"Wouldn't a prisoner head away from people?" Patrick asked.

"He needs clothes and money to get home. He wants to take ours."

"There are two of us."

"He's desperate. And Germans are ruthless, you know."

Patrick noticed a faint, shimmering wall; infinitely thin, it was best seen out of the corner of his eye. He was surprised to be able to detect a Primary World feature while anchored to silhouette. He remembered the tunnel-like interstice he had seen from his airplane and felt reassured. It paralleled the road; it would guide them to the mine.

"The German Army overran neutral Belgium because it was in their way," Jack said as he plowed ahead. "They rounded up civilian hostages and shot them. They raped girls. They're monsters. They…"

Jack stopped. He looked behind himself and then all around. "Something terrible…" The demonic presence was overpowering. Trembling, Jack lifted his gun and pointed it in the direction he had last seen the man. But when a minute passed and there was no break in the fog, he began walking again.

Two minutes after that, they caught another fleeting glimpse of the gray figure. He was very close, now, lumbering across their path. Jack took aim and curled his finger on the trigger. He hesitated only a second, but it was long enough for the mist to congeal and conceal his target. "Blast it!"

The next time they saw him, the man was ahead to the right. Jack aimed.

Yet again, the fog intervened.

Patrick gazed northeast. "Wolf's Tor Mire is over there, somewhere."

"God grant the Boche be sucked into the bog!" Moisture dripped from Jack's face. "Into the hungry ground." He adjusted his grip on the revolver and cocked its hammer. He had stopped praying; he was concentrating on his enemy. When he began marching again, he kept his gun aimed into the vapor. The demonic presence was terrible.

"We've wandered off the road," Patrick said.

"There's no way to tell."

"It follows the line of the interstice."

"Interstice?"

Patrick tried to locate the interstitial seam, but it was not to be seen.

"The German must be the demon." Jack's voice quavered.

"Pardon?"

"The German." Jack pointed the muzzle of his revolver to indicate where he thought the soldier was. "I think the German is the demon."

"What demon?"

Jack looked at Patrick as if he were daft. "What else is that presence?"

Patrick was bewildered. "Presence?"

"You can't feel it?"

"No." Patrick studied Jack's face. "You sense them. Demons."

Jack stared back. "Can't…you can't, can you?"

Patrick shook his head. "And you can't see interstices."

"No. You're the only one who can do it." Jack laughed bitterly, huffing strangely. "We have particular talents, you and I."

Patrick looked down. "I wouldn't want yours."

"Aye. I'm *cursed.*" The last word burst out as a bitter cough. He looked about for an escape that wasn't there. "We're turning back." Except that no trace of the road could be seen. "Which…which direction do we go?" The ground was the same everywhere. "We have to get away from here!"

Jack bent his knees and leaned forward as if about to run.

Patrick stepped in front of him. "Mind! We're near the bog!"

Just then, a swatch of blue appeared, then a rough horizon, and, miraculously, the fog lifted. The clouds drifted from the field, revealing the uplands to the north and a descending hillside to the southeast.

The defunct mine spread out before the two boys. The German was nowhere to be seen. He had gone to ground when the fog lifted. Gullies, pits, and stone ruins provided any number of places to hide. The only sign of recent human occupation was a solitary house to the north.

"There's the shaft!" Patrick set off across the pocked field. The smoke he had seen from his airplane had issued from a depression near the waist-high remains of a stone building.

Jack hastened after him.

There was no smoke, but when Patrick came to the depression, he discovered it was capped with rusted metal sheets.

"Colonel Sir Geoffrey! Colonel Sir Geoffrey!" Patrick pulled on a section of the thin, corrugated steel. The metal was so corroded it cracked. "Colonel Sir Geoffrey?"

"Yes," came a weak reply from below. "I'm here."

Patrick couldn't quite believe they had been so lucky as to actually find the colonel. "Sir, it's McCray. Lord Mayfield and I are here to help you!"

Taking care to avoid jagged edges, Patrick shoved and bent a corner of the cap to create an aperture wider than his shoulders. Then he pointed his flashlight down into the darkness. What he saw was a jumble of rusted metal frames and broken ventilation equipment fallen on top of an elevator platform frozen in position. The defunct elevator was some yards below the surface.

Patrick noticed a ladder attached to the timbered wall of the shaft. "Sir, I'm coming down."

"Take the lantern," Jack suggested. "Light it when you get down. I'll hold your torch while you climb." He carefully lowered the Webley's cocked hammer, put the gun into his coat pocket, and directed the flashlight beam through the hatch Patrick had made.

The Irish boy eased himself past splinters of metal sheeting and took hold of the ladder. It felt secure. He swung onto it, paused to orient himself, and started down. Happily, the clutter of machinery defeated his sense of height, so he was able to descend without fear, though the sharp steel wreckage around him was of some concern. After he cleared the broken elevator, he still had a distance to go but no more obstacles. His eyes adjusted to the low light, and he climbed the rest of the way without incident.

"Hello, Mr. McCray," said the colonel when Patrick stepped to the floor of the shaft.

"Hello, sir. Are you all right?"

The colonel was sitting on the ground with his back against a wall. He did not attempt to get up. "I've been better, I must say." Stubble and shadow darkened his deeply lined face.

"I'm coming down," Jack called.

Patrick lit the kerosene lantern and set it on the ground.

"Do you have water?" the colonel asked. "There's been some rain, but the stuff that trickles down here is not particularly wholesome."

Patrick unslung his canteen. "Here you are, sir."

The colonel took several deep swallows. His hands trembled, but he paid no mind to what spilled on him. "You are no longer anchored to the Primary World. Where is Gwendolyn?"

"Safe at home."

The colonel closed his eyes and breathed a sigh of relief.

"Sir, how did you come to be here?"

"It's rather embarrassing. I was abducted."

Jack joined them. "Who would do such a thing?"

"I can't say for sure." Sir Geoffrey told of his encounter on the road. "Next thing I knew, I was bound, gagged, hooded, and bouncing around in the back of a lorry." He took another sip of water. "I hope your horse found its way home, Jack."

"Not yet. Can you climb the ladder, Uncle Geoff? I suppose not, or you'd have done it already."

The colonel's left boot lay at his side. He indicated his badly swollen foot. "I'm afraid I'm lame. Consequence of my escape." He set down the canteen. "The scoundrels took me to a house near here and demanded to know what I had been doing for the past few weeks. As a military officer, I politely declined to say." He smiled, and the boys realized that some of the shadowing around his eyes was bruised flesh. "They didn't like that." The colonel tried to make himself more comfortable, only to wince and return to his previous position. "They kept me hooded, so I never saw their faces. One of them did most of the talking. I'm sure I've heard his voice before. Melodious, with a cruel edge. It might have been at an anarchist meeting."

"Anarchist meeting!" Patrick blurted. "Why—that is…uh, sir…?"

The colonel chuckled dryly. "I'm not an anarchist if that's what you're wondering."

"Uncle Geoff is attached to military intelligence," Jack explained. "Before the war, he was in a special branch."

"Eh? Oh. Oh. I see," Patrick said.

"I can't imagine why they grabbed me. Perhaps they thought I was investigating whatever they're doing here in Devonshire. I must admit, I am quite interested now." The colonel looked thoughtful. "I suspect they would have eventually killed me. But they underestimated an old man." He smiled. "They searched my clothes but didn't find the knife I keep in my boot. When they left me alone, I cut myself free and slipped out a window." He waved his hand to indicate the mine shaft. "I presume this is Whitebarrow?"

"Yes, sir."

"So I was headed in the right direction." The colonel nodded to himself. "I came down the hill hoping to be out of view before they realized I was gone. I wanted them to think I had blundered into the mire. Unfortunately, they were alert. I had scarcely three minutes' head start and couldn't outrun them. But God answers prayers. I came upon an adit—a shallow access tunnel in the side of the hill. A few yards inside, I found a discarded sledgehammer. I knocked out a stanchion, and the tunnel collapsed."

The colonel pointed at his foot. "Falling timber did that." He chuckled dryly. "I'm lucky I didn't bury myself. Apparently, my abductors assumed I did because they gave up their search." He sighed. "I crawled here."

Jack began fashioning a harness out of the rope they had brought. He was getting good at making climbing harnesses.

"Yesterday, I tore off a bit of my coat and set it on fire along with some dry grass and twigs—you'd be surprised how much rubbish falls down here. I hoped someone other than those villains would see the signal. A thin hope, but all things are possible with God. And here you are!"

Jack nodded. "We flew over at the right time."

"Flew over?"

"It's a long story. Let's get out of here, Uncle Geoff. McCray and I will haul you up."

"First, tell me everything that has happened these past few days."

Jack glanced up the shaft. "What about the blokes who abducted you?"

"At the end of the interrogation, they talked of shuttering the house. I think they've abandoned the property."

Jack fidgeted. "All right." He set down the rope. "After you left Buckton, we...well, actually, it was McCray...realized that the Roman numerals in Sir Robert's drawing were mirror images. So we had the verses all wrong."

The previous evening, Jack had looked up and copied down the text of all the corrected scriptures on Gwen's list. He handed his great-uncle the compilation and recounted his and the others' adventures of the past three days.

It was a dry, abbreviated report. Patrick was impressed that Jack could summarize such complex events so concisely.

The colonel asked few questions but apparently understood a great deal. In conclusion, Jack explained that he and Patrick had followed the clue about Shadrach, Meshach, and Abednego.

The colonel nodded and read the rest of the vision verses. When he came near the bottom of the page, his eyes widened for a fraction of a second. Neither boy noticed.

Jack picked up the harness. "Let me help you into this, Uncle Geoff."

The colonel gazed upward. "There is a lot of debris wedged up there. It looks to be a tight squeeze." He pointed into a tunnel. "Perhaps Mr. McCray could explore in that direction. There might be another drainage adit. It would be better if I could hobble out. With you two supporting me, I could manage."

Patrick nodded. "Yes, sir. Certainly."

When the Irish boy was out of earshot, the colonel motioned Jack closer and said, "There is one verse that is the same. If the key were in the book of Acts, as I had believed, there would be no index sixty-six, twenty-two, four. I reckoned the second digit to be smudged—that the number was sixty-*five*, twenty-two, four. I was wrong—the book *is* sixty-six, but since the key has turned out to be the Gospel of John, the second mistake canceled out the first."

Colonel Sir Geoffrey pointed. "This is the verse in question, from the Gospel of Luke: 'And he went his way, and communed with the chief priests and captains, how he might betray him unto them.'" The colonel looked grave. "It troubled me before. Now doubly so. Jack," the colonel said, "someone is going to betray you, and I think it will be McCray."

"What?"

"Gwendolyn is at the center of more than our family's troubles. What happens to her will have much wider consequences. She must be watched over. I'm out of the game. You'll have to take over."

Jack stared.

Sir Geoffrey said, "Let me have the prism."

"It's not here."

The colonel stared. "Where is it?"

"I left it at home." Jack looked away. "I didn't want to lose it."

"You must keep it with you always!"

"But it's yours."

The colonel shook his head. "Not anymore. Your parents will have returned from London. I suspect I'm no longer welcome at Maham House. Beyond that, there's my injured foot, a rattle in my chest, and I'm extremely weak. I need medical attention."

They heard Patrick returning through the tunnel.

The colonel finished quickly: "One of you will betray the others. That is certain."

Jack frowned.

The beam of Patrick's flashlight came into the shaft, and shortly he appeared. "It's a dead end."

Jack studied his companion of the past few days. "All right." He turned to his great-uncle. "McCray and I will pull you up. I'll go first."

He tied the loose end of the rope to his belt. "McCray—make sure it pays out freely."

He climbed. The rope dangling around his legs was annoying, but that hardly registered in his consciousness. His great-uncle's conjecture made no sense. Betrayal? How could McCray betray them? Why did the ordeal never end? Finding Uncle Geoff was no relief at all.

He hauled himself angrily up the last rungs of the ladder. When he was within a couple of feet of the surface, he shoved a flap of corrugated steel out of his way. His action shook all the metal capping the mine, and the cap's severely corroded support beams cracked. The noise boomed down the shaft and across the countryside.

Jack knew immediately that he was in trouble. The entire cap dipped and slid toward him. The broken end of a support beam thrust at his side. He grabbed the jagged, rusted bar to keep it from running him through.

He managed to push the beam back an inch, but the full weight of the cap was behind it, and even with all his might, he couldn't deflect the chance-made spear. And he had nowhere to go. Back pressed hard against the ladder, one heel on a rung, he was threatened on all sides by jagged iron. He hardly noticed the pain in his injured hand.

"HELP!" he screamed.

He wrestled with the pointed beam. Nothing he tried could force it from its inexorable trajectory.

"HELP!"

He kicked himself upward and got his head above ground. But now the beam was pressing into his stomach, and he couldn't climb any higher without being impaled.

"I'm coming!" Patrick called. But it was no use. He couldn't get above Jack's feet. "I'm blocked."

"Go to the side!"

That was not possible. Sharp metal jutted all around. Patrick reached with one hand, unfastened the rope from Jack's belt, and let it drop out of the way. He pushed and shoved on everything he could, but every time he relaxed, the pieces sprang back to where they started.

Jack trembled from fatigue. "I can't hold out much longer." The beam dug into his stomach. He was going to be run through.

Then, unexpectedly, the cap backed away. Someone was shoving the metalwork.

Jack was free. He scrambled up and out of the hole, tripped, and fell next to the person who had saved him.

The man lost his hold on the cap. Released, the broken structure slammed into the spot Jack had been. Patrick ducked down and escaped injury but was unable to come up.

The man in gray was, as Jack had surmised, the escaped German. His uniform, somewhat worse for the wear, was that of a foot soldier.

The fellow sighed heavily and sat down, looking defeated.

Jack reached instinctively into his pocket but paused as soon as he felt the pistol. He withdrew his hand without the weapon. "Thank you."

The soldier nodded. He was young. He couldn't have been more than nineteen years old.

Jack noticed a contingent of English soldiers approaching along a scarp to the west. Now he understood why the German was so dejected. In helping Jack, he had exposed himself. His capture was certain.

"Well…I'm afraid you'll have to go back." It was all Jack could think to say.

The German nodded. Either he understood English, or what Jack was telling him was obvious. He sat still, resigned.

Jack stood up. He felt quite odd. He had never experienced such confused emotions.

Something whizzed so close to his ear that he felt the air pulse, and a fraction of a second later, he heard the crack of a gunshot.

Jack waved urgently at the soldiers. He cupped his hands to his mouth and yelled, "DON'T SHOOT! DON'T SHOOT! HE'S GIVING UP!"

The six soldiers stopped. None appeared to have a weapon raised.

A bullet grazed Jack's shoulder and ripped the fabric of his coat. He waved his hands crisscross over his head and screamed, "NO! HE'S GIVING UP!"

But the German soldier was looking south. Jack turned and saw two men positioned behind brush three hundred yards away. He couldn't make out their features at that distance, but the thin one had a rifle to his shoulder and was sliding the bolt forward.

Whether the result of an instinctive action drilled into him by his military training or some other element in his background, the German sprang up and knocked Jack to the ground. There was an odd thump when the man reached the top of his arc. As the sound of the gunshot reached them, the fellow landed on top of Jack.

The English soldiers came running.

"Stop!" The squad's sergeant pointed at the gunmen. "You out there, put down your rifle!"

Seeing the soldiers, the two gunmen fled.

"Stephens, Talbot, go after them!" the sergeant ordered.

Jack stared at the escaped prisoner. The German had a strange look on his face, half surprise, half agony. He rolled off. Jack tried to understand what had happened.

"Bitte. Bitte," the young man whispered. He fished an envelope out of a pocket and pressed it into Jack's hand. *"Bitte.* Please." His voice was hoarse and thick.

Jack looked at the letter. One corner was wet with bright red blood. The envelope was addressed to Frau Maria Brock of Hamburg, Germany.

"Mama," whispered the German. And with that, he died.

CHAPTER 7

Invitations and Incantations

8-4-6

The British soldiers did not catch the gunmen. They helped Patrick free his truck from the mud and get it back to the main road. A corporal and the sergeant drove Colonel Sir Geoffrey and Jack to Plymouth.

The colonel did not have the strength to say much, but what he did say made Jack miserable. "Gwendolyn will be lost without you, Jack."

Jack did not know how to answer. His great-uncle was wrong. He had been wrong about everything.

The colonel said, "You have to help her."

Jack was silent for a long time, and when he was finally about to speak, he saw that his great-uncle had nodded off. He looked at the dried blood on his coat and quietly began to cry.

After the colonel was admitted to the hospital, Jack went to the postmaster and arranged for Private Karl Brock's letter to be sent to his mother through neutral Netherlands. Jack composed a note to go with it, writing in English because he did not know German. He tore up four drafts before telling Frau Brock simply that her son had died saving a life.

When he went back to the hospital, he found Mrs. Holliwell at his great-uncle's bedside. They sat silently for some time, the ticking of a clock the only discrete sound amid the subdued hubbub of the ward.

Sir Geoffrey had slipped into a coma. The old man looked worn out. Mrs. Holliwell read a book.

Eventually, Jack spoke. "Are Germans evil?"

"Some of them."

"Do you hate them?"

"It's not easy to love people who slaughter your relatives and friends, but that is what I'm commanded to do."

"Uncle Geoff is in the army. He has to kill them. Would he say the same thing?"

"I think so."

Jack looked out the window at the quiet street behind the hospital. Vines trailed along the bordering wall. In a little park beyond it, rhododendrons bloomed pink and white, premature for the season, their colors muted in the evening light. "How do you love someone when you hate what they do?"

"It's not human nature, is it? But if God's spirit is in us, we can feel a little of what He feels and do it, perhaps."

"So we have to accept their cruelty."

"No. Never. That would be a grave error. Hate a person's sin, but love the person."

"What is love?"

"Treating others with consideration and care. Granting a person forgiveness when they ask for it. It doesn't require agreeing with them or enjoying their company." Mrs. Holliwell smiled. "We're not talking about romantic love."

She went back to her book.

Jack listened to his great-uncle's wheezing breath.

"May I borrow this?" Jack picked up the Bible Mrs. Holliwell had put on the wheeled cart beside the bed.

"Of course."

Checking his list of vision verses, he turned to Philippians 4:6. It didn't mean anything to him. He kept reading. He snorted in derision when he came to 4:13. *I can do all things through Christ which strengtheneth me.* The derision was for himself. "Regardless, I can't do anything," he said out loud.

Mrs. Holliwell looked up.

"I don't want…" There were a lot of things Jack Maham didn't want. "Uncle Geoff says I have to help Gwen, or she'll be lost." He shook his head. "There's nothing I can do."

Mrs. Holliwell looked patiently at Jack. "What you are able to do isn't important. Doing what God asks is important."

He stared at nothing. "That's what the lieutenant angel said."

Outside, the street lights came on, and the sky deepened to violet as night settled. Jack was given supper and a cot.

He couldn't get comfortable and did not fall asleep until it was almost morning.

Gwen was alert the moment she woke up. She lay still, watching the red spot of sun on the eastern horizon expand into a disk, unstick itself from the ground, and rise into the pale sky. Everything in her room glowed golden. The night had been tranquil. She was at peace. The sound of footsteps in the hallway outside her room ended that.

A skeleton key clanked in the lock, and the mechanism clicked. Immediately, the door swung open.

Gwen remained motionless and kept her eyes closed. Harkless crossed the floor. Gwen didn't need sight to know what was happening. Rummaging and tinkling sounds provided a clear mental picture.

"Get up, girl."

Gwen pushed herself clumsily to a sitting position and mumbled incoherently like one befuddled.

Harkless sloshed what she supposed was narcotic into a tumbler on the butler's table. Then she pushed Gwen's head back and tipped the glass into her half-open mouth.

Gwen sputtered and coughed. But she gulped down the rust-tainted water without speaking a word. When the glass was empty, she sank down in bed and closed her eyes.

Harkless didn't remain long; the clatter of the latch signaled her departure. But the smell of her French eau de toilette lingered.

Gwen sat up in bed. What had happened to Jack and Uncle Geoffrey? And also Patrick—she supposed it was common Christian courtesy to be concerned for someone's well-being, even if that person was exasperating and not much more than a servant.

For no particular reason, Gwen believed the boys' search had been successful, but the outcome unhappy. Where were they? If they had come back, Jack would have barged in to see her no matter what Miss Harkless did. A cascade of fears gnawed her. The evil spirits scuttling around the house were weaving traps.

She worked up the courage to remove the blanket from her mirror. She got out of bed and swept it away.

The quiescent surface showed nothing out of the ordinary. Still, the room was unnaturally cold. She put on her housecoat.

She went to the door and peered through the keyhole. Bedroom locks were for privacy, not security. Freddie could pick them with a bent piece of metal. Could she do it?

Forming the end of a hairpin to the correct length and angle was not easy. She rummaged in her desk drawers and found a pair of pliers. With a few adjustments, her makeshift pick fit the keyhole. The next challenge was moving the mechanism that drew the bolt. She was about to bend the outer end of the pin for more leverage when she heard voices in the hallway outside.

Miss Harkless sounded crisp with cheerful assurance. "Lady Gwendolyn should be refreshed after so many hours' sleep."

Gwen scowled. It had been scarcely twenty minutes since the woman had forced the brown liquid down her throat. She shoved the bent hairpin into a pocket, sloughed off the housecoat, and threw the garment into the closet. Then she dove into bed and hastily arranged the covers.

"You locked her in?" Mrs. Nellis sounded shocked and angry.

"To keep the boys from bothering her. She needed undisturbed rest."

The two women came into the room.

"Oh!" Miss Harkless said, feigning surprise. "Not awake, m'lady?"

Gwen felt a human body next to her bed. A hand shook her shoulder. Fingers pinched hard, presumably out of Mrs. Nellis's sight. Gwen stayed limp.

"Oh dear. She's taken a turn for the worse."

Gwen heard Mrs. Nellis set something down—likely a breakfast tray.

"Lady Gwen? Lady Gwen?" The cook-turned-housekeeper hadn't used the diminutive for years.

Gwen felt bad, knowing the kindly woman was frightened, but did not respond.

"I'll call Doctor Foley," Mrs. Nellis said. "He should come after all, as Lord Buckleigh requested in his telegram day before yesterday. You shouldn't have told him not to."

"A moment."

Gwen was rolled onto her back and had one of her eyelids pushed up.

"She's groggy. Nothing more. Not in danger. No need for a doctor." Harkless spoke confidently. "Sleep and a little—"

Gwen heard a short intake of breath.

Her eyelid was forced back open. She did her best to stay unfocused and unmoving. What did the eye of a drugged person look like? She prayed. The blink reflex was nearly insuppressible. She couldn't have held out if a wandering cloud had not dropped the light level in the room.

Harkless tilted her head to one side, considering. "Hmm. She needs rest. That's all. Come."

Despite the housekeeper's protest, Harkless locked the door when they left.

Gwen did not dare move for half an hour. When her stomach growled, she slipped out of bed and considered the food on the tray Mrs. Nellis had left on the butler's table: watered-down milk and dry toast. Her heart skipped a beat when she saw the pliers lying next to the tray—had Miss Harkless seen them? Would she wonder what they were doing there?

Gwen had an even worse turn when the lock snapped and the bedroom door opened. She spun around.

"Christopher!" She sagged in relief.

The boy quickly shut the door, dropped the bag he was carrying, and ran to her. "You're all right! Mother said you were dying. You were in a coma yesterday."

"I was drugged."

Christopher balled his fists. "Miss Harkless has to be sacked! Mother *has* to do something."

"Mama won't believe it. The witch has her completely fooled."

"Then I'll pour out her nasty medicine."

"I already did. Out the window."

"Ha! Good for you!" Christopher grinned but then sobered. "But I suppose she'll just make more."

"She did. I snuck to the end of the house where she was mixing up the batch and tossed a hornet's nest into the lab."

"A hornet's nest? You didn't!"

"I did. The hornets were frightfully upset. Miss Harkless ran for a fumigator. Meanwhile, I replaced her potion with water."

"Marvelous!"

"She thinks I'm incapacitated." Gwen picked up the pliers and looked at them contemplatively. "I am, sort of. She's got me locked in."

Christopher handed her a skeleton key. "It works on all our bedroom doors."

"Bless you!"

"And here." He opened his bag.

It was the snacks he had gathered before their journey to Buckton: apples, cheese, and the tin of nuts. There was also a nice hunk of fresh bread and a dish of butter.

"Double-bless you! I'm famished."

"The north end of the house—" Christopher pondered while Gwen spread a great quantity of butter on the bread and ate it greedily. "Workmen are making something there. Mrs. Nellis said they started right after we left and have been at it off and on."

"Making what?" Gwen remembered the construction materials in the courtyard.

"I couldn't find out. Two scary men kept me away."

"Mr. Killen and Mr. Wye." Gwen violated a cardinal rule of etiquette by talking with her mouth full.

"I suppose it has to do with the party."

"Yes, and it can't be good if Miss Harkless is involved."

"I'll get past them next time."

"No, Christopher. Stay away from those men. They're evil. I'm not exaggerating. They'll hurt you."

"I'll be careful."

"Stay *away* from them!"

"If you say so."

"What's happened to Jack?"

"He's in Plymouth with Uncle Geoffrey."

"Good! They found him." She paused. "Plymouth?"

"Uncle Geoffrey's in the hospital. He has pneumonia."

"Oh no!"

"He was abducted, but Jack and Patrick found him at the mine, just as you said they would."

"Abducted?"

"It means kidnapped."

"I know what it means. By whom?"

"I didn't hear. Somebody died."

"Patrick!" Gwen clutched at her chest.

"Not Patrick," Christopher interjected quickly.

Gwen's heart wouldn't slow down. "Then who?"

"I don't know."

Christopher could only say what he had overheard when Mrs. Nellis delivered the message to Lady Buckleigh.

Gwen felt more in the dark than ever.

Christopher opened the window, leaned out, and looked down into the kitchen yard. He wanted to look to the south but couldn't see past the East Tower. "There are autos and lorries in the drive, and all sorts of people are arriving. You can see some of it from here."

"I wish I knew what was going on," Gwen said.

"I'm going to find out."

"Stay away from Miss Harkless and her men," Gwen warned again. "I'm telling you."

Impulsively, Christopher hugged her. "Don't worry."

He let himself out of the room, and she locked the door using the key he had brought her.

She gobbled down the cheese with the toast Mrs. Nellis had brought and then had the apple and some nuts. Then she paced, restless and perplexed. How could she have felt such happiness and confidence three days ago but now be unsure of *anything*? Had she really gone with Freddie to that magnificent city? It was all so vague. The one thing she knew with certainty was that she had placed herself in the Lord's service. Would she come to regret that? And what about the sword and shield? Her memories had lost their precision, but the depictions on Sir Robert's drawing kept her from forgetting.

She picked up her Bible and leafed through Ephesians to find the instructions regarding the full armor of God. The shield represented faith, and the sword the word of God. She couldn't see how metaphorical, spiritual weapons would help in a fight against flesh-and-blood adversaries like Miss Harkless and her men.

Gwen closed the Bible, held it up, and stared at it as if she could learn something from its cover. "Lord, I came back to you. Where did you go?"

She reopened the book and turned to Philippians 4:6. *Be careful for nothing.* That was the language of the King James version. She supposed a more modern translation would say *Don't be anxious about anything.* That wasn't possible in times like these. The next part had its own difficulties: *By prayer and supplication, with* thanksgiving *present your requests to God.* How could anyone in Gwendolyn Maham's circumstances be thankful? Well…the Apostle Paul was imprisoned and beaten many times. It was odd that he could be thankful.

She read the first part of Luke's gospel, because the Christmas story brought better times to mind. The shepherds' reaction to the angels made her smile. Yes, angels were *intimidating*—no doubt about that! Skipping forward, the account of Jesus's resurrection and subsequent meetings with his disciples triggered a peculiar wistfulness. Perhaps she could, after all, pray with thanksgiving. She put down her Bible.

The pliers were still on the butler's table. When she opened a desk drawer to put them away, her attention was drawn to an ordinary prism among the contents. It was one of the scientific gifts her father had given his children, believing everyone was interested in such things. *Patrick would be interested,* she thought to herself. When she took it out and held it in a sunbeam, it glinted and cast swatches of the spectrum. In its facets she saw odd-angled reflections of things in her room. But ultimately, her prism was just a piece of glass.

She retrieved her great-uncle's prism from the pocket of her overcoat and compared the two objects, one in each hand. Uncle Geoffrey's had extra weight. It was more substantial. When it reflected images of the room, those images were more detailed in a way she couldn't put into words. That was the prism's first use: to reveal concealed things.

Show me, Lord. She held the prism between thumb and forefinger and placed it in sunlight. Her room took on the now familiar vibrancy of the Primary World. When she directed the spectral light toward the windows, she saw the interstitial mountains.

The prism glittered brightly. If she turned herself sideways, she would be able to engage its second function and step across the plane to interact with the real substance of things in the Primary World. Or, if she rotated the glass, she could move the plane of demarcation so that it swept past her, as she had done with the hornets. That must have been what had happened on Saturday—Jack had used the prism to create a plane of demarcation. He had done it just before he put the prism on her desk. Except...was that right? Had the glass been shining when she picked it up? She had been too focused on Jack's bullying to notice.

The prism lay exposed but dormant in her palm. She pondered. There were three rectangular facets. Was there a third use? She prayed long and deeply, asking for guidance, and the prism began to radiate a puzzling form of light. The luminance made things it shined on very, very real. It was like the light in the place she had visited with Freddie.

She couldn't help experimenting, though she was wary of causing an accident even worse than trapping herself in the Primary World. At the edge of her consciousness, she was aware of her circulating blood. Or maybe it was the flow of warmth through her body. Randomly, she remembered how the Lord had smiled when she accepted His commission. As she recalled His approval, the prism flared with white incandescence. The light created something like the inverse of shadows: every corner of unused, empty space in her room glowed as if to proclaim that it was *not* empty but that it could, like everything else that had been made, show the glory of its Creator.

But it was no more than a light show. She was both disappointed she hadn't achieved anything and relieved she hadn't caused a calamity.

Then she looked in her mirror. The room reflected in the mirror was lit differently. Depending on how Gwen turned the prism, the room was shades of late afternoon, sunset, or even twilight.

Next, reorienting the prism, she watched the world ripple as if an interstice were forming or shifting from its original position. Each time she lowered her arm and the prism lost the light, however, reality sprang back to what it had been before.

"Lord, I don't understand what it's doing." She lowered the prism out of the sun, and it stopped shining. She set it on her desk beside the ordinary one and compared them closely, looking for differences. In both, she saw the angle-reflected image of her clock. It was noon.

How had it got to be noon? Harkless would be back any minute to dose her. Gwen put everything away and climbed into bed. Sure enough, within minutes, Harkless came in.

This time, Gwen did not feign unconsciousness. Instead, slack-jawed, a bead of drool dripping down her chin, she watched with lifeless eyes.

Harkless filled the drinking glass more than halfway. "Sit up, if you please."

Gwen was not pleased, but she obeyed. She coughed repeatedly. It was partly an act, partly a genuine paroxysm. Much as she hated to admit it, she was not entirely healthy. She reached out her hand and was given the glass. She swallowed the gritty liquid without protest.

The nurse was not so quick to leave this time. She sat down in the armchair and kept watch. Gwen lay down, closed her eyes, and rolled to face away.

Miss Harkless waited. And waited.

What was going on? Gwen began to think the hag intended to stay all afternoon. Finally, she felt a heavy presence lean over her bed. Fingers hovered at her nostrils. With effort, she kept her respiration shallow.

After five more nerve-wracking minutes, footsteps and the sharp snap of the lock signaled that Miss Harkless was gone. Gwen crept to the door and listened with her ear pressed against the wood. Hardly daring to breathe, she lowered her face to the keyhole and peeked out. The hallway was empty.

A little later, hair pinned, wearing the loaned blouse and skirt once more, Gwen slipped out to find her mother. The clothes had not been cleaned or ironed. Gwen had brushed off the worst of the dust and sponged away spider webbing, but the outfit still looked as if it had been worn in a barnyard.

She had no particular plan in mind—just an urgent need to redeem herself and be released from prison. Hearing unfamiliar voices filtering up the East Tower stairwell, she passed by, went to the end of the hallway, and turned right. From there, she padded softly to the library, down its stairs to the second floor, and back east to her parents' rooms.

Lord and Lady Buckleigh's master suite was on the south side of the house. Their private chambers included Lord Buckleigh's study, two dressing rooms, a spacious, modern bathroom, a sitting room, and a single bedroom that had tall windows with a fine view of the expansive front lawn. Upon a time, there had been two bedrooms, but the current master and mistress of the estate shared one, so Lady

Buckleigh had turned the other, which overlooked the gardens, into her day room.

Gwen did not come to these chambers often and felt shy of entering, as she had when she borrowed her mother's gardening dress. She lingered in the open sitting room doorway. No one was there, but a woman's voice came from the connecting day room.

"But, my dear, how have you gotten by without a lady's maid?"

"Mrs. Nellis assists me. And there's Anne when I'm in London."

"I can't see how you manage."

"Oh, I manage. *George* is the problem. He thinks he can dress himself." Lady Buckleigh snorted, making a surprisingly unladylike sound. "He's hopeless without a valet. I have to help him or he looks ridiculous. Everything loose and askew, if not wholly inappropriate."

Gwen gazed out the south-facing sitting room windows. As Christopher had reported, several vehicles stood in the plaza in front of the house. She watched a truck trundle down the service road that led to the kitchen yard.

"You haven't a single maid. Amazing."

"Two women come to clean, and Merrill takes the wash to Buckton. He rather resents using the Rolls as a laundry wagon, I think, but it can't be helped."

Gwen crept to the door to the day room and leaned ever so slowly to peek around the jamb. She was in no danger of being spotted. The two women had their backs to her.

Lady Buckleigh was standing next to her writing desk. The splendid mahogany piece was cluttered with precisely positioned stacks of paper—the birch and cherry inlays framing the leather writing surface couldn't even be seen. But the countess and her visitor, a fashionably dressed stranger, were looking at rows of dinner place cards laid out on a folding table that had been set beside the desk.

"You must trust Livingston," the elegant red-haired stranger said. "He is quite the best butler anyone has ever had. He has already finished his reconnoitering and has the staff jumping. I've kept my bargain and filled your entire order—six footmen and eight maids:

mine plus some of Jenny's and Lady Cheltham's. Livingston is very eager to meet the chef."

"Monsieur Léger arrives this evening," Lady Buckleigh said.

"Mrs. Nellis is a humble soul, but she takes no offense at being superseded?"

"None whatsoever. She is delighted to be sous-chef. It is a relief for her."

Gwen gazed around the day room, looking for clues that might reveal more about what was going on. Nothing had been placed on the low table where tea was served when Lady Buckleigh entertained guests. There were no handbags casually left on any of the cream, gold, and cyan upholstered chairs or settee by the table, on the ornate Turkish rugs, or anywhere else. Gwen glanced at the bookcase near the hallway door. It contained a variety of reference books: architecture, cuisine, jewelry, garden design, travel, and others. Its bottom shelf was devoted to binders with block-lettered labels. Incongruously, next to the elegant bookcase stood two filing cabinets more appropriate to a business office than a chamber where a lady welcomed close friends. Nothing was new or out of place; Gwen didn't learn anything.

Lady Buckleigh touched a menu card. "This will have to be redone. Major McCray has been promoted to lieutenant colonel. Happened the other day." She moved the card aside. "George is pleased. Lieutenant Colonel McCray was his chief engineer before the war."

Gwen's ears perked up. Were they talking about Patrick's father? She stood behind the door jamb, out of sight. She didn't mean to spy—well, actually she did, but had not expected to.

"Will Lieutenant Colonel McCray be staying in the house?"

"No. In Buckton, with his son."

"I did not see another McCray on your list. Is the son invited?"

"He's rather outside our social sphere." Lady Buckleigh tapped a finger to her chin. "Hmm. There will be a small contingent of young people, and his father *is* the guest of honor. Perhaps we should invite him, after all."

"His Christian name?"

"Patrick."

Gwen's jaw dropped. It was surprising that Patrick's father would attend a Cabinet dinner. That Patrick himself might appear was inconceivable.

Lady Buckleigh sighed. "Young McCray and Jack don't get along. Jack's fault, of course." She shrugged. "Oh, let's invite him. He's quite clever and polite, though a little awkward." She considered. "He might be overwhelmed by the company."

Gwen stood motionless and open-mouthed. Her pulse raced, and she felt hot. She revised her plan. She crept out of the sitting room and around to the day room's hallway door. She knocked.

"Yes? Come in?" The countess sounded puzzled—no doubt because servants only appeared when summoned and didn't knock.

Gwen opened the door.

Lady Buckleigh's eyes flew wide. "Gwen!"

Keeping herself stiffly erect, Gwen entered the room with all the calm and confidence she could muster. "Mother, I wish to speak with you."

"What are you doing out of bed?"

"Why should I be in bed at this time of day?"

The countess hastened to her daughter. "You collapsed. Have you forgotten? Sit down. I'm going to ring for Mrs. Nellis to help you back to bed." She steered Gwen toward a chair. At least, that is what she tried to do. Gwen planted her feet and held onto the heavy bookcase.

The stranger watched, curious.

"Mother, I'm quite recovered."

Lady Buckleigh nearly replied that Gwen looked pale, but her daughter's skin was a healthy color. Her concern fizzled. It was as if her inner voice of counsel was no longer there to push.

"I'm strong again, Mother. Really, I am."

Lady Buckleigh stopped tugging on the solid and immovable girl. She did the only thing she could. She made introductions.

"Miranda, do you remember my daughter? Gwendolyn, this is Lady Hamilton."

Gwen nodded. "I'm very pleased to see you, Lady Hamilton." She finally placed the woman. "Oh! Leona and Pamela's mother!" But she bit her lip. Defining a lady in terms of her daughters was discourteous. To avoid an awkward moment, she asked the first question that came to mind: "Will Pamela be coming to the party?"

"Yes, she will."

Gwen covered her mouth and pretended to cough; otherwise, she would have laughed. Jack was going to be mortified. Gwen had heard a very funny story about Jack and Pamela Hamilton.

"It is so nice to see you, Gwendolyn. You are looking well." Lady Hamilton spoke the formulaic politeness out of habit. Then she smiled but winced slightly. Given the mother-daughter exchange she had just witnessed, the comment was perhaps inappropriate.

Lady Buckleigh's brows knit together. "Well, perhaps…"

"Mother, it's about my dress."

"Dress?"

The countess seemed only then to notice what Gwen was wearing.

Lady Hamilton stared openly at the dingy, wrinkled blouse and skirt.

Instead of trying to explain, Gwen attacked. "My party dress has not been ordered."

"You will not be attending the party."

"Has Miss Harkless told you that I'm still sick?"

"Miss Harkless has given me detailed reports of your condition." Lady Buckleigh pressed her lips together tightly. "And irresponsible behavior."

Lady Hamilton became especially interested in the paperwork on the card table.

"You mean leaving my room? Why should that be irresponsible?"

"Because you can barely sit up in bed!" The countess frowned, realizing her statement was not supported by current evidence.

"Perhaps I am truly on my deathbed. If so, let me have a final happy memory. Please order me a gown."

"There isn't time."

The visitor couldn't help herself. "Gwendolyn could borrow one of Pamela's."

Gwen looked at Lady Hamilton and then at her mother.

The countess closed her eyes. She could have pointed out that Gwen was too young. But that should have been said first—it would sound argumentative at this point.

"Pamela has a blue gown that would go marvelously with Gwendolyn's eyes." Lady Hamilton studied Gwen's thin figure, especially her chest. "It might have to be taken in a little…" A lot, actually. "But my Agnes is a wonder with a needle. Shall I have her see to it?"

Gwen lit up. "Oh, would you? I'd be ever so grateful!"

Lady Buckleigh chose not to fight. It was a strategic move. There was no need. Her daughter would not be able to keep up the pretense of health for long. "Very well. I won't stand in your way. I fear you'll regret it."

"Thank you, Mama! I'm fine." Gwen backed to the door, retreating before her mother changed her mind.

"Perhaps at this moment, you are. Because of bedrest and medicine."

"I haven't taken any of Miss Harkless's so-called medicine in the last twenty-four hours. I put water in her bottles. I—"

Gwen was suddenly aware of a presence behind her. She turned.

Her tormentor was there, in the doorway. The smile on the woman's face expressed benevolent concern, but the fury in her eyes was terrifying.

"Lady Gwendolyn, you must come back to your room." Miss Harkless's fingers curled around Gwen's arm. "I'll help you."

"Mama…!"

"Go, Gwen, or I'll withdraw my permission. If you're strong enough, you can attend the party."

"Mama, she's poisoning me!"

It was futile. There wasn't even any leave-taking. Fingernails extended, Harkless pulled Gwen out the door and down the hallway. The woman did not look muscular but was strong.

Gwen blinked stinging tears as she stumbled along. All her efforts had been for naught. Why wouldn't her mother believe her? Where was God?

Mr. Wye met them in the East Tower. He had Miss Harkless's black medical bag. "Someone's been misbehav'n."

They took her to her room. The nurse uncorked one of the brown medicine bottles and sniffed. She put it to her lips and tasted a drop of the contents. The fury distorting her face was extraordinary.

"How? How did you do it?" The bottles had been in her possession the entire time.

"*Magic!*" Gwen cried, inspired. She laughed derisively. "*Real* magic. I wove an intricate spell that a feckless charlatan like you could never fathom, much less cast. A warding that turns witches' potions into water!"

Harkless drew back her arm to slap and barely stopped herself from leaving evidence of abuse. Who did this naïve little twit think she was? How dare she! Had she spent years deciphering obscure and arcane texts so dark that even a hard man would quail? What did the witless brat know of the self-denial and iron discipline required to control spirits? The child was insignificant. She had no ability whatsoever to perform magic.

Use a spell to change a narcotic to water? Even a novice knew that was impossible. Everything had a fundamental nature that did not change. Certainly, there were remedies and elixirs, even neutralizing agents, but they had to be taken as antidotes. An incantation was useless for such purposes. But…could it be the work of a spirit? Harkless herself was the master of several powerful beings. However, turning a narcotic into water did not seem like the deed of a spirit. How had the girl done it?

The woman recovered her wits, opened her bag, and produced an alarmingly large hypodermic syringe. She slid its long needle through the wax top of a vial and drew the plunger to fill the glass reservoir with yellow liquid.

Wye pinned Gwen's arms behind her back.

"I'll put a curse on you!" Gwen yelled, kicking.

"Keep still or this will hurt." Miss Harkless smirked. "More than it has to." She held the syringe like a weapon.

"No!" Gwen screamed. She stomped hard on Wye's foot. He stumbled backward. Snarling, he slung her against her desk.

Wrenching an arm free, Gwen thrust her hand down on the desk to catch her balance. Her fingers tightened around something hard, angular, and hot: the prism. She had left it on the desktop.

"*Hey! You!* Let go of my sister!" Christopher stood in the doorway, flaming mad.

Harkless whirled around.

Wye was distracted, and Gwen pulled free. She grabbed her fountain pen and waved it like a wand at her mirror. "Mirare, mirare," she intoned. "Lumen optimus orthograph!"

The ersatz wand and pseudo-Latin nonsense were a show to distract attention from her other hand.

It worked. Harkless looked into the mirror.

Gwen extended the prism into a sunbeam. Light of all colors flared and bloomed, setting walls, furnishings, and persons aglow.

Harkless let out a strangled gasp; Gwen was radiating an intense aura. More than a blinding glare, the light from the mirror was a cascade of gleaming darts. The woman convulsed as if something in her was sparking and writhing like an electric eel. She staggered backward. She dropped the syringe, needle pointed down. The hypodermic stuck in the floor and stood there quivering.

"Come," she screeched at Wye. She snatched up her doctor's bag and shoved Christopher aside to get out the door.

Wye gulped and followed on her heels.

"Did you see her, Christopher?" Gwen asked in a low voice. "Did you see what Miss Harkless looked like in the mirror?"

CHAPTER 8

Lost

1-16-33

Jack skimmed the Bible to know the character of its heroes, thinking it would give him hope. It didn't. Many of them were unwise and petty. Quite a few were seriously flawed and poor choices for their roles. Why had God relied on them?

There were exceptions, of course. Daniel was able and faithful. Ruth was praiseworthy. But Abraham and Jacob were deceivers, and Moses and David were murderers. Solomon permitted and even abetted idolatry, triggering corruption that led to the obliteration of the kingdoms of Israel and Judah. Archeologists had dug up plenty of artifacts from their ruins.

Could not better men have been found? True, individuals somehow rose above their failings. Esther saved her people despite her fear. The obtuse and often weak-willed apostles grew competent and bold after Jesus rose from the dead. Yet all of history was woven around mediocre human beings.

What on earth was God doing? The present was murky and the future frightful. More than ever, Jack wanted to run and never stop. He put the Bible down and stared out the window.

Mrs. Holliwell watched Jack from her chair. The haunted look in his eyes concerned her. She urged him to go home. She said, reasonably, that Lord and Lady Buckleigh should be given a firsthand account of

Sir Geoffrey's condition.

An administrator arranged a car to take Jack to Maham House.

Gwen sat at her dressing table brushing her hair. There were too many puzzle pieces still to find. The party was being held to clandestinely gather the prime minister's Cabinet members for an undeclared and unrecorded meeting—that was obvious. Most likely, the agenda had something to do with Maham and Carter's business. Medicines were hardly controversial. Her father's company had never manufactured chemical weapons; perhaps it was going to start. But why would that require high-level attention or extraordinary secrecy? All countries were using poison gas on each other's soldiers.

Miss Harkless was tangled up in whatever was going on. The woman's head was an animated collage of mouths and eyes put together like a Picasso—that's what Gwen had seen in her mirror. Had it been a symbolic vision or the woman's actual Primary World appearance? Whatever the answer, Miss Harkless was warped. Were she and her men planning to assassinate the prime minister? Perhaps his entire Cabinet? To what end? Miss Harkless had always claimed to consort with spirits…

Patrick might be able to figure out what was going on.

Arrrg! Why did it always come back to Patrick? Gwen closed her eyes tightly. She absolutely had to make him understand about the kiss. It meant nothing.

Where was Jack? What about Uncle Geoffrey? Gwen needed information. The party guest list might provide insight. She should have a look at it. She pinned her hair and prepared to sneak out. But as she was about to leave, Killen and Wye barged into her room.

"What do you think you're doing?" Gwen demanded.

"None o' your concern," Mr. Wye said.

Killen lifted the mirror, took it to the doorway, and rotated it ninety degrees to carry it through.

"How dare you? That's mine!"

It was a heavy piece. Killen handled it as if it had no weight at all.

Gwen was speechless. Theft of her property was clear grounds for Miss Harkless's immediate dismissal. Mr. Wye's creepy gaze lingered on her.

She had an unpleasant notion. Her mother was anxious and preoccupied with complex preparations. Miss Harkless was helping with some mysterious part of it. The nurse wouldn't be dismissed. She would claim to have asked and obtained permission to use the mirror for some purpose associated with the party. She would call Gwen's accusation a wicked lie. Gwen was sure that would happen.

Wye followed his partner through the door. Out in the corridor, Killen strapped the mirror to a dolly and rolled it away. Gwen went after the big man. Wye blocked her. She sidestepped. Wye matched her move.

"Get out of my way." Gwen looked into the man's eyes and wished she hadn't. He was as cold-blooded as a reptile.

"You're to keep to bed. Nurse's orders." Wye smiled congenially. "Like me to tuck you in?"

Gwen backed into her room and shut the door.

Miss Harkless paced in fits and starts around the mirror. Per her instructions, Mr. Killen had brought it to a locked and barred room on the second floor of the North Wing. Her innards seethed; it was as if corrosive bubbles were roiling around her organs and under her skin. Gwendolyn Maham had some power, after all. But the brat could not possibly understand what she was doing. She had blundered into something.

Harkless was furious that her plans had been disrupted. She was even more furious that she had been threatened. Absolutely, mind-bending furious.

What, she thought, if the girl should have an accident?

The theft of her mirror and inability to do anything about it made Gwen as fidgety as a cat in a wire cage, so the arrival of Lady Hamilton's maid was a welcome distraction. Agnes was no more than twenty years old. She had a pleasant face and slender fingers.

The gown she brought was gorgeous. The silk flowed like water, and its royal blue color matched Gwen's eyes. But the garment was very loose on Gwen, especially around her chest. The décolletage opened like a cavern.

Agnes was quick and sure. She pinned and marked the borrowed gown in a dozen places and stepped back to study the result. "A little more, I think." She pulled the material tighter and adjusted the pins until the dress draped perfectly. "It's beautiful on you, m'lady."

Gwen admired herself in her dressing table mirror. She felt effervescent. It had been years since looking at herself had given her any pleasure. The dress really did look beautiful on her. Now the loss of her full-height mirror made her especially upset.

"You have lustrous hair, m'lady," Agnes said as she helped Gwen remove the garment. "Like spun gold."

"Thank you."

"I'll have the alterations done tomorrow morning."

"That would be splendid, Agnes. Thank you ever so much!"

"Will there be anything else, m'lady?"

Gwen was eager to talk with another young woman and wanted to ask about current fashions. It was evident, however, that the seamstress was keen to get on with her duties. "No. Thank you, Agnes."

Shadows of trees were lengthening toward the east when Jack caught sight of Maham House. Arriving home should have been comforting, but his mood remained dark. He had not decided what he would say to his mother and father. He couldn't tell them where he had really been or what he had done for the past four days. They would think him insane.

The car drove past the wrought-iron gates into the long tree-lined drive that bordered the front lawn. Near the plaza in front of the house, Jack directed the driver to turn onto the road to the service entrance.

Patrick and another man were unloading an ice truck in the kitchen yard. For a few seconds, Jack felt lighter and less alone. Then his great-uncle's warning of impending betrayal brought him back down.

"Thanks for the ride," Jack said to his driver, letting himself out of the car rather than waiting for the door to be opened for him. "Kitchen's through there. Cook will give you tea if you ask."

"Thank you, sir. I will."

Jack walked to the ice truck. How would McCray betray him? His impulse was to ask Patrick why he had come to Maham House. The question was almost from his brain to his mouth when he realized how stupid it would sound—obviously, Patrick was delivering ice. Instead, Jack said, "There are two of you." It sounded almost as stupid.

"Yes, m'lord." Patrick addressed Jack formally since an adult was present. He inclined his head toward the other deliveryman. "Bill gave me a lift. I've come for my airplane."

"Ah. Quite." Jack glanced at Bill. The man could have been in his early twenties, but it wasn't easy to tell his age. The skin on one side of his face was bizarrely stretched and waxy. After the initial shock, Jack didn't know where to look.

"Would you like me to help you start your airplane?" Jack asked Patrick.

The disfigured man waved at Patrick. "Go on, Paddy. I'll finish up."

"Thanks, Bill. I'm much obliged for the ride." Patrick deposited his work gloves and tongs in the truck. "See you tomorrow."

The two boys set off toward the field where they had tied down the F.B.5.

"What happened to your mate's face?" Jack asked when they were out of earshot.

"Mortar shell. Close thing, but Bill was lucky. He was down in a trench. Didn't lose any limbs, and his eyes are fine. Bit deaf, though. That's common."

Jack didn't think Bill was very lucky.

They walked in silence. Jack, not watching where he was going, stumbled over a root. Should he tell Patrick to stay away from Maham House? The order would seem hostile and petty. He couldn't give the reason—calling a man a traitor was no light thing.

They emerged from the trees onto the open field and walked to the airplane. Patrick checked it thoroughly, inspecting the engine, struts, wires, and control mechanisms. Jack unfastened the tie-downs.

Patrick reached into a compartment and handed Jack a flashlight. "This is the one the angel gave you."

"Thanks."

Patrick climbed into the cockpit, this time with some confidence. The weather was good, and there was still an hour until sunset. He donned his flying helmet.

Jack stood next to the airplane. "Listen, McCray…"

Patrick waited.

"Don't crash."

Patrick smiled. "Thank you, m'—Mayfield. I'll see you soon."

Jack ducked under the struts and heaved the propeller. He had to spin it several times before the engine started. He ducked out and pulled away the chocks.

Patrick taxied a short distance, ran the engine to full power, and took off. He circled once, waved, and flew east.

Arriving in Buckton, he made the smoothest landing of his life. Actually, the only smooth landing of his life. He dragged the F.B.5 into its hangar, went to his house, and, as was his custom when arriving home, checked the mailbox.

The single envelope inside bore the Maham family crest. He slit it open and was amazed to find an invitation to the upcoming party. A separate note, written in beautiful script on expensive stationery, informed him that he would be provided with appropriate attire. The author had assumed, correctly, that Patrick had nothing suitable in his wardrobe. He was to come to Maham House on the morrow for a fitting. The letter also requested that, before the party, Patrick consult his father regarding protocols and the proper ways to address various guests.

He couldn't have known since it was unsigned, but the letter was written by Lady Buckleigh herself.

Mrs. Nellis made big pots of hearty mutton stew for the servants' supper. Christopher asked her to give Gwen some. It didn't take much to convince her. The cook-turned-housekeeper had never believed Miss Harkless's dietary orders were any good.

Christopher put a bowl of it on Gwen's dinner tray and took it upstairs.

Jack encountered the borrowed butler, Livingston, in the East Lobby and learned that his mother and father were in Lady Buckleigh's day room. He went up to see them.

His report took less than five minutes. Lord Buckleigh was sad to hear that his uncle's condition was deteriorating, and Lady Buckleigh was not entirely unsympathetic, but they were in the midst of approving menus, room assignments, and last-minute schedule changes. Anyway, English people were not supposed to be emotional.

Jack told them that Uncle Geoff had been kidnapped by anarchists, that he had escaped into a mine shaft, and that McCray had seen smoke from his signal fire. Soldiers assisted with the rescue and took Uncle Geoff to the hospital in Plymouth. Jack did not mention being shot at or saved by the German. And, of course, he said nothing about anything supernatural.

Judging by his parents' acceptance of his story, Jack's news didn't conflict with anything they had already been told.

After leaving his mother's day room, Jack went up to the third floor. When he entered the East Wing hallway, he saw a strange man peering through the keyhole in his sister's door.

"WHAT DO YOU THINK YOU'RE DOING!" Jack stormed at the man.

Wye jumped up and faced the irate boy. "I'm here to get—get a syringe that Nurse Harkless left behind."

"You were peeping at my sister!"

The door opened. "What's going on?" Christopher came out of Gwen's room.

"Who are you?" Jack demanded of Wye.

"Nurse Harkless's assistant."

Gwen, wearing her mother's gardening dress because she had sent her borrowed clothes for cleaning, took one look at Wye and strode purposefully toward the East Tower. "Jack—let's go see Mother."

She clutched the prism in her hand, having gotten it out to show Christopher what it could do.

"Hey!" Wye hastened after her.

"Get away from me!"

Jack formed up at her side.

"Stop!" Wye caught them as they passed through a flood of light from a west-facing room. He reached for Gwen's arm.

Christopher kicked Wye's calf. The man whirled on him. The little boy skipped backward.

Wye scowled but continued his twirl so that he had swung full circle in an instant. The hallway was empty. He froze. He looked into the open bedroom. The two kids were not there. He took a few steps toward the East Tower. The boy and girl were gone. Vanished. He spun and looked back.

The youngest child was grinning at him.

"Have you seen ghosts?" Christopher asked in a voice full of mystery. "Go tell the witch!"

When Wye had turned his back, Gwen had thrust the prism into the light, performed her sideways trick, and swept the plane of demarcation around herself and Jack. The two of them were on the Norman-era ramp inside the interstice.

"What have you done?" Jack asked apprehensively.

"It's all right. We have the prism. We can go in and out." Gwen pointed at Wye. "He's a tad unsettled, don't you think?"

The man was blinking and turning round and round at the bottom of the Norman incline.

Jack recovered his composure. "I've an idea!" He took out his flash-light and switched it on. He aimed its light into Wye's eyes and advanced down the interstitial ramp. He was careful to stay inside the interstice.

Faced with a spectral light from no apparent source, the man's jaw dropped.

Gwen joined her brother. "That's like what you did to Gideon Moran." She smiled. "This time, I approve."

Wye's face was fractions of an inch from the interstice. Gwen pulled a pin from her hair and poked his forehead. The man jumped and yelped.

Gwen laughed but an instant later recoiled when Wye lunged at her.

"*Ghosts,* are yer?" The villain charged around like a blind man trying to seize a disobedient child, appearing on one side of the interstice and then the other. "I don't think ye're ghosts. Come out of that spirit world if yer know what's good for yer!"

Inside the interstice, Gwen and Jack stood still, shocked. Christopher shrank away.

"We know yer game, we do, Harkless 'n' I." Wye strode toward the East Tower. "Go tell 'er ladyship whatever yer want. Yer won't like the result." He went into the tower and down the stairs.

"Good riddance!" Christopher yelled at his back.

Gwen and Jack stepped out of the interstice so their brother could see them. Gwen's face was bloodless. "Does he know about interstices?"

"I don't know." Jack stared after the man. "We better anchor back to silhouette."

Gwen handed her brother the prism. "Here."

Jack stared at the lump of glass. Slowly, he raised it until sunlight struck its facets. A small patch of color, mainly orange and red, appeared on the wall.

Please, God, Jack prayed silently, looking into the prism. *Please do something.*

The stillness in the hallway deepened.

Lord, show me what to do.

He stared into the prism. But instead of an answer, he saw his sister's confused face reflected in a facet.

Gwen didn't know why her brother was waiting. "What did you do when we came home on Monday?" she asked. "When I've used it,

I've thought of the way Jesus limited himself, and how I can do what he did. Then I've asked God to change me. Like turning sideways."

"Then…show me your way." Jack gave her the prism.

Just then, the last of the direct light disappeared, and the hallway dimmed. The sun was setting.

The prism cast an anemic spectrum. "This light isn't good," Gwen said.

"Hurry up." Jack glanced at the north end of the hallway, remembering the demons he had seen there on Saturday. "We're vulnerable."

"The prism is yours, Jack. You'll have to do it."

He made no move to take it. Instead, he pointed his flashlight at it.

Now Gwen saw an image of silhouette inside the glass. She created a plane of demarcation, turned it, and prayed. The world swung round. The interstice winked out, and the modern hallway was seamless.

Jack sagged in relief.

"Here." Once again, Gwen pushed the prism at her brother.

He looked at it as if it were a hand grenade missing its pin. "Tomorrow. I'll practice tomorrow. You keep it until then."

"Why?"

"Because demons know I can sense them."

Gwen drew back, brow furrowed, confused.

He walked toward her room. She followed.

"What are we going to do about Miss Harkless?" Christopher asked.

"I need to see Patrick," Gwen said.

Jack stopped. "I don't think McCray will be able to come here anymore."

Gwen waved her hands. "It's not what you think! It's not what you think!"

It was Jack's turn to be confused.

"Patrick's father will be the guest of honor at the party," Gwen said hastily. "So Patrick might know the real reason the PM and his Cabinet are coming here."

"I can tell you that," Jack said. "They're going to discuss a new type of chemical weapon."

Gwen frowned. "Why do they need to have a secret meeting for that?"

"It's how they're going to use it. Father wants to drop it on German cities. Uncle Geoff told me."

"The Germans have been bombing London," Gwen said hesitantly. "I suppose it's the same."

"Uncle Geoff doesn't like it."

"Neither do I, but it's the sort of thing everyone is doing." She went into her room. She was strangely irritated. Jack knew all about the Cabinet's business. There was no need for her to speak with Patrick, after all. She didn't know why she was irritated. She was irritated that she was irritated.

Jack wandered to Gwen's desk and stood there. "You were right about Whitebarrow." He related what had happened at the mine. He included details he hadn't told his parents, the soldiers, or the constable who had taken his statement in Plymouth.

Gwen dragged her desk chair to the butler's table and sat down to eat the mutton stew. She had never seen Jack so completely adrift.

Everyone was quiet for a long time after Jack's somber account of the German's sacrifice.

When it was apparent that her brother would say no more, Gwen said, "I stopped Miss Harkless from drugging me." She explained what she had done. "Oh," she said offhandedly, "Mother has invited Patrick to the party."

Jack stared. He sighed and shook his head, defeated.

They talked about the construction in the North Wing. It was a short conversation because none of them knew anything about it.

Jack gave Gwen his flashlight. "In case you need it." Then the boys said good night.

Gwen locked her door and left the key turned in the keyhole so no one could peep through. She took a long hot bath and felt almost good, though exhausted. She said her prayers, climbed into bed, and was asleep in no time despite the anxieties whirling in her head. Neither Harkless nor her henchmen came to bother her.

She woke up at two o'clock in the morning. After tossing for an hour, unable to get comfortable, she got out of bed and put on her housecoat. Not bothering to pin her hair, she took the prism and Jack's flashlight and quietly slipped out of her room.

The East Tower stairwell was cold and riddled with pockets of deep shadow; happily, the flashlight dispelled the darkness. She waited for more than a minute on the second-floor landing. Her mind played tricks on her—she imagined she saw motion out of the corner of her eye.

Exiting on the second floor, she half expected Mr. Wye to jump out at her. But the corridors were unwatched.

The door to her mother's day room was locked, and Gwen's skeleton key would not open it. She stood there, thinking. Using the flashlight and prism, she viewed the Primary World, hoping to find an interstitial gap to slip through. No such luck. She dropped the prism back into her pocket—and heard a light clink. She had forgotten that her makeshift lock pick was there.

She tried using it. It slipped neatly into the keyhole but wouldn't turn the mechanism. She kept working, praying for success, glancing nervously down the hallway. Miss Harkless's bedroom wasn't too far away.

Just when Gwen was about to give up, the lock clicked. She grinned triumphantly.

After carefully shutting the door behind herself, she peered into the prism, checking the day room for interstices. She saw one: a spiral staircase in the southwest corner of the room where the modern dwelling intersected an ancient turret.

She worked by flashlight. She found the party guest list on the writing desk and used her mother's fountain pen and stationery to make a copy. When done, she slipped the paper back into place and left everything as it had been.

Surveying the room, her eyes were drawn to the table normally used to serve tea. She noted the items lying there: Freddie's medals, photographs, and a stack of envelopes.

Gwen sat on the settee by the table and read through Freddie's letters. She had never seen them before. They were confident and cheerful, as expected of a good English soldier, but here and there a term or phrase would strike a strange chord. In one letter, Freddie mentioned that he had participated in a foot beauty contest. In another, he reported drinking toasts to comrades who had left his regiment. In a third, he praised his cat Lilah's outstanding hunting techniques. His droll prose invited the reader's mind to fill in between the lines: skin disease, corpses, and rats.

Gwen was so absorbed that she didn't hear the soft footsteps until it was almost too late. She jumped up. With no time to spare, she shoved the letter she was reading behind a cushion, yanked the prism from her pocket, placed it in the flashlight beam, turned sideways, and hid in the interstice she had seen in the corner.

Lady Buckleigh entered and looked around the room.

Gwen perched on the narrow, wedge-shaped steps of the Norman-era spiral stairs. But her foot slid when she shifted to ensure she was entirely hidden within the interstice. She flung out an arm to catch herself and fumbled the flashlight. It fell on a step and came to rest with its beam pointing directly at the photographs on the table. She stayed perfectly still. If she slipped a second time, she would topple into the day room.

Freddie's photographs glowed with an ethereal aura. Lady Buckleigh stared at them for nearly a minute. "Freddie…" the countess whispered, full of wonder. "Darling…" She held out a hand as if expecting to touch her son. "I'm going to see you in two days, you know. We'll be able to speak with one another."

Gwen went rigid. What was her mother saying? Slowly and carefully, she reached down, got her hand on the flashlight, and switched it off.

The photographs stopped glowing.

"Oh!" Lady Buckleigh stood silently for a time and then, to Gwen's dismay, settled onto the settee.

Ten minutes later, the countess had not moved. She stared at the photographs, giving every indication of staying all night.

Gwen hugged herself. She gazed up the spiral staircase. Perhaps there was an exit on the third floor. With utmost care, she climbed. But she did not find a way to the third floor. Instead, after four and a half revolutions, the stair opened onto a platform.

Gwen was atop the highest tower of the Norman fortress. The cold wind found its way up under the hem of her housecoat and down its collar. Her nightgown provided little insulation. She had a clear view in all directions. The moon had set, but by starlight she made out the roof and towers of the house, the turrets and battlements of the Norman fortress, and the moorlands and mountains beyond.

Something black undulated along the eastern horizon. Gwen shivered, not liking it. She scanned the sky, watching scudding clouds.

Then she looked north, toward Whitebarrow. There, the fabric of the Primary World was different than elsewhere. Mended? Improved, somehow?

It crossed Gwen's mind that the German soldier's actions to save Jack had done something. She needed to talk to Patrick after all. Patrick understood interstices. She needed to ask him if they could be altered.

She took another long look and then crept back downstairs.

Lady Buckleigh was still on the settee.

"Go to bed, Mama," Gwen muttered.

As if hearing the plea, the countess set down the picture she had been holding. She sighed, blinked tears from her eyes, and rose. After a minute, she quietly left the room.

Gwen moved quickly, re-anchoring herself to silhouette as she walked. She retrieved the letter she had stashed behind the cushion and set it with the others. She opened the hallway door quicker than she should have; the hinges produced a short but sharp squeak. The lock made even more noise. To her oversensitive ears, the sound of the bolt was as loud as a gunshot.

She hurried to the East Tower and climbed its stairs. Three minutes later, she was in bed. Five more, and she was asleep.

She had one prophetic dream that night. Its meaning was clear. Jack had to be in the North wing at half past three o'clock the following afternoon.

Hi Lara,

No depressing news this time. Instead, a little backstory, since you asked.

English family estates and assets passed, along with titles (duke, marquis, earl, viscount, and baron), from father to eldest son. There was a reason for that. If inheritance were divided among all children, the land and money would have been sliced into smaller and smaller pieces until the Duke or Marquis or Earl of Somewhere or Other would have been the Duke or Marquis or Earl of Nowhere. So this system, known as primogeniture, ensured the continuation of the nobility. Younger sons went into the military, or the government, or perhaps some prestigious business. That was the expectation for George Maham, second son of Richard Maham, the Sixth Earl of Buckleigh. To the slight annoyance of his parents, George wanted to be a research chemist. He was always happiest in a laboratory.

George's mother tried to arrange a marriage, but her headstrong son would have none of it, declaring that arranged marriages were a relic of the feudal past long dead, and he had not the slightest intention of disturbing its grave. He was pleased to learn that the object of his mother's matchmaking designs was of the same mind. Lady Cecilia was the third daughter of a duke, and her mother thought George suitable matrimonial material. However, as the youngest daughter, Ceil was given more leeway than her sisters. Furthermore, her father was secretly willing to indulge her desire to elope with the man of her dreams—who she expected to find at any moment—and live adventurously ever after. So George and Cecilia conspired to foil their mothers' plans. Corresponding secretly through friends, they avoided encountering each other.

But after graduating from university, George went to tour the Far East and then the United States where, while a guest at the estate of a wealthy industrialist, he by chance encountered Lady Cecilia. They had a roaring good laugh over the coincidence, spent the afternoon bemoaning the machinations of matchmaking mothers, and, having had such a good time, spent the next day together and every next day after that. George was not the most luminous conversationalist, but wandering the rugged New England seashore, trees aflame in autumn gold and red, he outdid himself with Lady Cecilia, who brought out the best in him. They were married in 1895 to the everlasting merriment of their mothers.

In 1898, George's elder brother William died childless in the Sudan on one of Lord Kitchener's exploits. George became Baron Mayfield and, upon his father's death a year later, the Seventh Earl of Buckleigh. So, in the end, Cecilia's mother got precisely the match she wanted for her daughter.

Had things been different, Lady Buckleigh would have been seeking to steer her own daughter toward a suitable marriage—preferably, a man with a title. The brilliant son of a high government official or military officer would have been acceptable so long as he was from an upper-class family. But with Gwen's deteriorating condition and the war, in 1918 there was no thought of steering her anywhere.

Best,

Kirk

CHAPTER 9

Dartrun

3-12-17

Work around Maham House proceeded in a whirl of purposeful skirmishes. Maids aired out bedrooms, prepared fireplaces, turned mattresses, and spread fresh linens on beds. Footmen cleaned floors and polished silver.

Before the war, servants had performed their jobs with smooth, well-practiced skill. But the old staff was gone, the house in a general state of neglect, and the temporary help not a well-oiled unit. Livingston, the butler, was everywhere, organizing, instructing, and helping when necessary.

Bathrooms were scrubbed and stocked with towels and soaps, rugs taken outside and beaten, clocks wound. Formalities of class were strictly observed. Each group had its place and status.

The construction materials Gwen had seen in the North Wing courtyard were gone; only piles of sawdust remained. Carpenters and plasterers had finished their work; now hangers were trooping in with rolls of wallpaper and buckets of paste.

Mr. Wye lurked balefully about the house on unspecified business. Mr. Killen was absent.

Patrick arrived at half past eight and was sent to Agnes. She had the jacket, pants, and shirt that had been ordered for him. She marked them and promised they would be ready midafternoon.

Patrick hoped to encounter Lady Gwendolyn. Overhearing a maid grumble about faulty lights in guest bedrooms, he offered his services. He made four trips between the second floor and the electrical boxes in the servants' quarters, replacing fuses and triple-checking every circuit even though he didn't need to. Perhaps Lady Gwendolyn would appear by chance on a stair or in a corridor. But she didn't, and he did not dare go near her bedroom.

Gwen was not in her bedroom. She was not anywhere in the house. She had snuck out to spy on Jack, who had gone to practice with the prism by himself.

Patrick, preparing to leave disappointed, ran into Christopher.

The little boy lit up. "There you are, old chap! Good. Gwen wants you."

Patrick's heart hiccupped. "Sorry? What?"

"She wants to ask you something." The boy lowered his voice conspiratorially. "About interstices."

"Oh." But Patrick's pulse didn't slow.

He was directed to a place down by the Dartrun River. Gwen had escaped the house through the secret tunnel; Patrick took an aboveground route through the gardens and woods. It was late enough in the morning that the grass and boxwoods had shed their dew. He followed a quarter-mile path between elm and spruce trees. Then, emerging near the bank of the narrow, storm-swollen river, he came to a private amphitheater.

Rather small, the theater had four semicircular rows of stone benches. Its stage was backed by an Ionian colonnade with marble statues at either end. To the left, shaded under the branches of a thick yew tree, perched a robed woman holding flaming torches—one in each hand. But Patrick's attention was drawn to the figure on the right. A goddess in a knee-length tunic stood beside a balustrade bordering the river. She was caught in the act of drawing an arrow from a quiver on her back.

The sun glinted brightly off the Dartrun. The sky was flawless blue save for a line of effervescent clouds on the eastern horizon. Two larks sang to one another above the cadence of the gurgling river.

Wearing her freshly cleaned and pressed white blouse and navy skirt, Gwen stood beside the goddess with the bow. The sun edged her golden hair with silver; a few loose, glittering strands drifted in the breeze. She was looking downriver. Beyond her, the rippling stream splashed a thousand sparkles of light. Patrick remained perfectly still, memorizing the scene. Gwen reached over her shoulder to scratch her back, unconsciously duplicating the goddess's pose. It was as if the statue had a living copy.

She turned, suddenly aware of his presence.

He jumped; any woman would be alarmed by a man lurking silently behind her. He had to say something quickly—there was a finite amount of time before even the most logical of explanations would sound suspicious. As the window of opportunity closed, he said the only thing that came to mind—exactly what he had been thinking: "Lady Gwendolyn—I thought you were the goddess come to life."

It was a horribly stupid thing to say, but the silly words had left his mouth. He pursed his lips in a pained smile. Any attempt to retract or modify the statement would draw greater attention to the inanity of it. Which was worse—a lurker or an idiot?

Made conscious of her pose, Gwen dropped her arm. "Which goddess?"

He glanced at the statue. "Isn't that Diana?"

She studied the marble goddess. She was being equated with a cosmically unapproachable woman. "You know, when a hunter saw Diana naked, she turned the man into a stag. His own dogs tore him apart."

"Well, I hope I shall never see you naked."

Her jaw dropped.

Patrick wanted to jump into the river.

"A girl might have mixed feelings after being told that by a boy."

"I…" He was now so off-balance he didn't know what to say.

She watched him flounder and enjoyed it very much. She had been wondering how to explain to him that the kiss had meant nothing. Suddenly, she had no desire to bring it up.

"Diana is very beautiful," he said.

She looked at him, considering. Patrick was a mix of awkwardness and natural ability. He had unconscious style—not conformance to trends or popular chic, but an intuitive ability to select and fit things together in the right way. And here suddenly, unpredictably, he was bold. She wanted him to comment more directly on her appearance.

Patrick squirmed. He, a commoner, had approached the daughter of an earl unchaperoned and was now speaking with her in a familiar, even flirtatious fashion. This situation was so improbable, astonishing, and inappropriate he didn't know what to do next. He stood up straight, coming to attention. "Master Christopher said you wanted to discuss interstices. Something to do with them. With interstices."

A rather sour expression crossed her face. There was a short silence. She blew out a breath through her nose. "Jack says you can see Primary boundaries even from the silhouette side. Did you notice anything odd at Whitebarrow?"

Patrick thought for a while. "There was a flux. Did your brother tell you about the German soldier?"

She nodded.

"When we left, the interstitial geometry of the vicinity was different—not a lot, but it was noticeable. Like the Defile of Ash after our battle."

Gwen walked in a slow circle. "Considering what you saw at Whitebarrow and what I noticed when experimenting with Uncle Geoffrey's prism, I'm led to believe there are times and places the Primary World can be reordered. Altered, I mean." She stopped under the colonnade. "The party tomorrow might be one."

She turned and stared at the river for the time it took the current to carry a floating branch in and out of view. Then she nodded as if she had gotten the answer she required. "Thank you."

She wandered so close to Patrick that he stepped backward. Lady Gwendolyn Maham might be willowy, but her presence was enormous. He smelled the scent of perfumed soap. He swallowed; it sounded like a great gulp. He was afraid he would lose his balance. She was gazing with curiosity around the amphitheater, taking an interest in the moss growing on the stone benches, the carvings of charioteers on the frieze of the colonnade, and the trees around the periphery.

Patrick contemplated a belt of pale yellow flowers emerging from the grass along the riverbank. Should he say something more about interstices? Lady Gwendolyn seemed to be done with the topic. He didn't want to continue with a closed subject and be a bore, but the silence was unendurable. He looked at patches of purple near the water.

"'I know a bank where the wild thyme blows, where oxlips and the nodding violet grows…'" He couldn't stop himself from saying stupid things.

"Pardon?"

"From *Midsummer Night's Dream*. We read it last term. Don't mind me."

She sometimes forgot he was the educated son of an engineer. "You memorize Shakespeare?"

"I read slowly." Why had he said that? It was true—positions of letters could shift mysteriously before his eyes on pages, and Shakespeare was particularly hard to follow. By the time he had worked through a scene, he had often learned it by heart.

But he was making himself out to be a moron. "I take my time to enjoy the language. Occasionally, I end up committing it to memory." He hoped that made his dullness sound like a virtue. "Without meaning to," he added quickly, not wanting her to think him a snobbish academic.

"I see." She felt compelled to compete with him. She tried to remember *A Midsummer Night's Dream*. "Should we perform Pyramus and Thisbe?"

"Then you'll be Thisbe?"

"No. Wall. Wall was the most sensible character in that act. Maybe the whole play."

He laughed. "'Thou wall, o wall! O sweet and lovely wall!'" It was the dialogue, faithfully rendered, but seeing her dismay, he realized how awkward it sounded, regardless of being on a stage. "I didn't mean to put you on the spot."

"'Out damned spot!'"

"Oh. Lady Macbeth..."

Oops. She had taken the part of a conniving murderess. But at least she hadn't asked wherefore he was Patrick. "Perhaps the lady doth protest too much?" Wait—that was Hamlet's mother—another unfortunate choice.

Patrick tactfully tied off the mess: "I suppose one should neither a borrower nor a lender from Shakespeare be."

Gwen smiled faintly. "'Well, of course I know nothing about these things, but I've no objection if it's usual.'"

"I...don't recognize that."

"Said by a little maid who all unwary came from a ladies' seminary."

His face stayed blank.

She stepped backward dramatically. "'If you please, I think you had better not come too near. The laws against flirting are excessively severe.'"

"I wasn't...I didn't mean—"

"The Mikado."

"Oh. Gilbert and Sullivan."

Now she was an ingénue in a romantic comedy. Had that been wise? She couldn't stop herself. "'If it were not for the law, we should now be sitting side by side, like this.'" She touched down on the nearest bench, then immediately ran to one on the other side of the amphitheater. "'Instead of being obliged to sit half a mile off, like this.'"

As far as Patrick could recall, the comic operetta was about impossible love. Aside from difficulties presented by anti-flirting laws and a recent shortage of executions, the young man and woman were both engaged to other people, and he was below her station. Except that he turned out to be the son of the emperor, so it all worked out in the end. Was Lady Gwendolyn making some veiled association with their own circumstance? Patrick would not turn out to be the son of a baronet, much less an emperor. "I saw *The Mikado* in London at the Savoy with my father when I was six or seven. I don't remember it very well."

"We have it on phonograph records. I must have listened to them a hundred times. The music is wonderful."

She took an interest in the river and drifted over to the balustrade. Patrick wondered if he had been dismissed. He was tempted to fall back on Shakespeare to fill the void, but the only lines that came to his mind were from Macbeth, and he couldn't get past them. *All hail, Macbeth, thane of Glamis!* The banter and mock play with Lady Gwendolyn had excited and terrified him. *All hail, Macbeth! Hail to thee, thane of Cawdor!*

But it was impossible.

Jack was less than a hundred yards away in a green spot amidst trees bearing new leaves that dappled the ground with shadows. He contemplated the prism in his hand. He hadn't tried to do anything with it; it lay smooth and hard in his open palm.

He had read through Sir Robert's vision verses again the previous night. Romans 12:17 stuck in his mind. *Do not repay evil for evil. Do what is right.* He had opened his Bible to see what the subsequent text was about. *If it's up to you, live at peace with everyone. Don't take revenge. Overcome evil with good, not evil. It is mine to avenge; I will repay, says the Lord.*

At one point, Jack thought of hurling the useless prism into the river. No prayer of his would be answered the way he wanted. His brain was filled with fantasies of Germans being shot and bayonetted. Weren't the things one thought about day and night one's real prayers?

He had met and been saved by a German. He was still shocked and confused by what Private Karl Brock had done. The man's death had brought Jack profound anguish. He felt bewildered gratitude, but it hadn't generalized. His desires hadn't changed. He could not pray for people he hated. Not except in the most shallow, mechanical, insincere way.

So God would never answer Jack Maham's prayers. They weren't His will.

Well…Jack was able to pray righteously for God's aid when he was in danger, as during the battles with demons. Terror, it seemed, was a concentrating lens.

He thought of the phantasmal spies spinning malevolent webs around the estate. There were at least four. Jack couldn't localize their positions, but he felt their activity. During the night, he had shivered every time he heard a creak, drip, or tap in the darkness. The powers of Hell seemed ascendant. Was he on the losing side? Lately, he sensed he was being invited to change his allegiance. Ha! How could anyone who had seen devils in their true forms and witnessed their viciousness have anything to do with them?

Still, God seemed to be little more than a disinterested entity viewing a sordid show that He had grown bored of. His angels had provided only marginal help to the Mahams. Was God ceding this world to new overlords? Would it be better to bow to them than be slaughtered in a futile fight?

Jack held the prism in streaming sunlight and studied the results—or rather, the lack of results. The glass didn't even cast a spectrum. Wanting what God wanted was impossible. No, the prism would never work for him.

His mood changed instantly when he looked northward. Patrick and Gwen were together, unsupervised, standing so close they were practically touching.

He balled his fists. All of his confusion cleared.

"It's a yew." Patrick gazed at the massive, ropy tree behind the robed figure at the north end of the colonnade. He pointed at the marble statue. "I think that's Hecate. Yew trees were sacred in her worship."

Gwen scrutinized the goddess with the two torches. The woman had keys hanging from her belt. "The goddess of magic?"

"Magic, night, witchcraft, and the dead."

"Why would she be here?"

"At one time, Hecate and Diana were associated with each other. Possibly opposite sides of the same person."

"Well, not anymore!" Gwen declared.

The intensity of her protest dismayed Patrick.

Gwen leaned on the balustrade, strategically positioning herself to trap him in the corner formed by the railing and its end post. She extended her arm carelessly. The slightest movement of his wrist would put his hand against hers.

She looked into his eyes. *Touch me,* she thought. She had no idea what she would do if he did. She held his gaze.

Patrick wanted to look away, but her eyes were insistent. He compromised, focusing to the side of her head on water that humped as it flowed over a sunken log.

"That's it!" He blinked as if coming awake. "A standing wave!"

"Huh?"

His face lit up. "How can wind blow past an interstice? Haven't you wondered? How can water flow across a boundary? I thought of magnetic fields within an electrical transformer. It's not a bad analogy, but it doesn't completely explain the phenomenon, you know?"

His animated speech masked the small strangling sound coming from her throat.

"We keep thinking of the Primary World as an extra dimension—I do, at least—but it's not. Primary and silhouette are different *aspects* of the same thing. It's a distinction of perception, not reality." He pushed past her to look more closely at the standing wave. "Fluids crossing boundaries—imagine a beam of light sweeping at an angle along a jagged three-dimensional surface. Think of the way the shadows move. Did you see it before? I didn't. I'm horribly slow!"

"Yes," she hissed through clenched teeth. "You *are!*"

Stunned by the acid in her voice, he turned to look at her. He went stiffer than the stone statues.

"Men are *idiots!*" Gwen stomped across the amphitheater.

At the same moment, Jack came racing in from the other side. Gwen passed him without even acknowledging his presence, her eyes scary.

Jack stopped, dazed. He swung to face Patrick. "What did you do to my sister?!"

"I—I said that fluids crossing interstitial boundaries are like beams of light shining over jagged surfaces."

"What?"

"I was pondering how air and water cross interstitial boundaries, and she just…" Patrick, entirely unconscious of Jack's fury, stood staring at the place Lady Gwendolyn had disappeared into the trees. "I have no idea what upset her."

His tone was so sincere, and he was so utterly crushed that Jack believed him absolutely. They stared after Gwen, equally puzzled.

Jack's anger dissipated. In its place was left something that might even have been sympathy. "Extraordinary." He patted Patrick on the shoulder. "Don't let it bother you, old chap. You haven't sisters, so you wouldn't know, but girls are crazy."

Gwen stormed toward the house. Clouds sailed behind her, clustered in thick lines like galleons with tall battle towers. Apparently, she was less interesting to a boy than a ripple in a stream.

Not bothering with secrecy, she crossed the yard below the terrace and entered the small kitchen. Two surprised maids stepped out of her way. She marched up the hallway, through the padded door into the East Tower, and climbed the stairs.

She cooled when she got to her room. Someone had been there. At first she thought nothing of it. Servants entered all the time. They had before the war, at any rate. But something wasn't right. The bed had not been made, nor the furniture dusted. Then the hair on the back of her neck stood up. Someone had searched her things.

She went quickly to the little jewelry box on her dressing table and verified that everything sentimental or valuable was there. Next, she opened her desk drawers. Some items might have been out of place, but nothing important was missing. Then she realized the prism was gone—the ordinary one her father had given her, not Uncle Geoffrey's.

Jack had Uncle Geoffrey's. She laughed. The fools had gotten the wrong one!

But her mood crashed down hard. Why would Harkless or her men be looking for Uncle Geoffrey's prism? When had they become aware of it? Could they know what it was? She thought of Wye's performance when she and Jack were in the interstice. She stood immobilized.

Patrick steered his truck around a large pothole and studied the threatening sky. He planned to stop in Buckton only long enough to eat some bread and cold meat before driving to Exeter to meet his father at the train station. His anticipation of reunion was overshadowed by the indelible memory of Lady Gwendolyn's outrage. He must have bumped her when, in his excitement, he stepped past her to look at the standing wave in the stream. If that were the case, then indeed, he had wronged her. He reviewed the event again and again, unable to conclude if he had jostled her.

His thoughts were interrupted when he came to the interstitial ridge that she and he had plunged through on horseback the previous Saturday. The boundary was indistinct, but he knew exactly where it was. His imagination invented a sensation of compression to accompany the instantaneous transit that he, anchored to silhouette now, couldn't actually feel.

Yes, he must have accidentally touched her.

Yet he and Lady Gwendolyn had touched before. Even *kissed*! But things that happened during extreme stress or relief were not evidence of deep or lasting emotions. She had given no indication she thought the least thing of kissing him.

Four minutes later, he passed through another scintillating plane. The sea was inside that interstice.

All at once, in a crazy leap of imagination that made his pulse race, he wondered if Lady Gwendolyn was angry because he had *not* touched her.

All hail Macbeth, that shall be King hereafter.

CHAPTER 10

Twists and Turns

24-16-14

Tall, lanky Inspector Thompson settled into a well-padded leather chair by a window so the light coming into the drawing room was at his back. Though he was merely a civil servant, he seemed surprisingly comfortable mingling with the aristocracy. His demeanor was not overly deferential. Jack didn't mind the man's casual attitude; in fact, it put him at ease. Thompson's face was sharp and intelligent, and the expression on it right then was mild and caring. "You had quite an ordeal at Whitebarrow, m'lord. Could you tell me about it?"

Jack took time to arrange his thoughts before replying, so his account was better organized and more chronological than the one he had given the soldiers. It included details he had forgotten to tell to the police in Plymouth. Of course, he omitted any mention of visions, interstices, or demons.

The inspector nodded frequently but said little, waiting patiently whenever Jack paused to recollect.

"That's all, I guess."

The inspector did not speak for some time. He turned pages of his notebook, searching for something he had written. Finally, he looked up. "Why did you believe Colonel Sir Geoffrey to be at Whitebarrow?"

Jack opened his mouth but then paused, sensing that the question was not quite as spontaneous or innocent as it seemed. "He told us he was going there."

"Indeed? Why did he go there?" The inspector leaned forward so slightly that the movement was almost imperceptible. "Why did Sir Geoffrey go to Whitebarrow?"

"Because…" Jack struggled. "To find the anarchists, I guess."

"Indeed? How did he know they were there?"

"He didn't say."

"Indeed?"

There was a long silence. The inspector waited.

Jack squirmed in his chair. "He saw one of them on the road to Buckton."

"He did?"

"Yes…he mentioned that there were two men in the farmhouse." Jack's eyes wandered here and there.

"I see. Sergeant Douglas said something about smoke?"

Sergeant Douglas was the leader of the soldiers who drove Jack from the mine to Plymouth. Jack had told the sergeant about his great-uncle's smoke signal.

"Oh! Yes. That's how we…another reason McCray and I thought we should go to the mine."

"Indeed? From where did you see the smoke? Not from here, surely?"

Jack looked at the window. All that could be seen from here right now was rain. He tried to remember what he had told the soldiers and the constable in Plymouth.

Inspector Thompson continued to smile good-naturedly as if the question had no more importance than asking the time.

"No, from…" Jack thought hard. Would the truth contradict anything he had already said? He stared at an empty chair. "From an airplane."

For the first time, Inspector Thompson was surprised into an expression other than benevolence. "A what?"

"An airplane. McCray refurbished a crashed Gunbus. He gave

me a ride."

"I see." Thompson penciled something in his notebook, his hand moving slowly as if preoccupation with his thoughts was interfering with the process.

"We saw smoke coming from the mine shaft and thought we should investigate."

"Lucky for Colonel Sir Geoffrey." Thompson gazed levelly at Jack. "Lord Mayfield, are you satisfied with his majesty's government?"

"What?"

"Do you back the prime minister and his majesty's government?"

"Yes, of course," Jack answered instinctively, with some surprise at the odd question.

Thompson let the silence lengthen.

"I mean, I don't know much about what they do, but there's a war, and we all have to do our part, don't we?"

"Tell me again, Lord Mayfield, how did you know Colonel Sir Geoffrey was at the Whitebarrow mine?"

"Because he said there were anarchists."

"I wonder why he told that momentous and urgent information to you but not any of his colleagues." The inspector watched Jack's face.

"I think it was more a hunch than a certainty. And he might not have told us he was going to Whitebarrow—not specifically. He told us there were anarchists, he went toward Whitebarrow, and there was smoke. So we believed he was there."

Thompson flipped backward through his notebook.

"Why didn't you allow Sergeant Douglas to speak with the colonel?"

"What do you mean?"

"Sergeant Douglas said you hovered over Sir Geoffrey until he lost consciousness on the way to Plymouth so no one else could speak with him."

"He's my great-uncle, and he was gravely ill. I stayed with him, naturally."

"Naturally." Thompson stared intently at Jack. "Did you know you are named in your great-uncle's will?"

Jack stared back. "No. I didn't."

"It seems you and Mr. McCray are close friends?"

"No. Well, I guess…we go to the same school and have some common interests."

"Indeed?"

"He has an airplane, and I…" Jack's face soured at the memory. "I wanted to fly in it." It was true. He had wanted to fly *in* it rather than on the wing. "Turns out I don't anymore."

The inspector smiled—actual amusement this time. "I see." He closed his notebook. "Is there anything else you would like to tell me, m'lord?"

"No, inspector."

Jack rang for a servant to show Thompson out. The summons was answered by a footman Jack had never seen before.

When the inspector was gone, Jack felt as if he were the one who had been dismissed.

A short time later, Jack was looking at the wreckage of the Beacon Tower stairs. He groaned. Gwen was right. There was no longer any way into the North Wing through the tower. He returned via the attic to his sister's bedroom.

"It's a disaster," he acknowledged peevishly.

"Let's use the secret tunnel," Christopher proposed for the second time.

"You said it was blocked."

Earlier in the afternoon, the little boy had explored the ominous northbound branch of the tunnel system but been thwarted by an unyielding door.

"Only for want of a crowbar," Christopher said.

Jack went to the window and watched rivulets of water stream down the blurry panes. "It's insufferable that common workmen won't let me go where I want in my own house!"

The workmen weren't the only obstacles. With the imminent arrival of the prime minister and his Cabinet, security personnel were everywhere.

Jack shrugged. "Well, that's that."

Gwen shook her head vehemently. "I told you, something will happen in the North Wing at half past three. You have to be there."

Jack faced her. "Exactly what is going to happen?"

"I don't know."

"Then how do you know I have to be there at half past three?"

"Don't ask."

"I *am* asking. How do you know? Tell me."

Gwen's face tightened in irritation. "Because last night I was inside the North Wing's Great Hall."

"You were inside…?"

"In a *dream,*" Gwen clarified testily. "Symbolic, not literal, this time." She paused to organize her thoughts. "I don't know what the North Wing's Great Hall actually looks like, but in my dream, it was pentagonal and out on the moor."

Jack stared at her.

"The interior was outdoors," Gwen explained. "Just accept the incongruity." She paused, remembering. "There was a stone circle… but that's not important. What's important is that the clock above the entry doors read half past three o'clock. As soon as I had marked the time, the hands began to wind around the clock face. Because it was a dream, I was able to see the clock's wheels and gears turning." Gwen waved her hand in a circle. "The wheels and gears in my dream symbolized intrigue." She looked at Jack. "Conspiratorial plans are going to be deliberated at half past three o'clock today in the North Wing."

"I see," Jack said. "You didn't hear voices?"

"*No,*" she snapped. "I didn't hear voices!"

Jack ran his fingers through his hair and took a deep breath. His whole body was taut. "All right. I'll go in through the tunnel."

Christopher brightened. "I'll get our torches and a crowbar."

Jack shook his head. "You aren't going." Intentionally putting his ten-year-old brother in danger would be unconscionable. Their adventures in the Primary World had been accidents and acts of desperation.

Two minutes later, Christopher followed his brother into the hallway. "You'll need someone to hold a light while you work on the door."

"No." Jack waved back to Gwen. "I'll let you know what I find."

She made no attempt to go with him. She was drained and faint. She changed into her nightgown and lay down for a nap, so distracted by worry that she forgot to lock her door.

Christopher pestered his brother all the way to the cellar. Jack, increasingly anxious, compromised. Christopher would come with him to the locked door but would go back once it was forced open.

The boys went into the utility closet and opened the secret passage. The air in the tunnel was saturated with moisture as if in supernatural resonance with the stormy atmosphere outdoors.

They turned left at the T-intersection. The mold-darkened bricks absorbed their flashlight beams. Jack shivered.

Some two dozen yards beyond the intersection, after a curve, they came to a stout oak door. Round-topped, it filled the entire width and height of the cramped passageway.

Jack wedged the crowbar between the door and its jamb, but the jamb was right up against the wall, so there was no room to move the bar. "I can't get any leverage."

"Pull the other way."

"That will only press the door tighter closed."

Jack pondered. The door's thick oak planks were held together with iron bands that, while rusted, were solid.

"Then again…" He did as Christopher suggested, attacking the wooden jamb instead of trying to pry the door open. The doorpost cracked, and a long piece broke off. "This will work." In no time he had reduced the jamb to splinters and forced the door ajar. He slipped his fingers around its edge. A dank draft blew into his face.

The hinges were nearly frozen. Jack heaved repeatedly until the opening was wide enough to squeeze through.

He looked at Christopher. "This is as far as you go." He kept his voice steady by force of will.

"You might need me again."

Jack gazed into the next section of the tunnel and then at his brother. Christopher's face was set. He was not going to listen. "You can go a little farther if you promise you won't argue when I tell you to go back. Do you *promise?*"

"I promise."

"And you'll go straight to our bedroom and remain there until I return?"

Christopher scowled. "No fair!"

"Ha! Thought I wouldn't define 'back' and you'd have me on technicalities, didn't you? Promise you'll go directly to our room and stay there until I return. If you don't, I'll seal the door behind me." It was an idle threat—he couldn't secure the door even if he wanted to. "And no crossing your fingers behind your back!"

"I promise," Christopher grumbled.

"All right. Come on."

It wasn't long before Jack regretted his decision. The farther they went, the less he wanted his brother to be in the murky passageway alone. But he believed what Gwen had said. He needed to observe something that was about to happen. If it weren't for the urgency, he would have escorted Christopher back to the house.

Unexpectedly, they came to a junction where another tunnel merged in from behind. "Straight on," Jack said. He had no reason for the choice except that it seemed the right direction, and there was no point agonizing over it. "Remember which way to go back."

"Right."

"No, left," Jack corrected.

"I meant 'right,' we should remember."

Jack stopped and stared at what looked like an archway ahead. "I think we ought to pray the way we did when we were in the mountains."

"I have been," Christopher declared.

"Ah. Of course."

A demonic presence had Jack's nerves jangling. It wasn't too far away. It eroded his self-control.

He tried to focus on something he had come across when looking for heroes in the Bible—something King Jehoshaphat had prayed: *We don't know what to do, but our eyes are on you.* But his thoughts kept turning inward on unknown threats.

Help me, Lord, he prayed. *Overpower my enemies the way you did Jehoshaphat's.*

"Jack?"

"Yes?"

"My torch…"

Jack looked at the dim beam of Christopher's flashlight.

"I think it's going out."

Jack shuddered. Every muscle in his body twitched. What would it be like to be trapped underground without light? If his flashlight also failed, the darkness would be absolute. "Turn it off. Save the batteries."

It was now impossible to send Christopher back by himself. Jack hesitated, but his watch read three-fifteen. "Let's press on."

Soon, the tunnel opened into a wide cellar corridor. The floor was glazed with water, and the place had a rank, mildew smell. The two boys passed open doors to empty rooms. One of the rooms appeared to have been a scullery, another a storeroom, and yet another a laundry. Narrow windows high on the walls must once have been above ground but had been buried by centuries of accumulated dirt.

Tiny pink eyes peeked out of the dark rooms. Jack's flashlight revealed dozens of albino rats as big as rabbits. He had read accounts of dead bodies stripped of flesh by rats. But rodents would keep their distance from living boys with lights…wouldn't they?

Once again, Jack paused to look behind him, memorizing the way they had come.

He gave a wide berth to a doorway plugged with bricks laid jamb-to-jamb, floor-to-ceiling. The masonry had settled, and the plug leaned precariously into the corridor.

But Christopher stopped. He stood on tiptoes and removed a loose brick.

"Watch out!" Jack swept his brother out of the way of two hundred pounds of falling bricks and mortar. Most of it landed where Christopher had stood, filling the air with billows of dust.

"What were you thinking?" Jack shouted. "You could have been killed!"

"I'm sorry! I wanted to make a little hole and see where the sealed-off passageway goes. I didn't know so much would fall."

Jack shined his flashlight into the big hole Christopher had made. "It used to be a stair. It doesn't go anywhere anymore. The top is boarded up."

Christopher bowed his head contritely.

Jack threw up his hands. "I should have sent you back! But now I can't. So come on."

How was he going to keep his brother safe? All manner of hazards might lie ahead: pitfalls, poisonous air, weak floors, and who knew what. He would have to spot each threat and shield Christopher. Would the two of them have to deal with Harkless's men? He might have to fight. He would use the crowbar. Would it be better to hold the straight end or the crook? Probably the crook. The bar was heavy… he would swing it up, down, around, and back up in a figure-eight pattern, using its inertia to his advantage. He would deal with the big man first.

With his full attention concentrated on protecting his brother, Jack's determination grew. And since his thoughts were outside himself, his composure grew as well.

The corridor took them to a cavernous space. Jack paused on the threshold of steps that descended into stagnant water. He pointed his flashlight all around. "It's flooded."

"We aren't going to let that stop us, are we?"

"We can't leave wet footprints and puddles. Harkless mustn't learn we've spied on her." Jack eyed the water, judging it to be about a foot deep. "I'll take you piggyback."

He took off his shoes, tied their laces together, and hung them around his neck. Then he rolled up his trousers and passed his flashlight to Christopher. "Take this." He crouched down. "Get on."

After Christopher was securely on his back, Jack stepped into the water. It was as if his legs had been slurped into cold, clinging sheaths.

Setting off across the coal-black pond, he tried to convince himself that nothing dangerous lived in the scummy liquid. The bottom was flat and level, but decayed boards and unidentifiable gelatinous things squished beneath the soles of his bare feet. He tested each step before transferring his full weight, twice saving himself from being punctured by something sharp. Was it his imagination, or was there a current where there should have been none?

Insects walked on the ceiling and convulsed their way through the stygian water. Everything either absorbed light or deflected it, so nothing was distinct.

Near the far side of the chamber, the boys passed a large opening on their right. A dirt and debris dam as high as Jack's chest kept water from flowing through. Jack surmised the dam resulted from wall and ceiling collapse rather than human excavation.

Christopher pointed the flashlight into the opening. The beam revealed a cavern that was dry even though its floor was ten to fifteen feet below.

"That must be the first cellar," Jack guessed. "The one that flooded."

"But it's dry, and this one isn't," Christopher said.

Jack had no answer.

The boys arrived at the far wall and entered the narrow corridor that continued from there. Jack had to bend at the waist to keep his brother's head from brushing the ceiling. He was acutely conscious of the little warm body on his back and how precious it was.

The tunnel sloped downward. Consequently, the water rose as they progressed.

"Blast. Hold tight." Jack stopped and rolled his pants legs up as high as he could. When he set off again, he created a wake that splashed against the walls. The water kept rising. He went up on his toes to keep his pants dry.

He had nearly decided they would have to turn around when the tunnel sloped upward, and the water became shallower. A minute later, relieved and thankful, Jack was on dry flooring at the bottom of a decrepit wooden staircase. He set his brother down, toweled his legs with his handkerchief, and unrolled his trousers. He donned socks and shoes. "I hate this place."

They climbed the stairs, and Jack pried open the door at the top. That admitted them to a bare-shelved pantry with grimy windows. Pouring rain limited visibility outside, but Jack saw enough to confirm that he and Christopher were in the northernmost part of the wing.

"Follow me, and don't touch anything that could fall over."

The next hallway they entered had a deep, undisturbed carpet of dust. The boys went south. Soon, they came upon the heavy door to what used to be the opulent parts of the North Wing. The door streamed cobwebs when Jack pulled it open.

They continued past rooms with elaborate wood and plaster ornamentations. The soaring ceilings should have made the chambers impressive and airy; however, the grubby, peeling paint and general dilapidation made them ponderous and sad. And eerie, Jack thought—places he had never been despite being near them all his life—a little like interstices. Outside the windows, rain fell harder than ever. The house was now sitting in a lake.

They found the Great Hall, but another room had been built inside it. They were confronted with the backside of a brand-new lath and plaster wall. Hearing a murmur of voices, Jack held a finger to his lips. He crept around the periphery of the room-within-a-room and found a place where two walls didn't quite meet. Through the gap, he saw an immaculately groomed, middle-aged man in a flawlessly tailored, charcoal-gray suit. The man was bending to look at a metal tray bolted to the underside of a twelve-foot-diameter round table.

"Fog?" the man asked.

"Yes, Herr Lehrmann." Miss Harkless confirmed. "Ice on the tray creates a chill, and fog floats on the floor."

"Yet you say your powers are legitimate."

"Such atmosphere is expected, and I confess I enjoy the theatricality. But my powers are quite real, I assure you."

The man glanced about, affecting nonchalance. "Is there a place we could speak confidentially?"

"Certainly. Come with me."

Jack lost sight of Lehrmann. Footsteps were followed by silence.

"She called him *Herr* Lehrmann," Jack whispered. "He's *German*!"

"German? *Here?*"

"He must be a spy!"

"Use the prism to get us into that room," Christopher urged. "Through an interstice, the way Gwen got into Father's laboratory."

"No, we can't. There are demons nearby."

Besides, Jack was unable to do anything with the prism. It would not work for him. And he didn't want Christopher to know that.

"We can anchor back to silhouette if a devil comes," Christopher said.

Jack took the prism from his pocket. Would he rather his brother think him a failure or a coward? Perhaps he should say there was a problem with the light or claim there were no interstices.

He put down the crowbar, turned on his flashlight, and pointed its beam into the prism. The glimmer in the glass was a mere suggestion of luminosity. He closed his eyes and pretended to pray, thinking about what he would say when nothing happened.

"There's a way in!" Christopher exclaimed.

Jack opened his eyes. He stared. An interstitial Norman passageway grazed the plaster wall, displacing four feet of it, creating a nice doorway. Back the way they had come, the interstice slanted downward into darkness. He had done nothing. The prism had done nothing. But he and Christopher were anchored to the Primary World.

Christopher ran into the breach. "Come on, Jack!"

"Wait!"

Jack stared at the lifeless prism, as bewildered as he was frightened. The lump of glass had not anchored them to the Primary World; God had done something different this time. His great-uncle said there was no such thing as magic. Jack should have taken that statement to heart. All along, he had been thinking of the prism as a magical relic that worked miracles if its user had the right knowledge, power, and skill. But he had been entirely wrong. And with that realization, Jack Maham guessed what the prism really was.

"Come on!" Christopher called.

Jack took a deep breath. "I'm coming." He stepped through the interstitial opening in the plaster wall.

The windowless pentagonal room was lit by Tiffany lamps. Panoramic wallpaper made the setting appear to be the middle of a Neolithic stone circle standing on a moonlit plain—what Gwen had seen in her dream. Twenty straight-backed chairs were jumbled temporarily in one corner and a grand piano in another. A candelabra and several photographs of a pretty, dark-haired girl sat on the piano. The place seemed like a stage setting—except the audience would be in its center.

A foyer connected the room to the North Wing's west-facing entrance. Concealed behind a fan-folded privacy screen, a door opened into a side chamber with two tables. Jack noted various articles on the felt-topped tables: tuning forks, bells, tubes with flared ends, and a gramophone. Those things would undoubtedly contribute to the "atmosphere" Miss Harkless had mentioned. But it was the eastern point of the pentagon that caught and held Jack's attention. There, in a four-foot-wide opening, stood Gwen's mirror. He was looking at its back side.

He walked to the opening, amazed by what appeared to be an infinitesimally thin, iridescent film between him and the mirror. He reached to touch the film, but there was nothing to touch; his hand went all the way to the backside of the mirror. He would have studied the phenomenon longer, but just then all the hair on his body stood out. An evil presence immobilized him. A door opened and closed within the dusty room beyond the mirror.

"The walls are thick."

Jack recognized Miss Harkless's voice, though he couldn't see her. "We won't be overheard," she said.

Christopher dove under the round table. Jack remained frozen behind the mirror. He had been caught. Herr Lehrmann was an arm's length away on the other side of the iridescent film. Yet the man gave no indication of seeing Jack.

Herr Lehrmann cleared his throat. "The directors have learned of the more aggressive aspects of the campaign and are concerned."

"Is that so?"

"They were under the impression the bank was preparing to take advantage of existing British plans. They did not know that efforts were underway to manipulate those plans."

"Oh? Please get to your point, Herr Lehrmann."

"The directors would be in an untenable position if your activities were to be reported."

"The risk is negligible. Nothing could be proved. The bank would issue outraged, unequivocal denials. Sue for defamation."

"Naturally. Naturally. But even unfounded accusations would be ruinous."

"There will be no accusations. Unless your ill-advised visit today is observed by the numerous British security men patrolling the estate?" Harkless spoke with clear contempt.

"The directors wish to call the thing off. Your fees will be paid in full, of course. We honor our agreements."

Although Jack could not see Miss Harkless, he was sure she was regarding Herr Lehrmann with scorn.

"Certainly, if that is your wish."

Herr Lehrmann smiled and relaxed. "I suppose you will still hold your little entertainment. You will not, however, put forth any, er, suggestions. We have an understanding?"

"Spirits will speak through me. I do not control what they say."

"I see. But we have an understanding?" Herr Lehman raised his eyebrows in emphasis.

"You should go back to Zurich."

"We will send payment shortly. Good day." The man bowed slightly and departed. Presumably, Harkless also left the room.

Jack was still trying to sort out what had happened when Christopher emerged from under the round table. The little boy pointed at the candelabra on the piano.

"What?" Jack asked. Then he recognized the sterling silver piece—it was the one from the gallery above the front hall. The one he had knocked over and Christopher had caught, anchoring it to the Primary World. But before Jack could do anything about the candelabra, he heard pairs of heavy footsteps.

"Out of here!" he croaked.

The boys darted into the interstitial corridor.

Jack stopped there, where they couldn't be seen or heard, to look back. He was staring at the candelabra, wondering what to do, when he heard Gwen calling, "Christopher! This way—*hurry! HURRY!*" At the same time, Jack became aware of a demonic presence very close by. He whirled around.

The ancient, interstitial fortress corridor had the appearance of a gray gullet, and Jack saw burning eyes within folds of shadow at its far end.

Christopher dashed down the corridor. "Gwen! I'm coming!"

"NO! STOP!" Jack commanded shrilly.

Christopher paused.

"IT'S NOT GWEN! COME BACK!"

Jack sprinted instinctively to save his brother. He almost peeled off when he realized he was rushing unarmed at a demon. But he loved his brother. He really and truly loved him in a way that was more than simple emotion. His love looked outward, not inward; it was not dependent on reciprocation or reward or anything else. And focused on Christopher, there wasn't any room in Jack's mind for panic.

Seeing the demon, Christopher froze.

Jack threw his arms around his brother, lifted him, and ran. He expected claws to rip his back, but that didn't matter. What mattered was getting Christopher out of the Primary World.

"Lord Jesus," he cried. "Forgive my unbelief. Save my brother!" It was the sincerest prayer he had ever uttered.

The boys were deafened by an explosive pop. They felt no movement but were instantaneously displaced several feet outside the interstice.

Jack stopped and released Christopher. Raising his arms like a boxer, he turned to face his enemy.

But the interstice had disappeared.

Jack stood uncomprehending. Only after many seconds of confusion did he realize the truth. They were once again anchored to silhouette; they were once again shadows that couldn't be clawed by spirits.

He sagged against the wall. "That wasn't Gwen calling you. It was a demon."

Christopher gulped and nodded.

Jack closed his eyes, bowed his head, and said a silent, absolutely heartfelt prayer of thanksgiving for his and Christopher's salvation. His awareness of the Lord Jesus was so strong that he would not have been surprised to find, when he opened his eyes, they were standing face-to-face.

But he could still feel the evil spirit. The cheated demon was lunging and whirling in a frenzy, seeming to be everywhere simultaneously. Jack had never sensed such overwhelming rage.

He thought for a minute. He had not been delegated power to change his or anyone else's anchoring. The ability to go into and come out of the interstice today was a once-in-a-lifetime gift to Jack Maham.

"*Oi!*" said a man inside the pentagonal room. "Over here. Somethin's in the walls."

"Let's go!" Jack whispered. He retrieved the crowbar from where he had put it down, made sure the prism was in his pocket, and led the retreat. He was so full of adrenaline that he could barely keep himself from running.

"Can those blokes get to us?" Christopher asked, jogging to keep up. "They won't break through their new plaster wall, will they?"

"They might have a door somewhere. Or they could come in a window." Jack glanced into a room they were passing. "But they'd have to be daft to go outside in that downpour."

The demon dogged them all the way to the pantry at the north end of the wing. Its caustic presence was like grit on a raw sore. The pervasive sound of gurgling water also troubled him, but Jack didn't realize why until, halfway down the cellar stairs, he saw a shiny, rippling surface below.

"The rain. It's all draining down here."

He stopped. The water was more than two feet higher than when they arrived in the wing.

"Someone's been here." The deep male voice came from the pantry. "There's tracks."

"Come on!" Jack plunged into the flooded tunnel.

Christopher glanced back. "I hope they don't have torches."

The frigid water was up to Jack's waist in no time. Pants completely soaked, shivering, he slogged on, crowbar in his left hand and flashlight in his right. The men who had been tailing them gave up, but the demon stayed with them.

When Christopher was immersed almost to his neck, Jack hooked his left arm around his brother's waist and carried him, careful not to poke him with the crowbar. Then Jack slipped on the slimy bottom and pitched backward. He instinctively thrust his right hand down to catch himself. He scrambled and got his balance, but his dunked flashlight fizzled out. The blackness was total.

"Jack!" Christopher cried.

"Switch on your torch," Jack said as calmly as he could. "Is it still dry?"

"I think so." The little boy had been holding it above his head.

Its beam was even dimmer than before.

"It will be all right." Jack hugged his brother tightly. He didn't want to think about the depth of the water in the tunnel ahead, but as the level rose toward the ceiling, he found it hard not to.

"Do you suppose…" Christopher began.

"Keep the torch dry. Hold it right up to the bricks. Mind your fingers."

Jack thought of the cellar's design. There were numerous rooms, but it was not a labyrinth. He and Christopher would get out so long as they did not panic.

Something ahead of them splashed in the dark.

Christopher shook. "What was *that*!"

"Something more scared of us than we are of it," Jack said as reassuringly as he could, hoping it was true. His mouth was bone dry. "Don't worry. We'll get through."

Was he telling Christopher or himself?

Shortly after that, the water rose to Jack's chin.

Christopher scraped the flashlight against the bricks. He bumped his head.

Jack used his free hand to paddle. Water sloshed into his mouth. He coughed and tilted his face up to keep his nose in the air. For a bad moment he became disoriented and wasn't sure which way was which.

But the tunnel finally curved upward, and the water level dropped. Joyfully, Jack drew in deep, even breaths. He broke into a big smile and laughed.

Then the flashlight went out.

Hi Paige and Lara,

In Victorian times and into the twentieth century, there was a saying: "The sun never sets on the British Empire." Great Britain controlled India, half of Africa, the Middle East, Hong Kong, Singapore, and more. Canada, Australia, and New Zealand were dominions. One-quarter of the world's population was ruled from London, and during the latter half of World War I, David Lloyd George, the son of a Welsh schoolmaster, was Britain's prime minister.

Lloyd George was intrigued by the practice of spiritualism. His fascination began after Mair, his musically gifted daughter, died at the age of seventeen. He was not alone. English people everywhere, suffering staggering losses during World War I, clung to the possibility of speaking with their loved ones across the veil of death. Hundreds of mediums took advantage of the longing, and several became quite celebrated. Those mediums used increasingly sophisticated techniques to convince their clients that they had contacted spirits.

Séance goers were predisposed to believe that the odd things they saw and heard were indeed the work of spirits. And mediums urged them to open themselves to those spirits.

Harry Houdini, the legendary escape artist, exposed tricks that several of the most famous spiritualists used to deceive their clients. Houdini never found credible evidence that any spirit was ever actually present at a séance. But it is impossible to prove a negative.

Yours,

Kirk

CHAPTER 11

Caught in the Current

43-18-16

Agnes circled Patrick, studying her work with satisfaction. "That will do."

Patrick nodded, only half listening.

"All in all, quite handsome." She flashed him a smile. Tilting her head to one side, she said to no one, "A smidgen too young." She tapped a finger absently against her lower lip, considering. "But only a smidgen."

He had no idea what his age had to do with the clothes.

Agnes hurried off to start the next chore on her long list.

The minute he was alone, Patrick made up his mind. He carefully folded his new clothes and packed them into his valise. Before his resolve could falter, he strode through the corridors to Lady Gwendolyn's room. He didn't think about what he would say—if he did, he might come to his senses and turn around. Visiting her bedroom unsummoned could get him expelled from Maham House forever. But he needed to know what was going on in her head. If she told him to go away, so be it. He would leave and never come back.

He raised his hand to knock. But before his knuckles touched the wood, a piercing cry came from within.

Patrick forgot everything. He threw open the door.

Lady Gwendolyn was sitting bolt upright in bed, eyes wide. "Get a torch!" she commanded. "Go to the secret tunnel. Take the north branch. Help Jack and Christopher!"

Patrick hesitated, confused.

"Now!" She yelled. "Go *NOW!*"

This, Jack thought, *is what it is like to be laid in a grave.* Robbed of sight, his mind invented terrible images to go with the demonic presences he felt. He concentrated on protecting Christopher. That kept him from panicking. One of Sir Robert's verses—the one from Psalm 18—gave him some encouragement: *He sent from above, he took me, he drew me out of many waters.*

"What are we going to do?" Christopher asked, trembling.

"Don't worry. We'll find our way back. It won't be difficult. It's dark, that's all." Jack tried to sound confident. But he sensed that another demon was coming. A demon full of demons.

Patrick hurried through the tunnel, propelled by Gwen's anxiety. He knew nothing of what Jack and Christopher were facing—only that he had to get to them quickly. He turned north and squeezed through the broken door.

At the fork, he stopped for five seconds before choosing, as had Jack, the route that ran straight on. He was unsettled by the growing number of rats following him.

He paused when he came to the flooded cavern. The shallow pond had become a murky lake. Having no choice, he went into the icy, chest-deep water and pushed his way across.

He stopped at the dam of fallen rocks and dirt. The surface of the lake was nearly as high as the dam. He climbed the debris and stepped onto a flat stone block at its end. As high as the dam, the huge rectangular block was probably a remnant of the Norman fortress foundation. There was no sign that Jack and Christopher had gone into the lower cellar.

Then he heard Christopher yell, "There's a light!"

"It's me!" Patrick plunged back into the water and directed his flashlight at the doorway in the north wall.

Christopher swam out with Jack right behind.

"McCray!" Jack clasped Patrick's hand.

Patrick shook it joyfully. "Lady Gwendolyn sent me."

"Thank heaven. Thank heaven! Our torches are dead."

It was the shortest celebration in history. All three boys, reacting to different cues, went quiet.

Christopher's ears perked to a cacophony of scratching sounds. "What's happening?"

Jack's pupils dilated to their full extent. "Something's coming."

"What?" Patrick aimed his flashlight across the lake. "What's coming?"

Jack pointed.

Patrick gasped. Hundreds of albino rats were pouring out of the tunnel from the southern part of the cellar. Plunging into the water, looking like a frothing mat of cottage cheese speckled with fiery red eyes, they propelled themselves toward the boys.

"Rats..." Patrick stared. "What's gotten into them?"

"Demons," Jack said. "Demons have gotten into them. They're possessed."

"That way!" Patrick indicated the tunnel from which the other two boys had emerged.

"No. It's flooded up to the ceiling," Jack said, dazed. "Too much water."

"Too much...too much...this way!" Patrick half lunged, half swam to the dam. "Hurry!" He scrambled on top.

Jack and Christopher clambered up behind him.

Patrick pointed at the massive, flat-topped stone block at the end of the dam. "We can stand on that. It will hold us." He tore into the dirt, digging with his hands like a dog since he didn't have a shovel. Catching on, Jack helped, driving the crowbar into the debris.

Seeing what the boys were doing, the rats went into a frenzy, swimming faster than Patrick would have thought possible.

In seconds, the boys had created a water-filled ditch across the dam. Only one large rock blocked the flow. Jack pried underneath; Patrick put his foot to the rock and kicked until it came loose and fell into the old cellar below. Water poured through the breached dam. The boys backed onto the flat foundation block.

The operation worked brilliantly—almost too brilliantly. The immense power of gushing water quickly eroded a deep channel, and the dam melted away. The boys backed against the wall, hoping their stone block would not go with the rest of the debris.

The rats scrambled madly to escape the current, but the water was too swift. The whole lake was pouring out. The demonic pack, frothing like popcorn on the lake's surface, was swept en masse over the falls.

But three rats clawed their way on top of their drowning neighbors and leapt onto the foundation block.

Wielding the crowbar, Jack smashed one and whacked a second with a swing that would have earned him a spot on his school's cricket team.

Patrick dealt with the third: he stomped on it. The demon-possessed animal was quick; it grabbed Patrick's shoe—which did not work out well for it. Patrick stamped the rat into the stone. After three bone-crushing thumps, it lost its grip on his shoe. He kicked it into the lower cavern.

In no time, nearly all the water had drained; only a couple of inches remained on the slimy floor.

Patrick was the first to speak. "I don't think we should wait around."

"I'm for that," Christopher affirmed.

The trio ran to the doorway on the far side of the cavern and pressed on southward without slowing down. Nothing—demonic or otherwise—chased them.

They went left at the fork and quickly arrived at the heavy oak door. Jack, last in line, shouldered the door closed and wedged the crowbar beneath it to keep it shut.

"Patrick?" Gwen's distant call echoed through the tunnel. "Patrick?"

"Gwen!" Christopher shouted. "We're here!" The little boy sprinted ahead. This time there was no doubt it was Gwen—they were not in an interstice.

Jack, an odd, embarrassed expression on his face, stood in Patrick's way. "Listen, old chap…"

Patrick felt embarrassed himself. Mayfield was going to thank him. It was awkward. It didn't need to be said. Anyone would have come to help.

"I think you should excuse yourself from the party."

Patrick literally did not understand the statement. Communication is based on situation and expectation as much as what is said; words provide details. What Jack said was so inconsistent with the situation that Patrick couldn't make sense of it.

"Sorry?"

Jack had been trying for two days to find the right moment to make the request. When his brain was relieved of other pressures, it just popped out. He had intended to lie—to say that Uncle Geoff suspected there would be demonic activity at the Maham and Carter chemical works and wanted Patrick to keep watch there. But that excuse seemed artificial and dubious, so Jack didn't make it.

Patrick was still struggling to understand when Gwen and Christopher appeared from around the curve.

"Are you hurt?" Gwen asked with real concern.

"No." Jack looked down. "We're wet…"

"I brought dry things. They're in the cellar."

"Very good," Jack said. "Very good."

Gwen led the way to the house. Christopher followed her.

Jack walked silently, looking anywhere but at Patrick.

In the cellar, Gwen showed them a pile of towels and dry garments and then went around a corner while they changed.

Patrick rolled his wet clothes in a towel. Christopher took his and Jack's things to the laundry. The maids ironing tablecloths paused and stared at his dripping armful.

"Fell in a puddle," the little boy said without further explanation.

He dumped everything into a wicker basket and left.

Upstairs in the third-floor sitting room overlooking the front lawn, Jack told Gwen and Patrick what he and Christopher had seen and heard in the North Wing. The first part of his narrative was terse and matter-of-fact; only his account of the rats in the storerooms was colorful.

"There was a German spy," Christopher blurted when Jack described the pentagonal room.

"Swiss," Jack corrected. "I thought he was German, but Miss Harkless said Herr Lehrmann was going to Zurich."

"What was a Swiss spy doing here?" Gwen asked. "I didn't know the Swiss had spies."

"He isn't a spy. He's a banker."

"Then—what was a Swiss banker doing here?"

"Looking under a table at an ice tray," Christopher said.

Gwen was bewildered.

"Miss Harkless said it was for atmosphere," Jack explained. "She has tuning forks and trumpets and a gramophone offstage. She said spirits would speak."

Gwen's eyes narrowed to a squint. "The witch is going to hold a séance."

Jack nodded. "Precisely."

Christopher looked back and forth between his brother and sister. "What does that mean?"

"A séance is a ritual to summon spirits of the dead," Gwen said.

"I know what a séance is. Why is Miss Harkless going to hold one?"

"To summon spirits," Jack said dryly. He glanced at his sister and knew she was thinking of High Tor.

Patrick was reluctant to join the discussion. More than ever, he was aware of the gulf between himself and the Mahams. Why should he excuse himself from the party? Why would Mayfield want him to? But he had strong opinions regarding spiritualism, so he spoke up. "Séances are vile trickery."

Jack squirmed uncomfortably. "I think this one will be genuine. There really will be spirits."

"Oh. I see what you mean. Except they'll be the demonic kind."

Gwen read the twenty-fourth verse of Sir Robert's vision. It was from Revelation 16. "'For they are the spirits of devils, working miracles, which go forth unto the kings of the earth and of the whole world, to gather them to the battle of that great day of God Almighty.'" She thought for a minute. "What do you suppose a Swiss banker has to do with it?"

"Switzerland is neutral," Patrick said. "A safe haven for wealth in time of war."

Jack nodded. "Yes…?"

"Money has been flowing into Swiss banks."

"It will come out again," Jack said slowly. "Eventually…"

"Not if the account holders are dead. Or there is so much chaos they can't prove they're the owners. Swiss banks have numbered accounts, you know? No names. And regardless, the banks can lend holders' money out at a premium during wartime." Patrick leaned forward. "What will happen when British and French forces cross the Rhine?"

"There will be an even greater rush to deposit in Switzerland," Jack said appreciatively. "There will be more gold in Zurich than in Germany."

"There may be a negotiated peace," Gwen interjected. "We may not have to invade Germany."

"That wouldn't be as good for the Swiss banks, would it?"

"Oh…You think they want Prime Minister Lloyd George to do something that extends the war?"

Christopher screwed up his face. "That's diabolical!"

"Which is probably why the bank had second thoughts and is trying to call it off," Jack said.

Gwen curled her legs on the sofa and tucked her skirt around them. "Except that Miss Harkless isn't going to call it off."

Jack put a hand to his forehead. "This isn't the time."

"What?"

"Uncle Geoff said Satan and his cohorts are searching for a way to exist apart from God, and they think they can do it by making a world He didn't plan. They're trying to cause creation to collapse from end to end. If they succeed, they'll contrive a reality of their own making without having to have performed any original creation."

"Demons are insane," Christopher muttered.

"It might not work the way they hope, but it would still be bad for everyone on earth."

Patrick looked at Jack. "What isn't this the time for?"

"According to Uncle Geoff, the present war is an echo of the end time. It isn't supposed to be the final apocalypse. If demons can manipulate men to cause the final crisis to begin before all prescribed conditions are met, they can make things really bad. Even worse than they would be, I mean."

"What do you suppose they want Lloyd George to do that will extend the war?"

"Accept Father's plan."

"What plan?"

Jack explained how a gelatinized mustard agent would make German cities uninhabitable.

Patrick grimaced. "Use of poison on civilians is—"

"It won't be deadly," Jack said in his father's defense. "Mustard gas blisters the skin." Jack looked at his lap. "Babies and old people might die, though."

"Your father believes it will force the Germans to surrender?"

"That's right," Jack said, then, quieter, "Uncle Geoff thinks it could make them madder than ever. But I say father is on to something. If the Germans have to abandon their cities, they'll surrender."

Patrick stood up and went to the window. The rain had stopped. The grass and trees glistened. "What will happen at the séance?"

Gwen had the answer. "Miss Harkless will pretend to summon our brother Freddie and Mair Lloyd George."

"Mair Lloyd George?" Patrick did not know who that was.

"The prime minister's daughter. She died ten years ago."

"And a demon masquerading as her spirit will tell Mr. Lloyd George to use mustard gas on German cities?"

Gwen chewed her lip.

"I don't think policy advice from a spirit would be welcome," Patrick said. "The PM will see it as a tactless attempt to influence him."

"I've heard the PM is superstitious," Jack said.

"The other Cabinet members will be more skeptical."

Gwen was not so sure. "At *this* séance, the spirits will be real. They may be *very* convincing."

Patrick stood still. "We have to report this to Lord and Lady Buckleigh."

Gwen shook her head. "Making German cities uninhabitable is Papa's idea in the first place. He may not be happy about the sideshow, but he won't stop it. Mama will think we're delusional. And Papa's plan is supposed to be top secret. If they find out we've learned about it, we could be confined to our rooms."

"Or arrested," Jack muttered, thinking of Inspector Thompson.

"What are we going to do?" For once Christopher was more earnest than eager.

"Ruin the séance, if nothing else," Gwen said. "The interstice you found in the North Wing will come in quite handy. We'll pelt Miss Harkless with eggs and rotten vegetables from the spirit world." She smiled. "That should dampen her *atmosphere.*"

Jack blew out a breath through tight lips. "If we're in an interstice, the citizens of the spirit world can disembowel us."

"We'll pop in and out."

"How do you propose we get *to* the interstice? You don't expect Miss Harkless to invite us to the séance, do you?"

"Of course not. She won't let us within a hundred yards. We'll sneak in."

Patrick raised his hand. "The cellar tunnels are no good."

"Then you'll have to get us in another way."

He frowned. "How do you expect me to do that?"

"Find another interstice. You seem to be able to see them."

Patrick turned to Jack. "In that case, I'll have to be at the party."

"Of course you'll be there," Gwen said. "You've been invited."

Jack stared at the floor.

Patrick looked at Gwen. "I think you were right, Lady Gwendolyn. The party—or more specifically, the séance—is a point of refraction."

"A what?"

"A point where light bends. In context, where people make decisions that affect creation and reorder the Primary World."

"So you have to get us in there."

No one said anything for a while. When they spoke again, there wasn't much to discuss. Everyone wondered what Mr. Wye knew of the Primary World and what Miss Harkless and her servants would do when the séance went wrong. They speculated but came to no conclusions.

Jack left to dress for the family's evening meal. Christopher went to trap mice, thinking they might prove useful.

Patrick collected his bundle of wet clothes and followed Gwen into the hallway. "Lady Gwendolyn, I wish to say something."

She pushed him back into the sitting room. "Would you please stop that!"

He didn't want to stop; he wanted to have his say. But he bit his tongue and waited.

"When we're alone, call me Gwen."

He blinked. "What?"

"Calling me Lady Gwendolyn is stilted. It's *annoying*. Just call me Gwen, for heaven's sake. You did in the airplane."

He was beyond confused. He had no idea what was going on in the girl's mind. She was too inconsistent and erratic. Jack was right. Girls were crazy.

"Not in company, of course—that's another matter. But when there's no one else around, it's silly for you to be so *stiff*."

He couldn't think how to reply.

"What was it you wanted to say to me?" she asked.

"I don't know."

She stared at him.

"I've forgotten what it was."

"All right. Come to my room." She marched out the door.

"Pardon?"

"You left your valise in my room. Remember?"

"Oh. Of course."

Ten minutes later, Patrick was on his way out of the house, the unpleasant smell of the North Wing basement clinging to his skin and hair. Lady Buckleigh intercepted him on the first floor of the East Tower.

"Mr. McCray, I'd like a word with you if you don't mind."

"Yes, m'lady?"

"I understand that you were in Gwendolyn's bedroom." The countess emphasized the word *bedroom*.

She looked at his rumpled, ill-fitting clothes and knit her brow.

Patrick thought fast. "Yes, m'lady. Lady Gwendolyn was quite concerned."

"Concerned?" It was Lady Buckleigh's turn to be caught off guard.

"Mr. Wye and Mr. Killen have been taking her things."

The countess frowned. "What things?"

"Her mirror and something personal."

"The mirror was borrowed with permission. What else was taken?"

"You will have to ask her, m'lady. She wanted me to inspect her lock." The statement was intentionally misleading but not a complete lie. He had shown Gwen how to wire her skeleton key in place after jamming it in the lock. No one on the outside would be able to get in, even if they had their own key.

"I see. Who else was with you and Gwendolyn when you were in her bedroom?"

"No one."

"Patrick, you've received an invitation to our party."

"Yes, m'lady, thank you."

"It's because your father is the guest of honor. It would be best if you did not associate with Gwendolyn so freely. People will talk. Do you take my meaning?"

Patrick took her meaning. "Yes, m'lady."

"Let us hope tomorrow will be an enjoyable evening. Oh, and Patrick?"

"Yes, m'lady?"

"You do plan to bathe before you come, I hope?"

Patrick walked glumly toward his truck, his shoes clacking on the damp paving stones. Just then, the sun winked out. In the span of a few footsteps, the last red rays disappeared, and the landscape smeared into cold blue-gray. He drew a quick breath, fighting a dizzy feeling that the material world was melting into a void.

Sensing an animal presence, he turned his head and saw an exotic, raven-haired beauty standing beside his truck. He hadn't seen her before because her black dress blended with the dark woods behind the kitchen yard.

"Mr. McCray, I presume?"

"You would be Miss Harkless." He made not the slightest attempt to be cordial. She was older than him, but they were on the same level socially—if anything, he would, one day, be of higher standing than her.

"You must forgive me for eavesdropping. I can assure you it was unintentional. But you must also forgive Lady Buckleigh."

"All's forgiven." He stepped around the woman.

She deftly cut him off. "Lady Gwendolyn is ill."

"I saw her earlier today. She was quite well."

"She may seem so, but she has been sick and depressed. Girls her age are often moody. Their emotions change at the drop of a hat."

He couldn't argue with that.

"But that isn't the sum of her condition. She has a respiratory ailment and fevers, accompanied by mental distress."

"And you want me to stay away from her."

"By no means."

He stared at the bewitching woman.

"You have had quite a positive effect on her. Your continued company would do her good."

"What are you saying?"

"I have some influence with the countess. I could recommend it."

He said nothing.

"I presume you would like that?"

"It's not my place to like it or not."

"Well, it is mine. I have a responsibility as a nurse, and despite what you may think, I care very much about Lady Gwendolyn."

"Then make whatever recommendation you wish."

"There are things I need to know first."

"What things?"

"Lady Gwendolyn has been dabbling in magic."

"Magic?"

"Yes. I know it sounds silly, but apparently she believes it, and it affects her mind."

"I wouldn't know anything about magic."

"I need to know what spells she casts. The names of powers she calls. How she uses her talismans."

Patrick looked at the woman for several seconds. "I'm sorry, but I can't help you with that."

She smiled. "I see. But if you do think of anything, please let me know. I'll be waiting. I am your ally. After I know what Gwendolyn has been doing, and I know how to help her, I'll put the two of you together. I can do it. I really can, you know."

CHAPTER 12

Parries and Pirouettes

3-7-19

The traits most important to the continuation of an animal's bloodline vary by species. For elephants, it is strength and bulk. Cheetahs, speed. For chameleons, stealth; wolverines, fierceness. Moose have antlers, but that is another story. For humans, it is intelligence; however, allure is also an advantage, and for that reason, Pamela Hamilton's bloodline was in no danger. Vivid hazel eyes and rich mahogany hair made her lovely face that much more striking. Her sixteen-year-old figure would not have been called voluptuous—not quite—but her small waist accentuated her bust and hips so that the overall effect was dazzlingly feminine.

At present, Miss Hamilton was standing in the Grand Hall pulling at her gloves, waiting for a footman to help with her luggage.

"Pamela will have a lot of suitors," Lady Buckleigh observed from across the room.

"Yes…well…my Pamela is sweet, but she intimidates boys," Lady Hamilton remarked in a strangely lost tone.

"I imagine so. She is gorgeous."

Lady Hamilton opened her mouth to clarify but changed her mind and simply smiled.

To say that Pamela intimidated Jack Maham was to grossly over-simplify a volatile interplay of yearning and trauma on his part. Their few encounters over the years had been one-sided; Jack knew she considered him a face in a crowd—or an idiot.

An incident in August 1917 was the apogee of, and from then on the greatest contributor to, the right side of the yearning–trauma equation. Gwen had never met Miss Hamilton but knew of the event through Jack's agonized confession, made because of his overpowering need to tell someone. Additional details were provided later by Pamela's younger sister Leona, an eyewitness, who had come to Maham house for a short visit.

Jack had accompanied his mother to the Hamiltons' home in Kent. Lady Buckleigh was there to attend a meeting of a benevolent society that provided pharmaceuticals, supplies, and services to hospitals. While the ladies discussed their business in the drawing room, Jack waited in the morning room with Pamela and Leona. Leona nestled in a well-padded easy chair in a corner, reading a novel.

Pamela, feeling it her duty as hostess, sat opposite Jack across a table inlaid with a chessboard of alabaster and dark jade. A maid brought tea, cucumber sandwiches, and pastries. Pamela endeavored to make small talk. Her attempts were futile.

Jack, unnerved by the immediate presence of the object of his secret desires, chiefly made odd noises in response to Pamela's monologue, managing only to comment about the muggy weather and to make one or two uninteresting observations about London in wartime. He picked up the book on the table beside his chair, desperate to find a topic of conversation, but it was full of mathematical equations. Finding a book with *Vector Calculus* in its title lying in a drawing room left him even more befuddled and tongue-tied than before.

Leona, sensing that the live action was better than her book, began paying attention. Her sister was prone to doing absentminded things without regard to where she was or who she was with, and this seemed to be developing into one of those delicious occasions.

Thrown by Jack's strangled attempts at speech, Pamela settled into silence. Contemplating the chessboard and its exquisite medieval-themed pieces, her eyes drifted randomly from square to square as if she were playing a game in her head.

Jack felt the silence to be an indictment of his incoherence and social ineptitude. The tea and sandwiches gave him a pretext for muteness, but it was only a matter of time before the plates were clean and the teapot empty. He was at the point of spontaneous human combustion. The void of sound was unendurable.

Leona leaned forward, anticipating.

Pamela reached out and adjusted the position of a gold-trimmed chess piece, centering it exactly on its square.

Jack resolved to open a new topic of conversation by saying: *You have a beautiful chess set.*

At that exact moment, however, Pamela, true to her absentminded nature, oblivious to the fact that she was with company—and male company at that—took hold of the bodice of her dress and pulled to straighten it. Jack's eyes followed her hands to her torso, and somewhere between his overtaxed brain and mouth a mix-up occurred and what he actually said was, "You have a beautiful chest."

Gwen suppressed a giggle when she encountered Pamela walking down the grand stairs on the way to supper. "Miss Hamilton—I'm Gwendolyn."

"Lady Gwendolyn. I'm so pleased to meet you. You are looking well." Pamela's voice pitched upward so that her observation was almost a question.

"Yes, I've recovered from my illness."

Pamela smiled honestly and happily. "I'm so very glad to hear that."

With the silver service polished and the crystal glittering, the formal dining room should have been cheery, but it felt empty. Extra leaves had been inserted into the table so it could seat thirty-five people. Tonight, however, there were only seven—the five Mahams plus Lady Hamilton and Pamela.

Jack sat in front of the enormous fireplace, centered between lions' heads carved into its magnificent mantel. He kept his arms close to his body so they would remain within the protection of the tall back of his chair. Pamela sat beside him, close enough to the blazing fire to be overly warm herself. Jack avoided looking at her glistening skin.

Christopher fidgeted. He pulled periodically at his stiff collar. For most of the war, the family had taken supper informally in the breakfast room, where a dress code was not enforced, so he had become accustomed to eating in comfortable clothes. Now he was trapped in a jacket and a starched shirt, his collar cinched with a tie. He decided that, after all, he was not sorry to be too young to attend the Cabinet party.

Pamela was splendid in a vibrant yellow gown and would have looked every bit as good in champagne-colored silk and muslin. Gwen, on the other hand, looked like a bleached moth in champagne-colored silk and muslin, which was what had been available to borrow for this evening's dinner. She had to be careful how she moved. Agnes had not had time to make alterations and had pinned the dress extensively.

Only four courses were served: soup, fish, beef Wellington with vegetables, and a dessert, all prepared by Mrs. Nellis. Knowing her mother was watching, Gwen forced herself to eat substantial portions. In addition to suffering an uncomfortable fullness, she worried that Miss Harkless had put something in her food. But she couldn't risk failing the evaluation and being cut from the party guest list.

The talk that night was not conversation so much as a pre-battle briefing. Lord Buckleigh lectured on the powerful guests: Lloyd George, Bonar Law, Lord Curzon, Lord Milner, Mr. Barnes, and Mr. Churchill. He spoke of their families, accomplishments, and current positions.

Gwen had done a little research of her own. When her father finished and two footmen brought the beef Wellington, she couldn't help herself. "I understand that Mr. Bonar Law is an avid chess player."

Jack choked on a forkful of meat and crust. Pamela, best situated to help, pounded on his back. He hacked violently.

"Are you all right?" Lord Buckleigh had risen and rushed around the table to his son.

"I...I think..." Jack looked at Pamela. Utterly defeated and with no dignity to be regained, he gave in to a perverse impulse to self-destruct.

"Something caught in my *chest*."

Gwen guffawed.

Pamela stared at Jack in surprise. Then, amusement in her eyes, she smiled and patted his shoulder.

Startled, Jack realized that he had somehow, inexplicably, come out for the better.

Gwen gasped for breath, tears running down her face, a reaction fueled as much by the release of days of tension as by Jack's quip.

Christopher didn't understand the joke but giggled in resonance. Lord and Lady Buckleigh wondered what madhouse they had stumbled into.

"Are you drunk?" demanded the countess, thinking the children had accidentally been served wine.

Lady Hamilton must have known something. She was holding her napkin over the lower part of her face, and all her attention had suddenly been captured by a painting on the wall: a landscape with cows.

That night, the wind gusted and Gwen's windows thumped against their frames. Lying in the dark, she imagined an ogreish army clapping together siege engines on the border of the estate. She had wired her key into the lock the way Patrick had shown her. She had the prism because Jack, for some reason, continued to insist she be the one to keep it. He had forced it into her hand when they came upstairs after dinner.

Her sleep was restless, and she dreamt of nothing except wandering a dark, featureless plain.

The Friday morning murder did not go as planned. In fact, it did not go at all. Poison having become problematic, Mr. Wye was supposed to have pushed the Maham girl down a flight of stairs and broken her neck, making it look like an accident. A plausible message supposedly from her brother would have drawn her into the East Tower at the right moment. However, with so much activity in the house, Miss Harkless had called it off, deciding that the risk of exposure outweighed the profit of eliminating a threat that was still ambiguous. Fredrick

Maham and Mair Lloyd George would not be joined by Gwendolyn Maham's spirit at the séance, after all.

Harkless blamed Wye for the business at Whitebarrow. Having Sir Geoffrey out of the way was extremely beneficial, so she hadn't punished her men for the spur-of-the-moment kidnapping, but the rest was a disaster. Wye should not have shot at Mayfield without confirming in advance that there were no witnesses—such as the squad of British soldiers around the corner.

Wye had accepted a savage slap and dressing-down with no attempt to defend his bungling. He wouldn't have been so passive three months earlier. Three months earlier he hadn't known Asmodeus or the other spirits. Meeting the six that Harkless commanded had transformed the man. The mescaline mixed into his drink was incidental but hadn't hurt. The confirmed atheist had become comically superstitious. He reported that Mayfield and the girl had physically entered the spirit world—an impossibility.

More disturbing was the insight from her midnight communion with Gnosarkiz and the others: the two brothers had broken into the North Wing. It irked her to near rage. Perhaps her ploy with the Irish boy would yield fruit.

The borrowed maids and footmen had settled into routines, and preparations were proceeding smoothly. Monsieur Léger, the French chef, had arranged things to his liking and overseen the preparation of stocks, sauces, and pastry dough. He was unsatisfied with the wines in the cellar and ordered several dozen bottles from a merchant in London. His assistants checked vegetables, fruits, truffles, and spices; however, Monsieur Léger also smelled and tasted everything himself. The big kitchen, alive for the first time since Fredrick's death, was suffused with savory aromas.

The weather held gray, but dry. Gwen took breakfast in her room and later, after beginning a new journal in a blank diary Christopher had found for her, a light luncheon. Upon request, Mrs. Nellis made and brought the food herself. The sympathetic woman was happy to do it, understanding without being told that Gwen was afraid of being drugged.

Mindful that her room could be searched again, Gwen hid her old diary in a dresser drawer instead of her desk. But the loose binding came apart, and pages spilled out.

"Bother!" She stuffed the pages back into the book—she would put it together properly some other time. But the drawer jammed. She shoved until it closed. She didn't notice that some of the diary pages had fallen into the rear of the dresser cabinet.

Jack went out the French doors onto the terrace. From the bottom of the steps to the garden, he sauntered north, scouting the exterior of the house. Workers were boarding up North Wing ground-floor windows. Soon there would be no way to get into the wing without making a terrible racket. He continued around the far end of the house and back south through the central courtyard. He kept his distance from the security detail at the North Wing's front entrance.

Inspector Thompson was there, giving instructions to his team. The inspector turned and watched Jack.

Jack smiled and waved.

There was nothing to be learned. His mind wandered to Pamela Hamilton. He desired her tremendously. Then he thought of Private Karl Brock. Love. The English language was illogical. The same word should not mean selfish desire on the one hand and entirely selfless sacrifice on the other.

With no clear destination, Jack continued diagonally to the fountain on the west side of the house. Water spilled in a cylindrical curtain from a three-foot-wide saucer at the top of its central spindle to a much larger saucer below it, to an even larger one below that, and finally into the pool at the bottom.

Who was Jack Maham? A person made to take vengeance on those who did evil. To annihilate Germans in order to bring peace and joy to the world. That was his reason for existing. It was the purpose that filled him so that he wasn't empty and useless.

He didn't want to be empty and useless.

He circled the fountain. It wasn't working out. Maybe God didn't want him to fight evil men. Then again, he was no longer convinced that Germans were entirely evil. Some of them were, but not all. Maybe not most.

He stopped and stood very still. He had not been praying for peace and joy. He had been praying for intensification of the war—Germans slaughtered, their cities poisoned. Exactly what Harkless was praying for. What Satan wanted. Jack was just like them.

In the falling sheets of water, he caught momentary, fragmented reflections.

Was it true? Was he so perverse?

He looked at the curtain of water splashing into the pool and imagined himself under it, in a storm-whipped sea, struggling to get back to air. For years he had fantasized about fighting Germans and believed his fantasies to be righteous. They were comforting: they allowed him to think that he, Jack Maham, not only knew how to change the world for the better but also had the power to do it. His beliefs were underpinned, he had been convinced, by absolute, indisputable facts that every person in England would affirm. But now he suspected that what Jack Maham wanted to happen would only cause more suffering.

"God, why did you make me like this?" Jack said out loud.

Jack knew what God would reply. God would say, *I did not make you that way. You bent yourself that way.*

He stared at the flowing water. The fantasies he didn't want to give up were pulling him down into the darkness he feared. Nevertheless, giving them up would take away the small amount of pleasure he was still able to feel.

He resumed his orbit of the fountain. The one and only God was in the distance—in all the vast universe, holding it together.

Light sparkled through the sheets of water. Jack Maham was bound to Jesus Christ. He was a child of God. If he accepted and defined himself that way, nothing could ever threaten his identity. Jack stopped struggling and let go of what he wanted. He didn't sink. The one and only God was walking beside him.

A gust of wind blew a spray, like droplets of fire that sprinkled him. He didn't need to worry about demons or even his own flaws and perverse nature. The one and only God was in him.

He walked back to the house, where he still sensed the demons, but their voices had been quieted.

The tempo of preparatory activity reached its crescendo when the guests' valets and ladies' maids began arriving. It tapered to an illusory calm at half past five when chauffeured cars began discharging Cabinet members. The domestic staff scurried out of sight.

It was not long before one or more of the bells in the servant's hall were ringing every minute.

At a quarter before six o'clock, Lord and Lady Buckleigh greeted Maurice Hankey, secretary to the wartime Cabinet. Prime Minister David Lloyd George and his entourage entered the front hall ten minutes later. Gwen watched the PM from the gallery above the grand stairs. He wore a bowler hat and a traveling cloak that, when doffed, revealed a frock coat and wide tie. He was not tall. After consideration, Gwen decided that he was handsome—or at least charming—though not stylish. His hair was graying to white, and he sported a bushy mustache. He talked with an attractive woman of about thirty as they strode across the hall. The woman must have been Miss Stevenson, his private secretary. Such was the PM's presence that space seemed to swell around him as he came up the stairs.

Gwen ducked around a corner. She went up to her room by way of a servants' stair, ignoring a surprised maid who nearly asked her if she were lost.

Agnes was busy attending to Pamela. A lady's maid named Mary came to help Gwen with her hair and gown. Mary spoke with a lilting Irish brogue that Gwen found pleasing.

"This is beautiful to work with," the maid observed, brushing

Gwen's hair. After hearing her client's preferences, Mary wove Celtic plaits into a circlet and left a fall that touched Gwen's back. Then she formed big, loose spirals that dangled past Gwen's temples.

Gwen was thrilled with the result. She wondered how Patrick would respond to the Irish elements. But looking into her hand mirror, she experienced a moment of doubt. She didn't want Patrick to think she selected the hairstyle to please him.

No. It was what *she* wanted. It had nothing to do with Patrick McCray. She left it as it was.

Patrick struggled with his studs and cufflinks. They kept slipping out of position. The bow tie gave him even more trouble. He redid it four times and still didn't have it quite right when his father declared it was time to set out for Maham House.

Gwen worried that she was too early, and then, as she left her room at ten past seven o'clock, that she was late. She found herself hurrying. There was no one on the landing above the front hall, so back straight and head high, she swept down the grand staircase unescorted.

She proceeded across the polished Grand Hall floor toward the murmurs and bits of conversation coming from the reception room. Inside, nineteen gentlemen and ladies, half of whom she didn't recognize, were talking in groups of two, three, or four. Her mother, wearing a bright hostess smile, was chatting with an elegantly dressed couple.

Lady Buckleigh saw Gwen, inspected her without seeming to, and gave a barely perceptible nod of acceptance. Gwen went to her.

"Lord and Lady Curzon, this is my daughter, Gwendolyn."

Lady Curzon was beautiful and greeted Gwen graciously.

"Delighted to meet you." Lord Curzon inclined his head stiffly. He had a thin, arched hairline, close-set eyes, and strong nose. Gwen had heard he was an intelligent and resolute man, but something about his demeanor led her to believe that he was also rather unfeeling. He had been viceroy of India and was now a minister without portfolio in the Imperial War Cabinet.

Gwen didn't know if she should offer her hand. Men often kissed women's hands upon greeting, but she was uncertain of the rules. Proper behavior was not only expected, it was compulsory. She decided to curtsy instead. "I'm happy to make your acquaintance, Lord and Lady Curzon. I hope you feel welcome in our home."

It seemed she had made an acceptable choice. The adults resumed their conversation, which was chiefly about mutual acquaintances.

Gwen scanned the room. In addition to Lloyd George, she recognized several men from their photographs. There was Andrew Bonar Law, chancellor of the Exchequer, whose expression right then was grim. It was as if the problems of the war were consuming him. He had lost two sons in it. He and Lord Milner were conferring quietly by themselves. Gwen also recognized Winston Churchill and his wife, Clementine. Gwen decided that the gentleman she didn't know must be George Barnes. He was talking with Maurice Hankey.

Patrick was not there.

Footmen in immaculate livery circulated with trays of Champagne, lemonade, and canapés with cheese or pâté. An amazing arrangement of orange, yellow, salmon, and purple flowers meandered down a long side table decorated with a white lace runner. Crystal bowls of colorful berries and chocolates were hidden throughout the arrangement to be found and enjoyed by the guests.

The room was filling up. Gwen took a glass of lemonade. She had no problem speaking with great men and women but lacked the background to contribute to any except the most mundane and trivial conversations. She was very conscious of being looked at. It was almost unprecedented for a teenager to attend an event of this type.

Lord Buckleigh had decided early on that Jack, as heir to the Buckleigh title, should be included. Lady Buckleigh invited Pamela Hamilton thinking—incorrectly—that Jack would be more comfortable if a girl he knew were there. Inviting Gwen had not even been an afterthought. In retrospect, Gwen was astonished she had wormed her way in.

She supposed her age was the cause of all the looks. Still, there might have been other reasons. Every woman was secretly assessing the gown and hair of every other, and Gwen liked to think she was included in the competition. Everywhere, colorful silk and taffeta were shaped and fitted to perfection. Gwen thought she scored acceptably. However, the glances made her horribly self-conscious of the pale skin exposed by the low neckline of her gown.

Every now and then a guest would comment on current or historical events that she knew nothing about. She heard furtive references to a new German offensive in France.

Jack pulled Gwen aside to whisper about the séance. They still did not know how they were going to stop it. Warning the guests would get them expelled sooner rather than later. Likewise, there was little chance they could break into the North Wing. It was well-guarded. Nonetheless, Gwen had faith that Patrick would find a way.

She still had the prism; Jack had never come to collect it. It was in her corset because her gown had no pockets. The hard, angular object pressed uncomfortably into her flesh. Wanting to pass it to Jack but unable to get to it with people watching, she was on the verge of suggesting that the two of them go to the library. Just then, however, she became aware that Lloyd George was in the group next to her. He turned, looked right at her, and smiled.

She was flattered, flustered, and delighted to have attracted the notice of the prime minister of England. He seemed about to speak to her when someone else caught his attention.

Gwen had never seen Miss Harkless in an evening gown. The woman was gorgeous and glamorous. Silk the color of black plums swirled sublimely around her legs and arms as she glided into the room. Pearls shimmered in her dark hair, and she wore a diamond necklace. Where she had got it, Gwen didn't know, but the diamonds must have been real because every lady in the room would recognize costume jewelry. Tonight, Miss Harkless's triangular face and small mouth were particularly fascinating. She had subtly emphasized her eyes with makeup in a fashion that made Gwen think of Cleopatra.

The prime minister was captivated.

When Miss Harkless moved among the guests, she caused oscillations and swirls like eddies in a boat's wake. She was quite aware of it—especially her draw on some of the men. Her eyes glittered. She affected to steer a random course but moved inexorably toward the prime minister.

Then, abruptly, the queen of the night's spell was broken. Behind her, Pamela Hamilton entered the room as completely without drama as Miss Harkless had come in with mystery. It was as if an eclipse had ended. The sixteen-year-old girl was stunning in a low-cut dress of gold and bronze, with rubies at her ears and throat—sparkling accents to her rich mahogany hair.

Harkless saw Lloyd George's gaze, and she turned to identify the disturbance. For a split second, her face contorted to irritation bordering on rage. Then the serene smile was back in place. Any smugness, however, was gone.

Pamela gave no sign of realizing she had caused a stir. After a quick survey, she proceeded toward Gwen and Jack. Before she reached them, however, it was Gwen's turn to be distracted. Patrick and his father had finally arrived.

Lieutenant Colonel McCray of the Royal Flying Corps was dashing in his dress uniform. His dark hair was impeccably groomed and shiny, every whisker of his jaunty mustache was perfect, and he stood straight and tall. But Gwen couldn't take her eyes off Patrick. Evening clothes transformed him. His hair, like his father's, was combed and smoothed with a little oil. He was the perfect young gentleman. She looked him up and down proprietorially. The only imperfection was his lopsided tie.

But Patrick was out of his league. Stiff and uncomfortable, it required no mindreading to know that he wanted nothing more than to find a corner and hide.

Gwen greeted Pamela. "How beautiful you are!" The compliment was a formulaic politeness, but in this case it was entirely true.

"Thank you. I can return the compliment. You look radiant." Pamela meant it, or she was a great actress.

Gwen waved discretely to Patrick, signaling him to come over. "Here's Mr. McCray," she said as if he were joining them by chance. "Miss Hamilton, this is Lieutenant Colonel McCray's son. Allow me to introduce you."

"How do you do, Miss Hamilton." Patrick bowed stiffly.

"Very well, thank you, Mr. McCray."

Gwen flushed and gulped. Patrick was so handsome! She felt such possessive pride she had to force herself not to grin. The problem with his tie didn't bother her. On the contrary, she realized with a thrill, it was a perfect opportunity for an act of domesticity. The joy of it filled her.

She considered: bend close to discretely confide an instruction or two that he could execute without leaving—or suggest he go somewhere and fix it…and go with him? It was the sort of thing a wife might do for her husband.

No, wait! She hadn't meant that!

Pamela tilted her head to one side, scrutinizing the tie. Then, without warning, she stepped up to Patrick, reached out, and worked the sides of the bow to even and straighten them.

Patrick went rigid. Up until that moment he had been scarcely aware of anyone but Gwen. Could he really call her Gwen? He was no nearer to knowing her mind—what she thought of him. He had not once seen a girl or woman look as breathtakingly lovely and enchanting as Gwendolyn Maham did that night. Everyone else was a dull, monochrome shadow.

Except that, impossibly, unbelievably, another girl was grooming him! Forced to focus on Pamela, Patrick saw that she was also beautiful—solid and real. He smelled her perfume and sensed the warmth of her body.

Gwen had never felt such emotion: a combination of outrage and fury. In full view of everyone, Pamela Hamilton was engaging in physical flirtation with a boy she had met seconds before. The rage didn't show on Gwen's face, but that was only because she was in shock. *Her* boy!

Pamela, the most serious competitor a girl could have, was revealed to be a predator with neither conscience nor soul. For Gwen, self-reflection and certainty were near instantaneous. What she wanted from Patrick was so much more than she had admitted to herself. Suddenly, she had a lot to lose, and she was afraid.

The expression on Patrick's face was unreadable, but at that moment he saw only Pamela—a girl of his own class or near enough.

"There," Pamela said with satisfaction. "That's better."

The butler, Livingston, appeared in the doorway. He held a gong suspended by cords from a handle. Struck gently with a mallet, it produced a long, majestically resonating tone. "Dinner is served."

Hi Paige and Lara,

I've taken a lesson from Mrs. Holliwell and Christopher and been praying a lot. I'm calmer and feel better. Also, I found the last of the missing documents. I know everything now.

Love,

Kirk

CHAPTER 13

A Cascade of Shards

66-22-4

As the guests made their way to the door, David Lloyd George came alongside the teenagers.

"Lord Mayfield, I believe?" The prime minister extended his hand.

"Yes sir." In other circumstances, Jack would have been tongue-tied. Tonight, emotions dulled, he was carefully deferential, but not overawed by the great man.

"I'm delighted to find four fresh faces in this grim old crowd." Lloyd George smiled at each of the young people in turn, his eyes lingering longest on Pamela.

"Prime minister, this is my sister, Lady Gwendolyn," Jack said.

"Delighted to meet you, milady." Lloyd George took Gwen's hand and touched it to his lips, eyes twinkling.

Distracted momentarily from her anger, Gwen blushed. "How do you do, sir."

Jack continued the introductions. "Miss Hamilton."

The prime minister kissed Pamela's hand as well, maintaining eye contact and smiling. "Charmed."

She smiled back serenely. Lloyd George appeared to be thrown off balance by her nonchalance. Did she know to whom she had just been introduced?

"And Mr. McCray, the lieutenant colonel's son."

Lloyd George shook Patrick's hand. "Mr. McCray, I am glad we have men like your father on our side."

"Thank you, sir." Patrick gulped audibly. He was as uncomfortable as Pamela had been unaffected.

"Ah—we are holding up the show." The prime minister glanced about. He offered Pamela his arm.

Ordinarily, escort responsibilities were prearranged. Couples would proceed to the dining room in order of precedence. The host would take the ranking lady, and the hostess would bring up the rear as the companion of the man of greatest standing. But etiquette was based on social, not political status. So perhaps Lady Buckleigh's failure to give the gentlemen advanced instruction regarding whom they were to escort and in what order was not an oversight.

Gwen reached for Patrick.

But Miss Harkless snagged him first. He flinched as if a giant tick had latched onto his arm. Gwen glared at the exotic woman, not bothering to hide her antipathy. Miss Harkless smiled back, dominant and smug about it. She maneuvered Patrick behind the Maham siblings.

Gwen kept glancing over her shoulder as she walked. The witch woman was speaking too softly to be overheard. At first Patrick marched stiffly, arm out to keep his body as far from hers as he could manage, but somewhere along the way, by the expression on his face, he began to give serious consideration to whatever it was she was murmuring.

Once in the dining room, everyone went to find the place setting with his or her name printed at the top of the menu card. Seating deviated from the usual protocol. Miss Harkless had been positioned in the middle of the table instead of with the teenagers—and they were thankful for that. Gwen sat between Patrick and Winston Churchill, the minister of Munitions, who had been put at the teenagers' end of the table because he was of lesser importance than some of the other Cabinet members. Jack faced Gwen. Lieutenant Colonel McCray sat to Jack's left and Pamela Hamilton to Jack's right, which meant that the mahogany-haired beauty was directly across from Patrick.

Eight courses would be served. Patrick studied the array of sterling silver forks, knives, and spoons to the left, right, and top of his place setting.

The china was lustrous, and the snow-white table linen even brighter. Light glinted from the crystal bowls, decanters, and glasses—and, of course, from women's necklaces, bracelets, and rings. Hothouse flower arrangements provided a colorful organic dimension.

"How lovely," someone said.

Gwen leaned toward Patrick and spoke in a low voice no one could overhear. "What did Miss Harkless want?" She knew it sounded like an accusation and didn't care.

He did not look at her. "She thinks you've been performing magic. She wanted…just wanted to know about it."

"And what did you tell her?"

"Nothing." He stared at his place setting.

"You talked a long time to say nothing," Gwen hissed through her teeth.

He refused to argue. "Did Jack find a way into the North Wing?"

"*You* have to get us in."

He winced very slightly. Gwen was the only one to notice it. She leaned away from him.

Not much of the conversation around the table was specifically about armies and battles, but references to hardships and losses made war the evening's backdrop. Gwen listened mainly. Children were to be seen and not heard.

Pamela was certainly seen. She gazed attentively at whoever was speaking. But it was an act—feigned interest. Perhaps she didn't understand what was being said. The girl was a simpleton. A vacuous ornament. Did Patrick realize that? He was a boy. Maybe that was what boys wanted. Gwen didn't mean to look at Patrick but couldn't stop herself. After every glance, she turned her head away with new resolve. But temptation grew second by second until she had to check on him again. Why did he never look at her?

Patrick knew that Gwen was watching him. He avoided her eyes.

They were colder than the ice in his delivery truck. He resented being made to feel guilty; he didn't know his crime. Had Mayfield's suggestion that he decline the invitation been, after all, a tactful attempt to save him from this misery? Why couldn't he just forget Lady Gwendolyn Maham and be done with her? Find a girl more like the one across the table. Miss Hamilton's easy familiarity had stunned him, but she was the only person in the place whose presence was calming.

She smiled at him reassuringly as if she understood his anxiety and lent him her support.

Then both Gwen and Patrick were distracted from their respective thoughts by a testy exchange between Churchill and the woman to his right. The two adults seemed to know each other well and were arguing about something to do with the United States—or maybe it was Russia.

The woman glared at Churchill. "Winston, if I were your wife, I would poison your soup."

Churchill thought for only a moment. "Marjory, if you were my wife, I'd drink it."

Gwen stared at her bowl. Jack and Patrick didn't know where to look. Pamela cleared her throat to hide a chuckle. Churchill beamed at her.

When the fish course was served—stuffed salmon—all attention turned to Lloyd George, who was describing a function held at the Guildhall when he was chancellor of the Exchequer.

"Our premier likes to recount this one," Churchill muttered. "The tale grows with each telling, like a reptilian appendage."

"I was obliged to attend in my privy councilor's uniform, complete with sword," Lloyd George said, his Welsh accent becoming pronounced. "It was an evening of pomp and feasting, and I probably wouldn't remember anything about it except that, on the way home, in the middle of nowhere, the car broke down. Mostyn, my chauffeur, pulled off the road to tinker with the motor, so I got out to stretch my legs. I couldn't have been more than ten yards away when I heard the door slam and the engine start. 'Stop! Stop!' I shouted at the top of my lungs. 'Mostyn, you are forgetting something!' All to no avail. Can you imagine? The fellow drove all the way home without noticing that I wasn't in the back!"

The prime minister sighed as if the event were happening then and there. "It was a long stretch of empty road." He scanned the imaginary distance, pondering. "No option but walk. Mind, I was in that outrageous uniform with knee-breeches, thin-soled shoes, and stockings—not exactly the attire for a ramble through wild, pitch-black countryside. Eventually, I came to a large residence." As if to himself, the storyteller said, "I believe that given the circumstances, I can be excused for failing to notice the sign identifying it as an insane asylum." He looked thoughtful. "I knocked. When the warden appeared, I announced: 'I require assistance. I'm the chancellor of the Exchequer.'"

Lloyd George paused and, keeping his expression serious to the end, concluded: "The fellow looked me up and down, beamed, and replied, 'Come right on inside! The rest of the Cabinet are expecting you!'"

There was polite laughter. Almost everyone at the table had heard the story before.

"The last bit about the warden was invention, I think," Churchill observed wryly. "And one wonders what our esteemed prime minister was really doing out in the bushes in the middle of nowhere."

Gwen looked at the plate with the next course: asparagus spears artfully arranged and topped with béarnaise sauce. She decided to eat a few of the tips and leave the rest. Asparagus was not her favorite vegetable, and she had to pace herself. According to her card, rack of lamb came next. That was followed by iced raspberry meringue, then apple tart, and cheese.

It was not a particularly adventurous menu, but Monsieur Léger produced delightful flavors, and his arrangements were as pleasing to the eye as to the palate. Several excellent wines complemented the food. The teenagers had to be content with water.

Gwen changed her mind a dozen times as the evening wore on. One minute, thinking Patrick felt nothing for her, she wanted to destroy him—tell him he was ridiculously stiff, or that his chewing was preposterously loud, or that he simply didn't belong in polite company. But the very next moment, remembering his shyness, the way he had stolen glances at her in the past, and the despair in his face whenever he thought he might have offended her, she was certain he must like her. Except now he didn't seem to be so worried about offending her. Had he given up? She should pet him—compliment and show him off and see how he reacted. Each impulse canceled the other in a circle. She ate in silence. The problem of the séance thrummed unpleasantly at the back of her mind, but she could not bring herself to think about it.

Churchill involved himself in numerous conversations. He was an interesting man. From what Gwen had heard, his insights and instincts were often correct, though they sometimes defied logic. His faith in the British Empire and the inherent virtue of the English people was rooted in past glories, but his ideas and inventions were ingenious and forward-looking. He was practically the father of the tank, the weapon that might end the stalemate on the battlefields in France. In the short time he had been minister of Munitions, he had increased British industrial output dramatically. But occasionally he was startlingly wrong, and he had a gift for making enemies.

Churchill gave firsthand accounts of various battles. He had been an army officer, a correspondent, and a politician in and out of Parliament. Learning that Churchill was one of the first British officers to pilot an airplane, Gwen saw an opportunity to fluff Patrick's pride and perhaps deduce from his reaction what was going on in his mind. "Mr. McCray has his own airplane," she said.

"He has?" Churchill was intrigued.

Patrick nodded.

"He repaired an old Vickers Gunbus," Jack said.

"And it flies?"

"Sometimes," Jack said more sourly than he intended.

Lieutenant Colonel McCray stared at Patrick. He frowned. He would not under any circumstances have given his untrained son permission to test-fly the F.B.5. Patrick lowered his eyes, knowing he would be disciplined later.

Gwen gnawed her lower lip, thinking perhaps she had made a mistake.

Lady Curzon was telling someone it was autumn in Argentina, the birthplace of her first husband. She turned to Pamela and explained slowly and carefully the way one would talk to a backward child: "Because Argentina is in the southern hemisphere, and the seasons are reversed."

A quick flicker of something that might have been exasperation or resignation crossed Pamela's face, but her cordial smile was back before anyone could read it. She nodded politely to Lady Curzon.

Gwen's mood rebounded immediately. She nearly laughed out loud. She checked to confirm that Patrick had seen Pamela's dull confusion. There was nothing at all in the dim-witted girl's head! But Patrick was staring fixedly at his plate.

Gwen looked over her shoulder. "Do you see that picture?" She pointed at a seventeenth-century painting of a gentleman conducting an experiment. The picture was crisp and precise, and the treatment of light was extraordinary, like something by Vermeer. Fixtures on a table held mirrors and lenses that directed sunlight through a prism, fanning colored rays onto an assortment of flowers. Half the yellow petals of a sunflower glowed red, the upper part of a spike of pale lupine luminesced pure green, and a scarlet rose appeared purple instead.

"I believe that is my ancestor John Maham," Gwen said, remembering what Uncle Geoffrey had told them about the first user of the prism. "I wonder what sort of experiment he is conducting there?" She wanted to say something about the scientific ingenuity that ran in her family but couldn't think how to do it without sounding artificial.

Lieutenant Colonel McCray contemplated the picture. "He appears to be investigating Sir Isaac Newton's theory of color. In Sir Isaac's day, it was believed that objects created color. He proved that the color was in the light that shined on them, instead."

Patrick twisted around in his seat and studied the painting. The sunbeam bent—refracted—when it entered the prism. The colors separated, and each of them refracted again when they exited the prism. His mind raced.

The conversation turned to relatives who had contributed to the sciences. Which by chance led to mention of Sir William Hamilton.

"My great-grandfather's cousin," Pamela said. "He was a mathematician."

This was received with polite nods, and nothing more would have come of it if Lieutenant Colonel McCray had not asked, out of politeness, "Sir William is best remembered for his work on vectors, I believe?"

"Quaternions," Pamela clarified.

"Oh yes, quaternions," Churchill said. "French whatnots."

Pamela showed no irritation at the poor joke. "They are sets of four numbers—three orthogonal identity vectors and a scalar for magnitude. Among other things, one can use them to calculate rotations in three-dimensional space."

Everyone stared at Pamela Hamilton as if she had just said something in Sumerian.

"They simplify the calculations, is that it?" Lieutenant Colonel McCray inquired after he had reset his perception of the girl.

"Exactly."

"When you say rotations, do you mean adding and subtracting angles?" Patrick asked as if this were a normal dinnertime topic.

"Imagine you want to define the relationship between vectors pointing in arbitrary directions so that you can transform one to another. How would you do it?" Pamela looked at Patrick.

Patrick frowned.

"Suppose you are given a diagram of two arrows, each with two gray tail feathers and one black," Pamela said. "The arrows point in different directions in three dimensions. A coordinate system is provided so that you can measure angles to each of the three axes. Imagine you want to write instructions for someone with an arrow in the first position to rotate it to the second so that even the orientation of the tail feathers is identical."

"I'd tell them to measure the angles from the axes and rotate about each axis in turn. First the x, then the y…oh…wait…oh!" Patrick's forehead crinkled. "I see what you mean. Each time you rotate around one axis, the other two axes change orientation. The tail feathers of the two arrows won't necessarily be aligned when you're done. It gets complicated."

"Correct. Aligning the arrows requires multiple operations and nine-term rotation matrices. You can't do it directly without computing an eigenvector. In any other case, the vector's coordinate system is different before and after each rotation." Pamela formed her right hand so that its index finger extended straight out, middle finger pointed to the left, thumb pointed up, and her ring finger and pinky were curled. She twisted her hand slowly, subconsciously depicting what she was picturing in her head, illustrating how the y and z axes would move after a rotation about the x axis.

The McCrays got the gist of the problem. No one else at the table had the least idea what she was talking about.

"Yes, I understand the difficulty!" Patrick exclaimed.

"I would like to rotate this year to get past the war," Lady Hamilton said, trying to redirect the conversation. But Pamela had found friends who wanted to talk about something interesting and could not be stopped.

"Quaternions can be added, subtracted, multiplied, and *divided*. Sir William's inspiration was that the identity vectors i, j, and k should be imaginary. Not Alice in Wonderland imaginary—imaginary as in the square root of minus one." She regarded Patrick meaningfully. "Do you see how that simplifies the matrix operations?"

Patrick was not familiar with imaginary numbers. Nor was he familiar with matrix operations, but felt he was close to understanding something important about Primary World geometry.

Other guests were bemused to have come across an exotic talking fox. Or a babbling lunatic. But the engineer and his son seemed to believe that what Pamela was saying made some sort of sense.

Pamela launched into a detailed explanation of quaternion algebra, which not even Lieutenant Colonel McCray understood. But Patrick was fully captured. He was not following the mathematics. He was visualizing the relationship between the Primary and silhouette frames.

Gwen set her spoon down so hard it clattered on her plate. She pushed the apple tart away, a desperate, hollow look in her eyes.

Patrick was gazing into the distance. Seams were joining in his mental model of reality. Colonel Sir Geoffrey's analogy of a shadow on a wall was completely inadequate. The truth was far more complex and actually different. The silhouette world was more like the intersection of two three-dimensional projections at a particular angle of incidence on a third. It all worked. It explained how beings and objects anchored and interacted. Picturing it in his mind's eye, he stared rapturously into space. Unfortunately, the space into which he stared so rapturously happened at that moment to be occupied by Pamela Hamilton.

Gwen let herself be swept along with the flow out of the dining room. Her face was impassive, detached, a mask. At the first opportunity, she separated from the group and made for the library. When out of sight, she ran, holding her skirt to keep from tripping. Angry tears blurred her vision and wet her cheeks. She bounded up the stairs to the second floor where no one could observe what she was doing and plunged her hand down the front of her gown. She couldn't think. The séance had become a backdrop instead of the focus of her concern. She saw no future for herself. She contorted her arm until she was able to reach the prism.

"What's wrong?" Christopher said.

Gwen was so startled she yanked her hand out of the dress, scraping the prism across her chest. "You scared me!" she shrieked.

"Sorry! Are you all right?"

"I had this stupid thing in my corset." Gwen waved the prism to explain what she had been doing. She pulled the back of her hand across her cheeks to wipe away the tears.

"Are we going to be able to get into the North Wing?" Christopher asked.

Gwen tugged the neckline of her gown to put it back in order. "I have no idea."

The boy, disconcerted by his sister's strange demeanor, tried to offer good news. "I have mice." He held up two small boxes.

Not having been in the battle on the mountain, Gwen didn't immediately connect mice with anything useful. Rather, the opposite. She was about to say something dismissive when inspiration struck.

"Let me have one of those."

Christopher gave her a box. "What are you going to do?"

"Create a distraction. We'll see what happens in the confusion." She was suddenly excited. One trick might solve all problems.

She rushed to the gallery above the front hall. Most of the guests had assembled below, waiting to be led to the séance. Gwen studied the crowd of men and women. Pamela stood beside the stairs. Perfect. Lloyd George and two other men were speaking with her, saying farewells since she would not be attending the séance. Patrick was in an excellent position to observe her hysteria.

"Stay out of sight," Gwen ordered Christopher. "There's going to be a lot of screaming and maybe fainting."

She glided smoothly down the grand curving flight of steps, hugging the banister. There was no danger her exploit would be noticed. The men's attention was on the girl in gold. Gwen kept the box with the mouse hidden within the shifting folds of her gown. Having no pocket, she had no choice but to clutch the prism in her right hand.

Five steps from the bottom of the stairs, she would pass next to and above Pamela. Gwen's plan evolved as she descended. Instead of dropping the mouse at Miss Hamilton's feet, why not into her hair? Her reaction would be sensational! She would never recover from the shock and humiliation. Patrick would see her as the childish and feckless creature she was, no matter her whatnots! The pandemonium would cause the séance to be canceled, or at least create sufficient chaos that Gwen and Jack and Patrick could sneak into the North Wing. The pleasure of being the master of destiny was intoxicating! And her timing was perfect!

Lady Buckleigh cleared her throat. "May I have your attention, please?"

All heads turned.

Gwen was giddy. No one would see what she did. The world had metamorphosed good and right.

"Miss Harkless has prepared a chamber insulated from psychic disturbances and optimally arranged for spiritual inquiry," the countess declared solemnly. "It is time to proceed there."

Gwen held the box with her left hand and removed the lid using the thumb and forefinger of her right hand—the other three fingers were curled around the prism. The frightened mouse pressed itself into a corner of the box. Gwen paused above Pamela. She leaned over the railing and, in a single serene motion, extended her arm and tipped the container.

It isn't amazing that plans go horribly wrong. It is amazing that those who make the plans are surprised when they do.

The falling, flailing mouse did not go into Pamela's hair. It dropped down the front of her gown. Pamela shrieked, jumped, and clutched at her dress.

An electric jolt of maniacal joy rippled through Gwen's body. This was better than her wildest dreams!

Only it wasn't.

Pamela's face drained of blood, but she did not go into hysterics. After the single understandable jump, she stood stock still, face frozen in a crooked smile—the kind that forms when shock temporarily discombobulates normal emotional responses. But she didn't lose her composure.

Lloyd George was the first to react. "What is it?"

"A…mouse," Pamela said in an ironically mouse-like voice. Then she laughed weakly because there was nothing else she could do. She looked down. "In my gown."

Gwen realized only then how slapdash her scheme had been. Pamela was not coming off badly. Instead, she was the focus of great sympathy. Her self-control was admirable. She did not race around shrieking in terror, never to live down the humiliation. In fact, she was more composed than most of the other guests, one of whom appeared about to swoon.

"In your *gown*? How on earth…" Lord Buckleigh was aghast.

"It seems to be raining rodents," Churchill muttered.

Several of the ladies glanced nervously upward and shrank backward. All the men's gazes remained locked on Pamela Hamilton's chest. Pamela squirmed, either because a frightened mouse was trembling inside her clothes or because a dozen men were staring with fascination down her dress. Or probably both.

Pamela was prone to unconscious social blunders, but tonight it was Patrick's turn. Fixated on an occurrence so strange that it caused him to lose all connection with reality, he reached out. "I'll get it."

Anyone watching would have sworn there was a collective gasp, but there was really only stunned silence as Patrick's hand extended toward the deep V of Pamela's gown.

Utterly horrified, Gwen lunged to prevent the unthinkable and slipped. She stepped on the hem of her gown, tripped, and toppled. She threw out her arms and grabbed the banister. The prism flew from her hand, hurtled to the marble floor, and shattered with a loud crack.

A thousand shards of glass cascaded across the cold stone floor.

CHAPTER 14

Mirror

64-17-20

Gwen hauled herself upward hand over hand, gripping the banister because her legs wouldn't stay underneath her. The air was so dense she thought she was drowning. She imagined she heard echoes of laughter. There was no color; everything around her looked like an afterimage of a camera flash.

She had broken her vows. Broken all trust. Thrown everything away. She was afraid to draw God's attention. She wanted to hide from Him once again.

She made it to her bedroom before collapsing. She crawled to the middle of the floor and lay there coughing violently, so nauseated that her hacking nearly became vomiting.

Jack charged in and demanded something. She didn't understand or care. But he wouldn't shut up. He pulled her to her feet. She fell sideways onto her bed and curled up in her crumpled gown.

He tugged urgently and angrily and shouted, "We have to go!"

"I don't have it," Gwen said. In all the confusion downstairs, everyone thought the broken glass was a wine goblet. Gwen could not bear the thought of telling Jack what had really happened—that she had destroyed the prism.

But he didn't ask for it.

"We have to go *now.*"

She coughed until the spasming was little more than panting. "I can't."

"You're coming!"

Blood pounded in her ears. "I *can't!*"

"You will!" He scooped her up and was not gentle about it.

"Put me down!"

"If it's the only way to get you to the North Wing, I'll carry you there."

He marched to the East Tower and stomped down the steps. She was tempted to throw up on him.

"Put me down," she repeated when they reached the first floor, this time in resignation. "I'll manage."

Patrick and Christopher were waiting by the French doors to the terrace—Patrick by arrangement, Christopher because he couldn't be gotten rid of.

Gwen was unsteady on her feet, so Jack kept hold of her when they went outside. The night was cold and gusty. A gibbous moon drifted westward over the house, in and out of ragged cloud banks.

"What are we going to do?" Gwen asked. Her skin was noticeably ashen even in the semidark.

"Stop that evil woman from practicing her cursed magic."

"There isn't any such thing as magic," Christopher said. "Only the power of God and the power of Hell."

"Well, we know which power claims her allegiance." Jack pointed at the black shape of the North Wing. "And right now it's in there."

Gwen didn't ask where God was. God had given up on her. She let herself be escorted to the end of the terrace and down the steps.

Christopher tugged on Jack's sleeve as they turned north. "What are you going to do with the prism?"

Gwen answered for him. "Nothing." She lowered her eyes. "We can't."

"Why not?"

She ached to confess. But she couldn't do it. "Evil spirits would rip us apart."

Christopher looked at each of the others in turn. "So how do we get in?"

"Patrick is going to…" Gwen's throat closed up. She couldn't look at him.

"I've arranged it," he said flatly.

Surprised, she glanced at him. The only thing she could read in his face was determination.

"Follow me," he ordered.

The wind blew hard against them. Their clothes flapped, and they had to lean forward to balance. The walkway beyond the kitchen yard was treacherous. Over the centuries, some of the cobblestones had settled, and others had pushed up. Gwen clutched at Jack and stumbled along.

They neared the small courtyard where she had seen construction work. Patrick stepped off the path.

"Where are you going?" Gwen peered into the inky recesses where moonlight didn't reach.

"That door, there."

"It's bolted," Christopher said.

"Not tonight."

Wet, overgrown grass and weeds snagged Gwen's skirt. Jack guided her through. The wind sounded almost human, the way it whistled and moaned. Patrick went straight to the door. It opened when he turned the knob. He made a remark to Jack, but Gwen couldn't hear it because of the wind.

Patrick waved everyone inside and shut the door behind them. A lit kerosene lantern had been left on the stairs at the end of the dilapidated hallway. Jack picked it up.

A big man stepped out of a doorway.

Lady Buckleigh led her guests into the pentagonal chamber. Nobody spoke. What did one say to greet the dead?

The visitors looked curiously at the mystical décor. Churchill was wryly amused. Bonar Law appeared to be unhappy about the whole thing. Lloyd George's expression was a mixture of skepticism—the sentiment he wished to project to the others—and the hope he hardly dared.

Everything was premeditated to create a mood that opened the mind. Music drifted in from a remote location, evoking memories of another time and place. Traces of incense wafted in the air. Mair's photos and personal things had been pleasingly arranged on the piano, Freddy's on a small, lace-covered table beside it. The chairs had been positioned around the round table. The candelabra had been moved elsewhere; it was not in sight.

Harkless was radiant. The souls she called would come. Years of disciplined, fearless, and sometimes ruthless work had gained her absolute mastery over every kind of spirit. Her every movement manipulated Gnosarkiz's submissive actions; she wore him as if he were a garment. And soon, she would control the men who steered the British Empire.

She bade them sit. "The prime minister shall be at my right hand, Lord Curzon to my left."

The gentlemen and ladies settled into their assigned places. Harkless clapped her hands, and a roll of thunder rumbled through the house as if by command. "We begin!"

Gwen couldn't have made it up the narrow staircase if Jack had not pulled her. In her imagination the house was swaying, the turbulent weather making it roll and pitch like a ship on a stormy sea.

"Up! Up!" The cheery tone of Mr. Wye's voice made the sound of it especially chilling. Mr. Killen came behind the children, ensuring that none of them escaped.

They were led a short distance to a heavy door whose frame had been reversed so that it opened into the hallway. It was barred by a steel rod laid in cradles bolted to the jambs. Wye unlocked a padlock and lifted the bar out of the way.

The room had a plain wooden table and four stout, straight-backed chairs. Gwen's mirror stood in a corner. The floor had been swept, but it was a shoddy job. One-hundred-year-old dust caked the creases and recesses of the east-facing windowsills. Jack recognized the room as the place Miss Harkless and Herr Lehrmann had come to converse in private.

Wye set his lantern on the table. He swept aside various objects: one of Gwen's monogrammed handkerchiefs, an old doll missing for two years, the ordinary prism her father had given her, and a book of the occult. A half-consumed candle burned in a holder heavily splattered with drippings.

Wye smirked. "Nicely done, McCray. Let's get them tied up."

"What?" Gwen swung around to face Patrick.

He took her shoulders and maneuvered her into a chair.

"What are you doing?" she shrieked.

He had a length of rope with a loop already formed. He closed it around her left wrist and, in a quick motion, forced her other arm behind the chair. She was restrained in seconds.

Killen had hold of both Maham boys. Jack did not struggle much, apparently too stunned, but Christopher pounded furiously with his free hand. Killen hardly noticed the ten-year-old's punches. Christopher's piercing screams, however, were painful to the ears.

"Save your breath! The walls are thick. No one can hear you." Wye stuffed a dirty sock into Christopher's mouth and tied a strip of cloth around the boy's head to keep him from spitting it out. The kidnapper nearly got bitten, but he gagged the little boy so effectively that the only sounds Christopher made after that were furious humming noises through his nose. Gwen feared he would suffocate.

Killen marched Jack to a chair.

"Just one thing," Patrick said, voice high with emotion. "A debt I owe Lord *Mayhem.*" Patrick punched Jack in the stomach.

Gwen gasped as loudly as Jack grunted. Mr. Killen had been ready for Jack to struggle. He was entirely surprised by Patrick's move. Jack twisted out of Killen's grip and lunged at Patrick. The fight immediately became a wrestling match on the floor. The two boys grappled and punched, knocking over the unoccupied chairs.

Killen pinned them both.

"I haven't finished!" Patrick sputtered.

"Yes, you have." Killen lifted Jack and slammed him down on a chair. Jack thrashed wildly. Killen balled his fist to knock him unconscious, but Patrick was ready with rope, making further violence unnecessary.

"I've got him." Patrick secured Jack's hands.

"Tighter," ordered Killen. "And his feet."

Patrick did as instructed.

Wye beckoned to the Irish boy and pointed at the empty chair. "Your turn."

"That's not the deal. Miss Harkless…"

"You'll see the mistress later. For now, you're to sit there and shut up."

Killen lashed Patrick down.

Wye smiled. "Don't worry, my friend, you'll have your reward soon enough."

Killen checked the ropes around Jack's wrists and ankles. He pulled, twisted, and completely retied the cords until they were so tight that Jack could hardly wiggle.

"What's going on?" Gwen demanded.

"Mr. McCray offered his services. His pay will be a love potion."
"*What?*"

Wye winked. "Young love. Ain't it grand?" He snickered until he and Killen were out of the room, and the door was barred and locked behind them.

The stub of candle flickered.

Gwen turned on Patrick with animal rage. "Love potion! *Love* potion! Are you *insane?*"

"You ordered him to get us in," Jack said grimly. "He got us in."
"*What?*"

Patrick stared at the floor. "I couldn't tell you. I wanted your reaction to be genuine." He licked his cut lip. "Mayfield was quite convincing."

"You told me to fight. That's one thing I know how to do." Jack scowled. "I hope there's more to your plan, McCray. I'll never get out of this." His hands were turning a deep shade of purple. "What comes next?"

"I wedged my pocket knife under this chair during our fight." Patrick searched for forgiveness in Gwen's face.

She was still digesting the news. "This is the most idiotic plan I've ever heard of."

"Do not let go hands," Harkless commanded. "The circle must remain unbroken." She closed her eyes and turned her head in a slow arc as if using paranormal senses to search a hidden landscape. "Those who have died young and unexpectedly are often confused. They linger and search. Mair and Fredrick wander lost. Call to Mair, Prime Minister. Guide her. Let her know she is welcome in our circle."

Patrick wormed his hand under the seat of his chair.

"I suppose you'd like one," Gwen snapped.

"One what?"

"Love potion. To use on Miss Hamilton."

"I agreed to whatever the witch offered. All I cared was to be brought here." He thrust his hand as far as he could; the ropes dug into his arm. He paused, confused. "Who's Miss Hamilton?" Then he remembered. "Oh. Why would I give *her* a love potion?"

Gwen snorted. "I think your performance at the dinner table explains that."

He was taken aback. "She's not the one—" He stopped himself. "It was a way to get in here."

"You didn't have to try so hard. Miss Harkless *wanted* us here."

"Of course. But she thought she was fooling me, so her men weren't so careful."

"You *were* fooled. We're tied up and locked in!"

He almost had it. Shoving with all his might against the ropes, he touched a finger to the pocketknife. It came loose and fell to the floor.

Out of reach.

Everyone stared at it.

"What do we do now?" Jack asked no one in particular.

"MUHHH! MUHHH!" Christopher bounced madly in his chair. The others turned to see what he was looking at.

The mirror had become an oval window into the séance.

"HELP!" Jack shouted. "OVER HERE! OVER HERE! WE'RE PRISONERS!"

None of the men and women in the other room paid the least attention.

"They can't hear us," Patrick guessed. "It's a one-way image. Not an interstice."

"But there *is* an interstice," Jack exclaimed. "There was iridescent film. Christopher and I saw it."

Patrick studied the space around the mirror. "Haven't seen this before—two separate silhouette locations joined back-to-back in Primary. The interstice is the plane between them."

"We can use the prism to go through," Jack said.

Gwen went rigid at mention of the prism.

Jack heaved himself violently, trying to loosen the joints in his chair. It was constructed of sturdy oak; he had more chance of loosening the joints in his body. He threw himself about until his chair tipped over and came down on its side, crushing his arm. He gasped.

"The knife's less than a yard behind you," Patrick advised.

Jack rocked and pushed with the side of his foot.

"A little to the left. The direction of your head."

Jack's arm throbbed.

"Stop. It's at your fingertips."

Jack had to fumble for some time before he was able to position the knife to cut the rope binding his hands. He sawed for several minutes and nicked himself but ultimately sliced through the rope and staggered to his feet. Bruised and bloody hands tingling painfully, he cut clumsily through Patrick's bonds. Patrick freed the others.

Christopher pulled the gag over his head and spit out the wadding.

He ran to the mirror. "There are devils all around you!" he yelled at the unhearing participants. "Can't you tell?"

Patrick tried the door. It was thick and solid. There was no hope of getting through it without a battering ram.

Christopher gasped. "Miss Harkless is a demon."

Her body appeared to have been cut apart and spliced back together around the perverted organs of a demonic being. The woman had more than one jaw. Her skin writhed.

"She's possessed," Gwen clarified. They were looking at a hideous thing: a human being who had utterly debauched and damned herself.

"Mair? Mair?" Lloyd George stared fixedly at the piano.

"You sense her, don't you?" Harkless cooed.

"She's here!" The prime minister's eyes filled with wonder and joy.

Haltingly, as if struggling to regain a half-remembered skill, an invisible performer began playing the piano. It was an ordinary baby grand, but the keys moved up and down on their own. The top of each key was coated with a white substance.

After a minute, the music smoothed and swelled into a haunting tune. It was not a parlor trick. A spirit was indeed sitting at the piano, and to Gwen it appeared to be the seventeen-year-old girl in the photographs—albeit starved, stretched, and twisted. Gwen knew she saw the demon that way because it was pretending to be Mair Lloyd George. The white substance coating the keys was wax from the candelabra that Jack and Christopher had accidentally anchored to the Primary World. The spirit played by pressing on the Primary-anchored wax, which pressed down the keys according to the inanimate object rules Colonel Sir Geoffrey had explained.

The men and women participating in the séance could not see the entity, but they felt it. Lloyd George recognized the smell of his daughter's hair. Awe and longing mixed in his face. "Mair, you always played so beautifully."

"Go to her," Harkless said in a breathless voice. "Comfort her."

Lloyd George's chair began to move on its own. Harkless let go of his hand—apparently, the circle no longer mattered. The guests were astounded. Churchill and Milner stood up.

"Stay in your places!" Harkless warned.

A spider-like demon had secretly placed the Primary-anchored candelabra under the prime minister's chair and was using it to slide him slowly toward the piano.

"Be joined," Harkless implored. "Prime Minister, open yourself—open yourself to your daughter's spirit so she can be at peace!"

The children could not hear anything spoken in the pentagonal room because no sound came out of the mirror, but Gwen knew exactly what was happening. "We were wrong." She shivered convulsively. "They don't mean to *persuade* the prime minister. They mean to *possess* him."

Jack snatched the prism from the table and pressed it into Gwen's hand. "Get us through the interstice."

The demon possessing Harkless could both hear and see the children through the interstice, and he flinched so that Harkless flinched as well. Gnosarkiz had endured the extreme tedium of maneuvering the woman he possessed. The behavior of puppets did not affect creation. The woman had to act not only of her own free will but also from her own original ideas. Now all his painstaking work was in jeopardy. He had thought the Maham girl was the only threat. He should have paid attention to the boy.

Gnosarkiz took direct control of Harkless. Her left arm extended toward the privacy screen, and her fingers made a scissor motion. Mr. Wye, observing through a tiny hole in the screen, saw the gesture. It was one of several prearranged signals. It was an order to kill the children immediately.

"Get us through the interstice," Jack repeated. "I can't do it."

"I can't either!"

"You have to!"

"Jack—it…" Gwen choked back a sob. "You aren't able to make it work because—"

"Because God always meant it for *you!*"

"No, it's because…what?"

"God always meant it for you, not me."

She was stunned by the thought, but she recognized the truth of it. In her mind, she saw her commissioning before the crowd of witnesses. She shook her head violently and sobbed. "Choosing me was a mistake."

"You weren't *chosen*. You happened to be in a particular situation in a particular time and place. So it has to be you, and God is relying on you. If you don't act now, all of creation will be in jeopardy!"

Christopher gazed into the mirror. "What's the devil doing?"

The demon mimicking Mair was still playing the piano but was face-to-face with Lloyd George, embracing him with a second set of arms.

"The prime minister thinks that's his daughter," Gwen said through her sobs. "The PM is inviting the devil into himself."

Indeed, Lloyd George knew beyond doubt that it was Mair. He would have staked his soul without hesitation. He would have denounced anyone who denied it. He was about to have the reunion he so badly wanted.

Jack took his sister by the shoulders. "Use the prism!"

"I can't!" she cried.

"You must!"

She raised her fist and shook it, gripping the prism so hard it bit into her palm. "This isn't the real one! I smashed the real one! I was jealous of Pamela Hamilton and sorry for myself. I only cared what I wanted, and I smashed it!"

"I know!"

"No, you don't! This is just a piece of glass!" she screamed, trying to make him comprehend.

"So was the other one!" Jack screamed back at her.

"The other one?"

"Uncle Geoff's. The one you broke."

Gwen stared at her brother. So he had seen what had happened in the Grand Hall after all. "Then…you know this one won't work."

Jack held Gwen's shoulders. "Jesus healed blind men. He didn't always do it the same way. Once, he put mud on a man's eyes. Do you think it was the mud that worked the miracle?"

"But this prism…"

"It's no different than Uncle Geoff's. Have *faith*, will you?"

She shook her head. "I keep doing what I shouldn't, and now I've done something unforgivable."

"The only unforgivable sin is blasphemy against the Holy Spirit. Do you understand what that means? There's nothing God *won't* forgive—only what he *can't* because you won't let Him." Jack let go of his sister and stepped back. "Gwen— this is the point of refraction. It's now or never."

She looked at the prism in her hand. "But…"

"Have faith."

Harkless stared at them through the mirror. In fact, many eyes stared out of the human shell named Harkless.

A psychological wall blocked Gwen from acting. Its bricks were self-doubt and shame, but its mortar was her enduring desire for events to unfold in a way that would produce the world she wanted. It wasn't merely a selfish desire to have things her way—at least she didn't think so; she wanted what was best for all humanity. Just as her father was going to end the war. Just as Lloyd George was going to help his daughter find peace. But Gwen was forced to see that attempts to impose her own will had produced nothing but disasters. Even her small victories—replacing Harkless's narcotics with water and learning about the séance—would have been unnecessary if she had done what God wanted from the beginning. The way she wanted things to be—what she thought would be the perfect world—was imperfect.

She had tried to change herself; she had tried to do what she thought God wanted. Instead, she had done things she knew He *didn't* want. The only way to succeed and do what God wanted was to give Him control.

"I'm not good enough."

"It doesn't matter. Do what God asks. That's all He wants."

From Jack, of all people. Perhaps because the words came from a messenger Gwen thought so unlikely to have the insight, she was able to grasp the truth and take it to heart.

She heard the bar being removed from the door to the hallway.

"For goodness sake, do it *now*!" Jack pleaded.

The force of her brother's insistence pushed Gwen through. Her wall crumbled, and the fragments fell away. As she had five days earlier on High Tor, she saw creation the way it was meant to be and the way she influenced it by the choices she made. She let go of her dreams. She let go of control. She had faith God was with her and would save her.

Killen came through the door.

"Thy will, not mine, Lord," Gwen prayed. "I'll follow. I'll reflect. I'll be a mirror."

With that, her will conformed to His.

Submerged in God, Gwen had unbelievable power. But at the same time, she was wholly herself, not manipulated or controlled or diminished. She was what He had made her to be and always intended her to be.

Gwen asked for light. It was midnight. The sun was on the other side of the planet. But she believed that dawn would come, and it did. The sun rose beyond the mountains, and the mountains moved out of the way, and light streamed into the east-facing windows. Gwen stretched out her arm. Beams entered the third facet of her prism, refracted, and fanned out in all wavelengths to do the work of mending the tattered fabric of creation, transforming reality to what God meant it to be. Gwen was not in control of what was happening, but she was God's agent, and what she did glorified Him. There was not a shadow anywhere.

Well done, daughter. Your faith has healed you.

Killen threw up his arms to shield his eyes.

She blazed like a star. Now completely free of doubt or hindrance, she did what she was supposed to do, fulfilling her role in creation. The interstice opened. The lead demon, poised to spring and devour her, pitched backward.

The sword was in her hand and the shield fastened in place, and now she wore a breastplate and gleaming helmet also. Metaphors, she knew, for her mind's sake, but they felt very real to her. She passed through the interstice and entered the séance room. Time had paused. That was not surprising—time is a notion, not a motion. Every bit of space, matter, and energy changes by God's power, and the result is the dream called time. All of the men and women in the pentagonal room were frozen in place. Only the demons moved, fleeing the girl who reflected God's intense light.

Jesus promised his disciples that anything they asked in his name would be granted. "I come in his name," Gwen called, her voice clear and strong. "I bind you in Jesus's name!" She said *Jesus,* but the Spirit in her spoke the true Name.

"I cast you down!"

And she was like lightning, striking with the sword. It wasn't her; it was the Lord using her, but there was no real distinction. She was radiance; she was joy. Her burnished armor deflected every counterattack. The creatures of Hell shrieked in terror and agony as their will was undone.

Gwen circled the room like a flare in a whirlwind, lunging, striking, and pivoting. First, she eliminated five demons standing in the corners of the pentagon—the spirits came apart as if sliced a hundred times at cross angles. Their flaming remains disappeared through holes into Hell. Next, Gwen eliminated the demon impersonating Mair. She cut it apart as she swept past and, with the next motion of her arm, did away with the spirit that had moved Lloyd George's chair.

Propelled by the light, Gnosarkiz, the demon possessing Harkless, flew across the room. Harkless hit the wall like debris flung by a storm and remained there, held by a force greater than gravity. Her human body could not escape through the wall. Gushing like vapor, the demon ripped itself out of her, attempting to flee. Gwen cut it down.

The forces of Hell had gathered on Dartmoor to escalate the war, famine, pestilence, and death wracking the human race in 1918. But instead of finding a weak point to exploit, they encountered a girl who, led by her brother, chose to be who her Creator wanted her to be. And they were utterly defeated.

Gwen lowered her sword.

EPILOGUE

The participants of the séance saw a tremendous flash of light, which afterward was attributed to a short in poorly-rigged electrical wiring. Miss Harkless was found crumpled and senseless, presumably having been electrocuted. At daybreak, still crazed and speaking gibberish, she was sent to a hospital in Plymouth. A week later, she was committed to a psychiatric institution where she stayed, suffering from what was diagnosed as schizophrenia, for the rest of her life.

Killen and Wye, stunned and dazed, were arrested by Inspector Thompson. They were convicted of the murder of Private Karl Brock and sentenced to life in prison.

Discussion of Lord Buckleigh's plan to poison German cities did not happen. The morning after the séance, the Cabinet's attention was consumed by alarming reports from France concerning a new German offensive code named "Michael." German advances were dramatic for a time but ultimately checked by English, French, and American forces. The Kaiser's armies were pushed back until the Germans sued for peace and signed an armistice. Hostilities ceased precisely at 11:00 a.m. on November 11, 1918.

The Allies did not have to invade Germany.

Colonel Sir Geoffrey Maham succumbed to pneumonia and died a week after his hospitalization in Plymouth.

Gwen regained full health and strength in the summer of 1918.

Later in her life she wrote: "Our first assignment may have had further-reaching consequences than we knew. Just as a vaccine teaches a body to recognize and fight a virus, Mr. Churchill may have been inoculated by his unknowing exposure to demons at the séance."

Churchill was one of those rare individuals who can be singled out as having singlehandedly turned the course of history. Very early, he recognized the evil in Adolph Hitler and tenaciously opposed him. His warnings were dismissed and ignored for years. In 1940, Churchill kept Britain in the fight against Hitler's Germany when resistance appeared futile. Had the British capitulated, the Nazis would have dominated the world.

World War I had profound effects on every aspect of life in Europe. In England, the class system began to break down, and social restrictions relaxed. It was no longer unthinkable, as an example, for the daughter of an earl to marry an aeronautical engineer. And there was at least one case in which it happened.

Saving the City of Light

A Novelette

by

W. F. Rogers

Saving the City of Light

August 1944

Paul Brock shifted to make himself less uncomfortable on the vibrating floorboard of the B-17's forward compartment. He was seated against the ribbed metal side of the droning four-engine bomber, a cushion behind his back, a parachute under his right arm. His thoughts were so deeply inward he hardly noticed the bitter high-altitude cold, the crick in his spine, or the numbness in his legs. The world was at war, and he was at war with himself. A German pilot who had been shot down over England in 1940, he was aboard an American bomber in a vast formation bound for Germany. But he wasn't going to Germany. He was going to France.

He adjusted his oxygen mask and glanced at the blonde woman sitting on the floor to his left. Was she really an assassin? He couldn't have imagined a more unlikely commando. She looked petite even wearing a bulky, fur-lined leather jacket. And Lady Gwendolyn must have been about forty years old—she had been in her late teens in 1921, when he first met her.

In the spring of that year, Paul had accompanied his father to learn about the mysterious death of his uncle Karl. Lady Gwendolyn and her younger brother Chris had shown seven-year-old Paul around the grounds of their amazing estate while his father spoke with their brother John, whom they called Jack. Uncle Karl had saved Jack's life.

Twenty-three years later, in the prisoner of war camp commandant's office, the hot July sun streaming through the open windows, Paul met Lady Gwendolyn and Chris again. Having tea with them at a conference table on the shaded side of the room, Paul replied warily to their questions about his health and conditions in the camp.

"Your English is perfect, Oberleutnant Brock," Lady Gwendolyn observed. "No accent. You spoke it at home with your mother, I suppose?"

He nodded. "My mother is English." He looked at the framed photographs on the commandant's desk: the man's wife and his two sons in their uniforms. "During the last war, my mother was suspected of being a traitor. We suffered because of it. But she would never betray Germany, and I will never betray Germany." He stared fixedly at Lady Gwendolyn.

She opened a portfolio. "We do not want you to betray Germany. We want you to deliver a letter." She handed it to him.

It was addressed to General Dietrich von Choltitz. As a boy, Paul had seen von Choltitz many times and called him "uncle" even though they were only distantly related.

"Next month, your relative will become the military governor of Paris." Lady Gwendolyn leaned forward, rested her arms on the table, and clasped her fingers. "Herr Hitler has ordered all of Paris blasted and burned to the ground if it cannot be held. The City of Light's beautiful architecture and monuments will be destroyed, its historical artifacts and French cultural heritage obliterated." She nodded at the letter. "That's an appeal to General von Choltitz to spare the city."

Paul looked her in the eye. "And you think you can convince me to take it to him."

"No." She smiled. "I think Chris can convince you." She patted her brother affectionately on the shoulder. "Chris is good at convincing. He was a trial lawyer before the war—a very successful one."

While Paul read the letter, Chris made the case. "British, American, and Canadian forces landed in Normandy on June 6, and our armies are pushing into German-occupied France." He enumerated the vast Allied resources, conjuring in Paul's mind images of a limitless arsenal, and then described battle outcomes and force momentum in language which made Paul feel the German army was being swept by an unstoppable wave. After establishing the perspective, Chris pointed out that Paris had no strategic value. Turning the city into a pile of rubble would not hinder the Allied advance at all. In fact, the Allies might bypass Paris entirely. Destroying it would serve no military purpose and not help Germany in any way.

Paul raised objections, but Chris neatly countered them all. The former barrister described the beauty of Paris in evocative detail, and then set the hook: "After delivering the letter, you'll be free. You can go wherever you want—even return and fight for Germany, though I hope you won't do that."

Paul didn't want to help his enemy in any conceivable way, and as a German officer, he didn't want to lie. But he had been in prison for four years. Was there any harm pretending he would deliver a letter? He sat silent for more than a minute.

"You asked about my English," he said. "My father moved our family to England in 1922 when I was eight years old, did you know that? Times were desperate in Germany. The war—and the reparations you British and French demanded—destroyed our economy. People were starving." He looked out the window at the wooded countryside beyond the camp's two barbed wire perimeter fences. "When I moved back to Germany in 1932 to attend university in Augsburg, it was like moving to a new country. But Germany is and always will be my home." He touched the pilot badge pinned to his uniform. "I joined the Luftwaffe in 1937 to serve my country. I flew over Poland and France." He smiled with some pride. "We were unstoppable." He looked down. "Then you British and your Spitfires…"

Lady Gwendolyn nodded. "My husband Patrick helped develop the Spitfire fighter plane."

Paul smiled dryly. "I thought you were here to make me more

comfortable, Lady Gwendolyn."

"No," she said. "I'm here because I'm going with you."

The B-17 bounced in rough air. Paul pressed on the floor to steady himself. He looked at the dark-haired man poring over the maps spread on the B-17's navigator's table. Wing Commander McCray and Paul had talked animatedly about the differences between the Messerschmitt 109E and Spitfire Mark II that opposed each other in the Battle of Britain. Not for the first time, Paul felt a stab of guilt. He liked McCray, and he was going to get McCray's wife killed.

He glanced again at Lady Gwendolyn. What was she, really?

He might have learned the answer in Scotland.

They had been lodged in a guest house separate from the commandos at the training base. McCray was there to help Paul plan the route he would take from the drop point in the French countryside all the way to the Hotel Meurice, where von Choltitz would make his headquarters. Lady Gwendolyn was glad for her husband's presence. She did not like jumping out of an airplane. She stoically did it without complaint, but each time, Paul saw her hands trembling as she hooked up the static line that deployed her parachute canopy when she exited the plane.

Chris Maham stayed in the same guest house. He gave Paul lists of German officers, summaries of troop movements, battle reports, and political news. He drilled Paul until Paul could answer questions automatically if challenged by German soldiers.

Jack Maham orchestrated preparations. He was the Earl of Buckleigh, a member of the British House of Lords, and a commander of covert operations. Taking personal control of this operation, Lord Buckleigh formulated the mission plan and schedule in great detail and made arrangements with the Americans. Paul learned that before the war, Lord Buckleigh and Lady Gwendolyn had been co-directors of Maham and Carter, their family's company, and traveled the world on business. They had met important people and, from what Paul ascertained, their trips often coincided with headline news, so perhaps they had served with British Intelligence even then.

Paul had nearly decided he would deliver the letter, after all. He liked these people. They were intelligent, considerate, hardworking, and sincere. On his last night in Scotland, however, everything changed.

Although he was kept under surveillance, he was allowed freedom within the guest house. That night, he was sitting in the corner of the common room studying a report cataloging German deployments in France. It was a good place to concentrate on facts and figures because it was quiet. Noise from the rest of the house was dampened. However, due to the geometry of the residence, sounds from one particular spot in an upstairs hallway were amplified instead. Even whispers there were perfectly audible down in the otherwise quiet corner of the common room. That night, Lady Gwendolyn and Wing Commander McCray were talking when they passed the spot.

"It's too risky," McCray said.

"Patrick, I'm going to drive out a demon. It's going to be risky no matter what."

Paul sat listening to a ticking clock. Lady Gwendolyn was going to Paris to drive out a demon? That was a euphemistic way of saying she was going to drive the German Army out of Paris.

He looked out the airplane windows. Hundreds of B-17's streamed white contrails across the blue sky. His stomach churned. All those airplanes would be dropping bombs on his country.

He had the letter in a German courier bag British Intelligence had supplied, along with a fresh Luftwaffe uniform and carefully updated identification papers. But the letter was probably a ruse. Lady Gwendolyn was being sent to commit sabotage. Or to assassinate General von Choltitz.

Why did it have to be her? She was fluent in French, but so were any number of English men and women.

Paul was one of few captured German pilots imprisoned in England—most had been sent to Canada. Was he caught up in a long-planned byzantine plot? He couldn't trust anything he had been told. He was certain of only one thing—whatever was going on was important. Lord Buckleigh said the mission had been approved by Prime Minister Churchill himself.

Paul recalled an odd interplay the afternoon before the operation, in the drawing room of the country home in Suffolk where he and the McCrays stayed, not far from the Ninety-Fourth Bomb Group's base. The room was elegantly furnished but had a businesslike feel. Memos, schedules, and checklists cluttered a large table, and a map of France was taped to the wall adjacent to the bank of windows. The surrounding green landscape was deceptively peaceful.

Lady Gwendolyn had gone to a tailor to collect the clothes she would wear in France. Paul and Chris Maham were waiting for her to return when Lord Buckleigh, wearing a Royal Navy captain's uniform, and Wing Commander McCray, also in uniform, arrived from the American Army Air Force base.

Lord Buckleigh tossed his umbrella neatly into the stand in the hallway. "Football. Energy and excitement."

"A game without focus and precision is a brawl." McCray strode into the drawing room. "Cricket. A thinking man's game."

Letting down his guard with friends, serious and methodical McCray revealed a wry sense of humor and passion for diverse subjects. But Paul had a feeling the wing commander was arguing this topic primarily because he liked to argue with his brother-in-law.

Lord Buckleigh looked at the two men already in the room. "Good afternoon, gentlemen."

"What about American football?" Chris asked roguishly. "How would you two rate it as a sport?"

"American football isn't football at all," Lord Buckleigh said.

The trim Maham brothers had clean features, strong jaws, and dark brown hair, though Lord Buckleigh's was graying, especially at the temples. Their attractive sister had an oval face, blue eyes, and golden hair.

She walked briskly into the room. "Well, Jack…are we set?"

Lord Buckleigh nodded. "Carlston briefed *Morning Glory's* crew last night." The Americans liked to name their airplanes; *Morning*

Glory was the B-17 that would fly Paul and Lady Gwendolyn into France. "The four escort pilots were given their instructions this morning and will tell no one. They understand the need for complete secrecy." He walked to the map on the wall and tapped a crossroads a few miles southwest of Soissons. "Our friends put the car in the garage yesterday. The building won't be locked, and you won't be challenged."

"I'm not Chris"—Lady Gwendolyn flashed her younger brother a quick smile—"but I can talk my way out of a mess if need be."

"You always do." Lord Buckleigh turned to Paul. "You'll have no trouble navigating, Oberleutnant Brock?"

"I've memorized the route and alternates all the way to the Meurice." Paul said.

"Good. Then we are indeed all set. Last chance for questions. Anyone?"

Paul had many questions but dared not ask any of them—and doubted he would be given straight answers if he did. He looked out the windows at the wrought iron gate in the lattice brick wall enclosing the flower garden. The path beyond it meandered into an adjacent woodland. Effervescent cumulous clouds piled in the east, their gray bottoms portending showers.

Lord Buckleigh saw his gaze. "Feel free to take a walk."

Paul had not expected to be allowed to ramble the countryside alone. He assumed he was still under house arrest. Perhaps Lord Buckleigh trusted him. Or perhaps the earl was willing to take a small risk to get Paul out of the way. Shortly after Paul left, it began to rain. He returned and entered the house through the garden room, which was connected to the drawing room by wide-open French doors.

The McCrays and Mahams were deep in discussion. They had been joined by a stranger with mahogany-colored hair. In her late thirties or perhaps early forties, the woman would have turned heads in any room. She had big almond eyes, a lovely mouth, and an excellent figure. She and McCray were hovering over a map unrolled on the big table. Even from the adjacent room, Paul could see that the chart was annotated with red circles, arrows, three-dimensional boxes, tubes, and other shapes.

Everyone looked at him. Lady Gwendolyn smiled pleasantly through the open doors. After a brief, awkward pause, they went on smoothly with their business as if to show Paul they weren't hiding anything. But they used cryptic words and phrases. Did they think he was insufficiently fluent in English to know they were speaking in code?

Brushing raindrops off his jacket, he went to the windows opposite the French doors and watched the scene reflected in the windowpanes.

The beautiful stranger tapped a spot on the map. "This is your best option. A half-mile wide and eight long. It's a toe-in interstice, so if you graze the side, prevailing winds will carry Gwen and Lieutenant Brock across the boundary to its interior."

McCray looked fixedly at his wife. "Anchor the plane and jump from inside the interstice."

"No." Lady Gwendolyn shook her head. "I might not be able to reanchor you after I jump."

"Then—don't get angry with me for saying it yet again—let the RAF take you in at night."

She touched the map. "Patrick, this is the plan."

McCray studied the markings. He looked at the mahogany-haired visitor. "I wish I had your ability to map interstices, Pamela."

She shrugged. "It's just calculations. I wish I had your ability to *see* them."

Chris Maham took his sister's elbow and held it firmly. "I don't understand why you won't let me go along. I've been into France so many times now it's second nature."

"I have Paul." Lady Gwendolyn looked through the doors and smiled at him.

That was a bad moment for him. He liked Lady Gwendolyn. Ach! He was a German and she was his enemy. How could he have so many doubts? Fealty to his country was paramount. Still…being part of a group—especially a group with a clandestine and dangerous job—created a sense of belonging and comradery. And these comrades were admirable and likeable. But his allegiance to Germany superseded all others.

Chris sighed so deeply it was almost a groan. "Well, the whole team is here to see you off. Except odd-bird Harold. You would think he could step out of a library long enough to be here for you."

"Don't worry about Harold. Let him stick to what he's good at. By the way, he confirmed the arrival time."

"And?"

"Eight past six."

"Precisely? To the minute?"

"That's what he thinks and it's consistent with my"—she hesitated, glancing toward Paul—"other information."

Pamela looked thoughtfully at Lady Gwendolyn. "This will be the first time in years we haven't been with you in an action."

"It's the right plan. Jack agrees and approves."

Pamela glowered at Lord Buckleigh.

The earl pursed his lips. "Too late for second guessing. Gwen and Oberleutnant Brock are the team this time."

"Jack has an uncanny ability to make right choices," Lady Gwendolyn said. "Trust him and trust me."

Paul pretended to study a hand-colored photograph left on a table by the garden room windows. Then he actually did study it. It was a snapshot of a painting. Superimposed on a fiery background evocative of Japan's rising sun, a female warrior with a trident and shield—Britannia—and a huge, determined bald eagle fought together against grim men in black uniforms bearing the double lightning insignia of the German SS. The drawing incorporated patterns from the flags of the Soviet Union, France, Italy, and many other countries. Groups of Arabic numbers formed a swastika. At the drawing's center, a symbol evocative of the Eiffel Tower was labeled with the Roman numerals I, VII, and XII.

Someone had marked the photograph with grease pencil, printing dates beside the Arabic numbers. The earliest was July 7, 1937. A few of the dates caught Paul's eye: June 22, 1941, the disastrously delayed start of Barbarossa, Germany's invasion of Russia; and June 4, 1942, when the Americans, their fleet deployed almost as if they knew the enemy's plans, defeated the Japanese at the pivotal battle of Midway. September 15, 1940, was of personal significance. That was the day Paul had been shot down over England and taken prisoner.

Following the chronologically arranged numbers inward around the swastika, the final date, at the very center of the drawing below the Roman numerals on the Eiffel Tower, was August 25, 1944—just over two weeks away. The penultimate date—tomorrow, the day of the mission—was appended next to the number sequence 5-9-6.

"Here you are." Pamela handed Lady Gwendolyn a Baedeker map of Paris.

Lady Gwendolyn unfolded it and laid it on the table.

From what Paul could see, it was annotated with the same strange red markings as the chart Pamela gave Wing Commander McCray.

"This is your best option." Pamela pointed to a three-dimensional tube shape.

"Is that a sneak door or rabbit run?" Lady Gwendolyn asked.

"Indeterminate. You'll have to see when you get there."

Lady Gwendolyn pondered. "I may not be able to get all the way to the Rue de Rivoli out in the open. What if I go through this crepe warren?"

"*Don't.* Harold says stay out of there."

"All right." Lady Gwendolyn thought awhile. "The hotel…interstices throughout?"

"Right. Comingled geometry. Offset fractures like Maham House and some fossil fill. You'll be able to slip almost anywhere undetected."

"Hmm. That's good."

Pamela looked at her watch. "I have to get back to Bletchley Park."

Lady Gwendolyn took the beautiful woman's hands. "Thank you, Pamela."

"Of course."

"Everyone together." Chris swept his arm in a circle, motioning.

Paul sensed he was included in the invitation but edged into the far corner of the garden room and turned his back.

There was a time of silence. Then Chris prayed, "Father, thank you for giving us everything we need. You are holy, righteous, and sovereign over all things. Forgive the frailties and weaknesses that cause us to fail you so often. Overcome those frailties and bless this endeavor so that your will may be done. We are confident you *will* bless it because we are following your guidance. Lead Gwen and Paul. Give them the skill, discernment, and fortitude to do what is right. Deliver them from evil and give them peace. We ask these things in Jesus's name—the name above all names."

Everyone in their group said, "Amen."

Paul did not feel at peace. The war within himself was raging as fierce as ever.

Pamela left and Lord Buckleigh went with her.

A little later, the McCrays' son George, who had recently joined the Royal Air Force, and daughter Susan, who was still in secondary school, came for supper. They did not know what was going on but clearly understood their mother was about to do something dangerous. They had no idea Paul was German. He could not look them in the eyes. He slept little that night.

McCray checked his watch, drew a line on a map, and gazed at the ground. Finally, he touched a switch and said something into his intercom microphone. A minute later, the sound and vibration of the engines changed. Paul watched the port inboard propeller come to a dead stop, fully feathered. *Morning Glory* slowed and banked left, dropping out of formation.

Bristling with a dozen heavy machine guns pointing in all directions, every bomber in a three-level American box formation protected its neighbors as well as itself. But an airplane all alone was vulnerable, so four P-51 Mustang fighters peeled away from the bomber stream to escort the supposedly stricken plane.

Did they need to? There was minimal chance a Messerschmitt or Focke-Wulf would find *Morning Glory* now that the Allies had air supremacy. The Americans no longer even bothered to paint camouflage patterns on their airplanes—sun glinted brightly off the Mustangs' bare aluminum skin. *Morning Glory* hadn't actually had an engine failure, of course. The dead engine was an excuse for the B-17 to be flying by itself in the skies over northern France.

Paul had a hard, acidic lump in his stomach. There was no turning back. He was about to betray the Allies and go home to fight them… or be shot as a spy. He really was Oberleutnant Paul Brock, as his carefully forged identification papers said. But he would be in France under false pretenses. What would Uncle Dietrich think when he saw the letter? No—von Choltitz would never see the letter. Paul would surrender himself and Lady Gwendolyn long before he got to Paris.

"Time," McCray announced.

Morning Glory had descended below eight thousand feet. The passengers no longer needed heavy clothing or oxygen masks. Paul put his mask into an equipment stowage box and rose, though there wasn't room to stand up straight.

Lady Gwendolyn climbed stiffly to her feet and shed her leather jacket. She embraced her husband. They put their foreheads together, closed their eyes, and whispered prayers. They were saying goodbye for the last time. Did they know that? A Bible verse came to Paul's mind—the one about Judas going to the priests and officers of the temple to betray Jesus.

He ducked down and went aft, passing below the cockpit into the space with the platform where Sergeant Doogan, the flight engineer, stood manning the top gun turret. Paul's senses were especially alert; he noted the rich quality of the engines' roar resonating in the cramped compartment, the hard, vibrating, green-painted metal he touched, and the smell of outside air displacing the odor of the oxygen mask. He glanced at the pilots. The copilot, Lieutenant Laskey, looked over his shoulder and gave Paul a thumbs-up.

Paul stepped into his parachute harness and pulled its straps up over his shoulders. He fastened the buckles and adjusted the straps so the rig was snug behind his legs.

Lady Gwendolyn fussed nervously with hers. She finished the job and was first through the bulkhead into the bomb bay. She walked carefully on the narrow beam between the racks, placing one foot in front of the other, holding onto the metal frames to keep her balance. There was nothing below her but the bay doors.

There were no bombs in the racks—*Morning Glory* was not going to the target—but there was a large backpack to be dropped with the jumpers. It had its own parachute.

Using her free hand, Lady Gwendolyn clipped her static line to a ring on the port-side bomb rack. McCray stepped behind her to verify its security, squeezed her shoulder, and returned forward to stand behind the pilots.

Paul attached his line and tugged to double check it. Blood pulsed in his veins. He had prayed fervently for God to bless his plan to hand Lady Gwendolyn over to the first German soldiers they met. But he had not felt God's blessing. Instead, he felt a hollowness in his chest. She would be questioned by the Gestapo. She was a spy, saboteur, and assassin; it would be a very rough, very ugly affair. Gestapo interrogators would go no easier on a woman than a man. In fact, they might do things to her that they wouldn't do to a man. Paul shuddered and tried to shut the brutal images out of his mind.

Didn't the English realize that the two of them would be spotted on their way down and arrested immediately upon landing? Jumping in broad daylight—were they utter fools? Paul would not have to betray Lady Gwendolyn—her capture was inevitable.

He was so engrossed in his thoughts that he was startled when the bomb bay doors opened underneath him. The engine noise became even louder and air swirled around him. A green and tan patchwork of French farmland slid by below. It was an oddly serene tableau.

Sergeant Doogan ducked his head through the bulkhead. He held up a hand signaling for the jumpers to get ready. He looked back at McCray.

Paul glanced at Lady Gwendolyn. She clutched something in her left hand—an angular chunk of glass. A lucky charm, perhaps? She stared intently at Doogan, alert for his signal.

Doogan chopped the air in a sweeping motion.

Lady Gwendolyn hopped off the beam and dropped into the sky below the airplane. Her streaming static line pulled out her parachute canopy; it blossomed wide and round.

Doogan gave the next signal; Paul stepped into thin air and fell out of the B-17.

He sighed with relief when his parachute opened, but tensed a moment later when a brilliant, multicolored light enveloped him. An antiaircraft shell? Had *Morning Glory* exploded? No—the sky was peaceful and the B-17 was flying away in the protective custody of its P-51 Mustang escorts.

A high crosswind yanked him sideways. That was unnerving. He looked down and saw that he was being swept over a gray, miles-long rectangle that looked like something out of the last war: lifeless ground blasted and churned by constant canon and mortar bombardment. Was there a battlefield like it in this part of France in 1944? The sight stirred a foreboding.

He was still confused and unsettled when he landed. Forearms together, he fell sideways and rolled to absorb the impact, as he had been trained. By the time he gathered his parachute's canopy, Lady Gwendolyn had already wound hers around her arm and was headed for the backpack.

He studied the blasted ground.

"Those woods over there—" Lady Gwendolyn dumped her parachute on the ground and pointed. "We need to bury our parachutes here and get to those trees quickly. I don't want to have to fight, yet."

"Bury them *here*?" Paul looked at her. "We're out in the open. Shouldn't we get to the cover of the trees first?"

"No."

Paul surveyed the barren gray landscape. No one was after them thus far. But surely their bailout had been observed and their landing point noted. "Very well." He unstrapped the small spade that had been lashed to the backpack and quickly dug a wide but shallow hole in the lifeless gray dirt.

Lady Gwendolyn stopped him from making it deeper. "That's good enough, Paul. We have to prevent the material from blowing away—nothing more." She shucked off her jumpsuit, tossed it on the pile, and did her best to smooth the wrinkles in the skirt and blouse she had been wearing underneath it. Now she was dressed like a Frenchwoman. "Hurry."

He did. He added his jumpsuit to the heap, shoveled dirt on it, and piled rocks on top of that. It was a poor job—it would be found in no time. As he stood contemplating the ridiculous business, there was another flash of light.

"That's a rather advanced technique," Lady Gwendolyn said proudly as if congratulating herself. "I anchored the parachutes and jumpsuits to silhouette while they're inside an interstice. They're untouchable." She gave Paul an impish smile, apparently enjoying his inability to understand her private joke. She put the glass object into her pocket. "Let's go."

He was dealing with an escapee from a madhouse. The mission was doomed from the start.

Lady Gwendolyn paused when they reached the tree line. The strange light flashed again. This time he saw its source—it had come from her hand. The glass she held was a prism.

He looked behind himself and went rigid. *He* was the one who had gone insane. He was deep inside a forest. The blasted gray field was gone.

"No, you're not crazy." Lady Gwendolyn said as if reading his mind. She put the prism into her pocket. "Come along."

Dressed as French provincials, they walked south until they were out of the forest and continued to a crossroads with a few houses, barns, and storage buildings. Paul saw a farmer working in a field but no German patrols.

Lady Gwendolyn went directly to a barn outside the village and opened the doors. The place smelled of petrol and motor oil.

Paul studied the Mercedes-Benz G4. It was a staff car, but had no flags or markings.

"Here we are," Lady Gwendolyn said. "Time for you to change, Oberleutnant Brock."

She had stopped calling him Paul. He felt strangely hurt.

"Ja." Paul went around the car to have some privacy. The long, elegant but masculine six-wheeled vehicle had a small dent in a fender. Otherwise, it was immaculate.

Happy to shed the rumpled French clothes, he removed his starched and pressed trousers, shirt, and jacket from the backpack. He carefully unfolded them and put them on. After adjusting his necktie, he sat down on the car's running board and pulled on his highly polished boots. Setting his peaked cap securely on his head, he went back around the car.

Lady Gwendolyn had also changed into fresh clothes. She now looked like a Parisian. The muscles in her jaw tightened when she saw him—an instinctive reaction to the appearance of someone in the uniform of a mortal enemy. But she said, "Very good."

He *felt* good in the uniform. He was himself again.

He gestured at the open car. "Should we raise the top? It might provide some protection from curious eyes."

"We won't have a problem. You look the part."

"I was thinking of Resistance snipers."

"Don't worry about them," Lady Gwendolyn said flatly.

He shrugged. Prearrangements must have been made. "What about cowboy fighter pilots? We could be strafed."

She chewed her lower lip. "Well..."

"Lord Buckleigh said our escort pilots were the only ones briefed."

"I don't think we'll be strafed. If we are, with the top down, you might see the planes in time for us to stop and jump into a ditch."

Shrugging again, he took the German courier bag out of the backpack and put it on the front passenger seat. When he turned around, Lady Gwendolyn was holding a pistol—a Luger. It looked large in her slender hand. He stiffened.

But she wasn't pointing it at him. She stepped up into the car, slipped between the middle seats to reach the rear, and opened the secret compartment that had been constructed beneath the bench seat. She slid into the space to make sure she fit. She left the gun in the compartment when she wriggled back out. "Not very comfortable. I'll sit on the floor until I have to fully conceal myself."

Paul nodded. They had sixty miles to drive. He hesitated. "When we're stopped and questioned…"

"You did fine practicing with Chris. You'll have no trouble passing the test."

He couldn't look at her.

The test came sooner than either of them expected. After taking one-lane tracks to a byway wide enough for two vehicles to pass, Paul had driven fewer than four miles through the rolling countryside when he came to an improvised checkpoint. German half-tracks sat on either side of the road. Each vehicle had mounted machine guns, and Paul counted more than a dozen men on the ground. He slowed.

Clearly, the gray-clad soldiers were looking for someone. How would they react when he told them there was a British spy in his car? They were Waffen-SS storm troops, not regular army. He did not see an officer—they would have to contact a superior for instructions. Did they have a radio?

He suspected Lady Gwendolyn had shown him the Luger as a veiled threat. She would start shooting. She would probably kill herself rather than be captured. More thoughts he didn't like.

God, help me do what I need to do, he prayed. *Should I do it now or in a more favorable place?* But God was not listening. Paul still hadn't made up his mind when the squad's sergeant held out his hand, palm forward, signaling Paul to stop.

The tight-faced trooper pushed up the brim of his steel helmet and came alongside the car.

A big corporal with a submachine gun stood watchfully by the side of the road, his weapon casually trained on the car's grill. If he moved fractionally, he could spray the entire car with bullets.

The sergeant saluted. He looked uncertainly at Paul's uniform and the car. "May I see your papers, please, lieutenant?"

Paul handed over his forged documents. They included instructions to deliver orders to General von Choltitz.

The sergeant's gaze wandered to the courier bag on the seat next to Paul. "You are going to Paris?"

"Yes, Paris."

The man looked again at Paul's Luftwaffe uniform and the car. "Lieutenant, sir—why are you in this car?"

The corporal with the submachine gun was paying close attention.

"I was flying to Paris but forced down." Paul pointed upward. "Mustangs. So I commandeered this vehicle."

A civilian truck carrying fruit rolled up behind him.

The sergeant indicated the side of the road beyond the checkpoint. "Sir, if you would please park over there?"

Paul drove forward. *They're going to find Lady Gwendolyn. I should have said something.*

He pulled off the road.

The corporal and two other storm troopers came alongside the car. "My apologies, lieutenant," the corporal said curtly. "You must get out and—"

Shouts and a gunshot sounded somewhere behind.

The corporal looked back. He motioned urgently to Paul and shouted, "Go on. Go on." Then he sprinted toward the commotion, his comrades on his heels.

Paul did not hesitate. He went on. Looking in his mirror, he saw the soldiers hustling to take up defensive positions. The hunters had become the hunted. Once organized, the disciplined, well-equipped SS squad would almost certainly decimate the Resistance fighters; however, Paul had no intention of waiting for that to happen.

He heard sporadic gunfire until he was a mile away. His heart beat fast with the thrill of battle even after that.

He followed a carefully planned route past vegetable and wheat fields. Some of the farms were separated by rows of trees. Here and there he came upon timeworn brick or stone houses. Once, he noticed a chateau on the horizon. Occasionally, he passed centuries-old churches. The few Frenchmen he saw either glared at him or deliberately ignored him.

He did not drive fast on the bumpy roads but made good progress. As he got closer to Paris and encountered heavier traffic, Lady Gwendolyn spent more and more time under the seat. She must have been uncomfortable in the airless, bouncing compartment but said nothing about it.

There was a sizeable checkpoint with barriers on the outskirts of the city. Paul waited in a line of civilian and military cars and trucks spurting exhaust, moving slowly in a walled lane past gun mounts, praying for God to help him serve his country. But when he reached the barrier, the overtaxed soldier in the guard shack merely glanced at Paul's papers, signaled that the barrier be raised, and waved him through. In that congested place, word of a spy in a vehicle would initiate quick, decisive, and probably bloody action. They might machine-gun the back seat—maybe the whole car—before they asked questions. Paul drove on.

Though he had never been to Paris, he had memorized the maps and was able to work his way south without trouble. He was constantly in the sights of German gunners in emplacements positioned for clear lines of fire down the wartime boulevards.

There was a traffic jam near the city center. Several trucks blocked the road. Impulsively, Paul pulled into a side street and parked by the curb.

Lady Gwendolyn stirred under the back seat.

He got out of the car without saying anything. It was time to find soldiers and turn her in.

He walked back to the corner of the boulevard but stopped there. Two dozen French men and women stood by the trucks, staring south. One of them spotted Paul, and they all turned. Every one of them scowled at his German uniform. Paul was stunned by the hatred in their faces. Several in the crowd cursed under their breaths. A man spit on the sidewalk.

Paul stepped backward involuntarily.

Lady Gwendolyn pulled his arm. "Come with me. Quickly."

"What's going on?"

She reached into her purse—for the Luger, he assumed, but she took out the prism. "Hurry, or there will be trouble."

Some of the Frenchmen advanced toward him. One held a steel pipe.

Lady Gwendolyn hastened Paul down the side street. They were about to pass a padlocked door when he had another hallucination: an alley ran through the middle of the building. He gaped.

"This way." Lady Gwendolyn stepped into the dark, narrow alleyway.

Paul's first instinct was to back away from the schizophrenic mirage, but one glance at the advancing mob changed his mind. He didn't need to understand French. The venom in their voices clearly communicated their thoughts. He followed Lady Gwendolyn into his hallucination.

She offered him the Luger, holding its barrel so its handle was toward him. "Take this."

Why would she give her enemy her gun? He stared at it and her. But he took it.

The French didn't come into the alley. They stopped to either side and looked every which way but at Paul. He saw them clearly; they must see him. What were they doing?

"We're not far from the Meurice. We'll walk the rest of the way," Lady Gwendolyn said.

The French began a heated argument.

"They—"

"Can't see or hear us. I'll explain later."

Had the British invented an invisibility ray? Paul didn't think he was invisible. And he saw Lady Gwendolyn just fine.

She walked to the end of the ally and stepped out into a small, shadowed square. Perhaps it would more accurately be called a court-yard because it was fully enclosed by ramshackle buildings squeezed together without gaps. Large swatches of their yellow, pink, and gray stucco exteriors had sloughed off, exposing weathered bricks. Only a few windows still had shutters—most were empty rectangular holes.

After consulting Pamela's red-marked Baedeker map, Lady Gwendolyn went inside one of the abandoned buildings and climbed stone steps to the second floor. Paul followed. It was a hot day, but the air inside the building felt stale and smelled…the only word that came to his mind was *frozen*, though that was obviously wrong. The air was not cold, and *frozen* wasn't a smell. But frozen stuck in his brain. And the texture of the building's plaster walls was equally confusing. It was…*hollow*? Or the opposite. It was immovably, unchangeably solid. It had tremendous inertia.

"Stay close to me," Lady Gwendolyn ordered. She had the prism in her right hand and a gleaming sword in her left. No—the sword was a figment of his delirium. He blinked and it was gone. What was happening to his mind? What had they done to him?

He followed Lady Gwendolyn into a long gallery that had gaping openings where once there had been windows. In the modern plaza below, German soldiers were marching five men, three women, and two teenage boys to the wall of the building opposite. One of the women resisted and had to be dragged. Paul heard a German officer command his men to bind the prisoners.

Lady Gwendolyn stopped at a window.

"You're exposed," Paul warned her.

"They can't see me."

So the British *had* invented an invisibility ray?

The officer read a notice loudly in French. Paul didn't understand what was said, but it sounded like a decree or sentence. "What's going on?"

"It's an execution," Lady Gwendolyn said. "Resistance fighters killed German soldiers in a skirmish."

Hands behind their backs, the men, women, and boys were tied to the railing.

"Those people killed soldiers?"

Lady Gwendolyn shook her head. "Probably not. They were in the vicinity. It apparently doesn't matter if they're guilty or not. They're being made examples."

"Oh." Paul felt a tightening in his chest. Killing enemy soldiers in battle was one thing. Even accidentally causing civilian deaths. War was war. But deliberately executing people for a crime they probably didn't commit—he didn't like it, even if it had to be done.

"I don't want to watch this," Lady Gwendolyn said. "Let's go." She stormed to the end of the gallery and down a flight of steps, not looking back.

Paul went after her, a lump in his throat. He winced when a volley of gunshots echoed through the empty rooms. Three coup de grace shots followed at four- or five-second intervals.

Loyalty, duty, doing what was best for his family and countrymen—he steeled himself to betray Lady Gwendolyn. When she proceeded down a tunnel-like street overhung by jutting upper stories, he darted left into a tiny alley he thought would take him toward the Rue de Rivoli. Running hard, he quickly left her behind.

He winced again. Shooting innocent people…

What was right? Helping his family was right. Helping his country and helping people throughout the world. But how best to do that? People were ignorant and needed to be led. That was why there were governments to control them and wars fought to place stronger nations over inferior ones. That was why the National Socialist party was trying to create a well-structured world—the Nazis were working for the greater good. It was unavoidable, regrettably, that individuals were hurt in the process.

He almost turned his ankle on the uneven cobblestones. It was dark in the warren of tiny streets. Where was he? There was nothing like this neighborhood on the maps. It was like something out of Dickens's *A Tale of Two Cities*—a place that existed before Paris had been replanned and reconstructed in the mid-nineteenth century. The roads were so narrow, crooked, and poorly paved that a modern vehicle would have had trouble negotiating them. That was probably why he hadn't seen anyone since he ran away from Lady Gwendolyn—the whole area was abandoned. Which was good. He didn't want to meet any French people. He wanted to find his German countrymen.

He came to a junction of six narrow streets and alleys. Every route looked like a dead end, but that might have been because the ascending and descending streets all curved so he saw only walls. He stopped. "Ach!"

While he pondered which way to go, he smelled something like decaying corpses and heard scratching footfalls. The hair on the back his neck stood up. He gripped the Luger and spun around.

The appearance of the five creatures staring at him from halfway up an alley made his heart pound so hard he thought he was being hit in the chest. The mangy, ropy-muscled bears metamorphosed into huge spiders blacker than holes in outer space, and then to long-fanged, ape-like creatures with multiple arms. He was hallucinating again, but whatever they actually were, the things were dangerous. Their jaws dripped saliva in glistening, gooey strands.

He was a highly trained and battle-seasoned German soldier, but his limbs failed him. For several seconds, he couldn't move.

The creatures looked at his gun and at each other, calculating, each of their eyes moving independently. One of them took a step. Then they all surged forward.

He fired but trembled so badly he could hardly aim his pistol. Not that pointing mattered—the things followed the gun barrel with their eyes and could have evaded his shots even if he had full control of his arms. But the seventh bullet ricocheted off a wall and miraculously hit one of the ape-like things in the head. Gushing black fluid, the wounded creature stumbled and careened into a stone doorjamb. Its four comrades skidded to a halt and stared at its injuries.

Paul turned and fled, choosing a street that went downward.

Two of the sinewy things remained with their wounded brother—to help it, Paul assumed—but the other two pursued him. They loped in measured gaits, biding their time, knowing he couldn't escape. And something else was shadowing him: lithe and liquid gray, it looked like a bead of dirty mercury streaming along the walls. In the single instant he caught sight of it, his stomach heaved as if his body were trying to reject poison.

"God, help me!" The utterance was an exclamation, not a prayer. But realizing what he had mechanically said, he embraced the words. *God, save me!*

He careened around the corner of a small church. On impulse, he ducked into its open entrance, hoping the hunters would not realize he had gone inside.

He might have made a mistake. There was nowhere to conceal himself; the building was a hollow shell without furnishings. It did not even have an altar.

On this murky day, the large stained-glass windows were dull and colorless. Looking down from the cross depicted in the window behind the sanctuary, Jesus appeared forgotten.

Paul went around the corner of the transept and stopped there, peeking back at the front entrance. He thought he saw movement on the tracery above the doors and looked closely at a stained-glass panel. It depicted a man, fallen on a road, illuminated by a beam of light from heaven: the apostle Paul on his way to Damascus to arrest Christians, just before his conversion. Just before God revealed what he must do.

The two ape-like hunters crept inside. They didn't have to move quickly; their quarry was trapped. They glanced warily at the stained-glass window behind the sanctuary, as if Christ might come down from it into the church.

Paul did not run or try to hide. He had nowhere to go. He had a single bullet left in his gun. He might be able to kill one of the creatures. His heart beat erratically. The other would rip him apart.

The larger of the two things opened its bottom and side jaws.

Then a shining figure surged through the door behind them—a woman in armor so bright it dazzled Paul's eyes. She wielded a sword with a white-hot blade.

"In Jesus's name, back to Hell with you!" she cried as she sliced through the creature nearest the door.

The monster was a void—that was the only way Paul could describe what he saw. The thing turned inside out and was sucked into nothingness.

The other attempted to flee, but the woman plunged her sword into its neck. Like the first, it was pulled into its own void.

Paul was so shocked he simply stared.

"Paul!" Lady Gwendolyn gasped for air, her chest heaving. She must have run all out to find him. "I told you to stay close!"

He tried to take a step but couldn't control his shaking and nearly fell. "What *were* those things?"

She finally caught her breath. "Demons."

"What do you mean by *demons*?"

"I mean demons. Spirits that rebelled against God."

"Spirits? Those creatures were solid." He scanned the floor, looking for remains.

"In this place, demons are quite solid."

"This place?"

"More precisely, our current state. I don't have time to explain. We have to get to the Meurice."

Whether warned by something she saw or pure intuition, Lady Gwendolyn jumped sideways. A stone hurled from the tracery above the church entrance missed her head. But it glanced off her shoulder with enough force to knock her to the ground.

The liquid-gray thing pounced like a leopard and pinned her sword arm under its long-toed foot.

Paul aimed the Luger, but only for a second. He was pointing his gun at Major Steinhoff, his commanding officer.

"Shoot it!" Lady Gwendolyn cried, straining to escape Major Steinhoff's clutches. "Paul, shoot the demon!"

Demon? Paul got a good look despite the dim light. The person standing over Lady Gwendolyn was the Fuhrer himself—Adolph Hitler, the man to whom Paul and all German soldiers had sworn personal allegiance. The man Paul owed loyalty above all others.

He couldn't think. His mind was fogged.

Hitler bent down and groped at the pinned woman. Her armor protected her from his jagged claws, but she couldn't thrust the sword she managed to tilt toward his chest.

"Kill the woman," the Fuhrer ordered. "Kill her *now!*"

There was no higher authority than the Fuhrer. Paul's finger tightened on the trigger.

But sunlight broke through the clouds and the stained-glass windows lit up. The large arched panel high in the window above the door dazzled him. It depicted the risen Christ sitting on the judgement seat, and its radiance burned the fog from his brain.

Men make mistakes, but God judges perfectly. When loyalties and duties conflicted, God would guide if Paul would listen. Paul had wanted God to bless the choices he made. That was backward.

He owed loyalty to God above all others, even above his family and country. And he owed nothing to the liquid-gray creature. He took careful aim and shot it.

The thing spasmed.

Lady Gwendolyn ran it through, shouting, "In Jesus's name, I bind you and send you back to your prison!"

The void took it.

"I hate apoks," she said, climbing shakily to her feet. "When they stalk solo, you never see them coming."

She had her prism but no longer held a sword or wore armor. She looked at the cross in the sanctuary. "You always save me, Lord. Forgive me for doubting."

Paul stared at her blouse and skirt. "Your armor…"

"Armor?

"You were wearing…" He shook his head again. He couldn't tell what was real.

"You saw armor?" That seemed to please her. "What did I look like?"

"Sir Galahad."

She snorted, but smiled.

Paul scanned the rest of the church, especially the tracery around the windows. He saw no more creatures. "I overheard you say you were going to drive a demon out of Paris. You meant that *literally?*"

"Yes, I meant it literally."

"I can't believe any of this." He pulled the magazine out of the Luger. All the bullets had been fired. "But I guess I have to." He looked around the church. Then he stared at Lady Gwendolyn. "Why didn't you tell me before?"

"That I was going to Paris to drive out a sure-enough, bona fide demon? A literal fallen angel? What would you have thought?"

He rubbed his face, shook his head, and closed his eyes. "I would have thought you insane."

"Exactly."

"So, you came here for those…" Paul waved his hand where the demons had been.

"Not those. I came for the one sent to influence your relative, von Choltitz." She looked at her watch. "I'll explain everything later. We have to be inside the Meurice in fifteen minutes."

"You won't be allowed into the hotel." He sighed. "I doubt I will be."

"We'll get in. You'll see."

He followed her out of the church. "And you'll kill the demon."

She set off at a brisk pace through the narrow streets. "Demons can't be killed. I'll order the pseustee—the demon—back to Hell with the authority I've been delegated." She gripped her prism and scrutinized every building, watching for dangers.

"Using your talisman?"

"This?" Lady Gwendolyn held up the prism. "This is a piece of glass. But it helps me focus. It's faith that allows God to work in our lives. And it's His power that defeats demons. I've been delegated that power—that's all."

"And you do it all the time? Fight demons?"

"No. Only a few times in my life. We avoid demons. My team's job is to redirect demonically manipulated circumstances. That means working with human beings."

Paul walked beside Lady Gwendolyn. "What will happen if you don't stop the demon in the Meurice?"

"The pseustee will influence General von Choltitz to carry out Hitler's orders to raze Paris to the ground. And the French may block American plans to rebuild Germany after the war."

"Victors don't rebuild their enemies. They take what's left." Paul thought of his youth.

"After this war, the Americans will do something different."

Paul stopped. "I can't believe that."

Lady Gwendolyn motioned brusquely for him to follow. "We have to hurry. This is a highly unusual opportunity. For once, we know exactly what will happen, and all demonic factions are in the dark. The pseustee is in for a terrible shock when it enters the Meurice at eight minutes past six o'clock."

"How do you know it will come?"

"God reveals things to me." She glanced at her map, turned a corner, and hurried down a winding street, her heels clicking on the stones.

"God talks to you? You can hear Him?"

"I don't *hear* Him," Lady Gwendolyn said irritably. "Usually."

"The picture with the symbols, numbers, and dates—does it have something to do with all this?"

"Ah, you saw the photo. Yes, that picture provided hints. It was drawn by our ancestor Robert Maham three hundred years ago. His visions relate to Maham family crises and commissions. Two of them apply to my life. The one you saw applies to seven years of my life—and a few weeks of yours."

"But I'm not in your family."

Lady Gwendolyn looked at him. "I guess you don't know your mother's genealogy. Your great-great-grandfather Henry Maham was my great-great-grandfather." She smiled. "We're cousins."

Paul looked at her, dazed. "We...are cousins?"

She stopped. "There it is."

They stood across a boulevard from a grand stone building.

"That's the Meurice," Lady Gwendolyn announced.

Paul looked left and right, confused. "What boulevard is this?"

"The Rue de Rivoli."

"It can't be. If this were the Rue de Rivoli, we would be standing in the Tuileries Garden."

"We're in an interstice—a place in God's creation you can't normally go. We're between the Jardin des Tuileries and the Rue de Rivoli."

Paul studied the fossil-like structures around him. They reminded him of bombed buildings but with smoother edges. He stopped trying to understand.

He raised empty hands. "I don't have the letter. I left it in the car."

Lady Gwendolyn chewed her lip and frowned. "Well…it's too late to go back for it."

She opened her marked-up map and fixed her eyes on a three-foot-wide strip of cobblestones that cut across the boulevard. "It's a rabbit run."

"What?"

"See that strip of old cobblestones? Patrick and Pamela would call it a lift-fault interference fringe. The rest of us call it a rabbit run—a long, thin stretch of interstice. Inside interstices, we can't be seen, heard, or touched, so we can walk unobserved and unmolested straight into the hotel. Which is good because I do *not* want to be seen. Please accept what I tell you and don't ask questions right now."

Paul studied the worn stones. They ran through a row of troop trucks and German staff cars parked in front of the Meurice. Several senior officers stood talking on the sidewalk on the other side of the vehicles.

"If you can get in without being seen, you don't need me anymore."

"You're supposed to be here." She looked at her watch.

Paul looked at his, also. It was four minutes past six o'clock.

She hurried out into the street. "Come on. Pay no attention to the traffic. It will go right past us."

She was not watching. Just before reaching the space between two parked trucks, she walked in front of an oncoming car.

"Look out!" He grabbed her and jumped between the trucks. Inertia carried them off the cobblestones onto the sidewalk with the officers.

"No! Paul!" She stiffened.

The startled officers stepped back. Two guards with submachine guns whirled and pointed their weapons.

"Pardon!" Paul said. "She—" He indicated Lady Gwendolyn. "She was not paying attention to the traffic and…"

The indignant officers stared at the Oberleutnant and Frenchwoman who had suddenly appeared among them.

"Paul?" General von Choltitz said in amazement.

"Yes, General, sir."

"What are you doing here? You were a prisoner of war."

"Yes, sir. I escaped."

The general looked at Lady Gwendolyn—by all appearances an attractive Parisian.

"She…" Paul hesitated. "She is…my woman."

Lady Gwendolyn didn't speak German, but her glare and crooked smile told Paul that she knew what he had said.

Von Choltitz turned to the other officers. "Please excuse me for a few minutes." He signaled Paul. "Come with me."

Paul gave Lady Gwendolyn a weak, apologetic smile.

Face blank, moving mechanically, she followed the two men into the hotel.

The general passed guards, who saluted him, and went into a side room. He addressed Lady Gwendolyn: "Miss, would you please wait in the lobby?"

She slipped a hand into a pocket.

"She doesn't speak German," Paul said. "We converse in English." He turned to her. "The general asks that you wait in the lobby."

As he said it, a wiry, multicolored creature slipped through a door at the back of the room. It had a long, thin snout.

The demon stopped dead when it saw Lady Gwendolyn, as shocked as she predicted it would be.

She pulled her hand out of her pocket, and a glove fell out. Even as the glove dropped, the prism she held flared with all colors. The air became as thick as frozen molasses. The glove hung midway to the floor.

"Hold!" Lady Gwendolyn commanded the demon. "Creature of Hell—"

"Wait!" it cried. "Great lady! Don't bind me! I will serve you. I will be your eyes and ears and mouth. Great Lady! Let me be your faithful servant! I am useful in many ways." It vibrated as if straining against shackles even as it tried to negotiate.

"No. Go back into the darkness."

"You claim to follow a merciful God—have you no mercy?" it wailed.

"I won't be fooled or shamed," she replied.

The thing hissed. "You are *foul*! At least let me go by my own hand."

"Very well. Your fate has always been yours to decide."

It snarled, disintegrated like a spray of inky shadow, and flew into the void.

Paul stared. "That's it?"

"You wanted something more dramatic?" Lady Gwendolyn looked at her suspended glove. "Listen, Paul. No time has passed. Only you and I experienced the last minute. Put your thoughts in order. When you're ready, I'll resynchronize and reanchor us. Time will pick up exactly where it left off. Continue with the general as if nothing happened."

After all he had just experienced, nothing could fluster him. He took a deep breath. "I'm ready."

The prism flashed and her glove finished falling to the floor. She retrieved it and nodded to von Choltitz. "Yes, sir, I'll wait outside."

The general closed the door. "Paul, tell me what has happened to you."

"I was released on the condition I deliver a letter—an appeal for you to spare Paris from destruction."

The general's eyes narrowed. His expression became stony.

Over the next several minutes, Paul explained his reasons for accepting the British offer. He recounted his journey to Paris—omitting mention of supernatural places and beings—and spoke of his conflicted thoughts. His highest loyalty, he concluded, was to God and his conscience. So he had come, though he had lost the letter. Sparing Paris was the right thing to do.

Von Choltitz said nothing while Paul was speaking, and for almost another minute afterwards.

"You should be court-martialed for what you've done." The general stared into a corner as if Paul were not in the room. "Never tell anyone what you said here. You're dismissed. Go away."

When Paul walked out of the hotel with Lady Gwendolyn, he felt as if a tremendous weight had been lifted from his shoulders, and the world looked brighter.

Gwen watched the river of American G.I.s marching from the Arc de Triomphe down the Champs Elysees. General von Choltitz had not carried out his orders to destroy Paris. He and twenty thousand German troops had surrendered on August 25, and the liberated City of Light had erupted in celebration. To Gwen's relief, Paul had not gone to fight for moribund Germany, pointlessly killing and probably being killed himself for Adolph Hitler and the other evil Axis leaders. When she discharged him, his obligation fulfilled, he went to act as a liaison for wounded German prisoners.

The major powers would be at peace for a while. Times would be tense, and there would be conflicts, but no world war in the coming decades. Unfortunately, Satan used peace even more effectively than war. He was happy for mortals to have safety, luxury, and contentment so long as they damned themselves for all eternity. So he made the road to Hell easy and pleasurable to travel.

She had had to cope with war. Her successor would have to cope with peace. In his time, the western world would begin turning its back on Jesus. Her successor…she knew more about him than he would know about himself in 1976.

A French girl of about eighteen was handing flowers to soldiers and kissing them on the cheek. One of the Yanks broke step and kissed her back—on the mouth. She skipped away, feigning distress, but broke into a grin, giggled, and waved.

Gwen let herself be swept along. She would enjoy the celebration while it lasted.

AUTHOR'S NOTE

It's probably rare for a fantasy author to say he relied on personal memories for things described in a story; however, in this case, it's true. I had the fantastic fortune to fly in a B-17 twice. I spent a good part of each flight in the nose compartment. The view from the bombardier's chair was spectacular. I thought of the dedicated, resourceful, courageous crews who flew during World War II and what they experienced on their missions. They deserve all the praise and credit they have received in history books and films. Inflight, I walked through the bomb bay on the beam between the racks and thought to myself that I better not fall because the thin doors below might not hold my weight.

I did not jump out of the B-17, but I did jump out of another airplane with the same type of round parachute described in *Saving the City of Light*. Unfortunately, my landing was not as good as Paul's. I came down in briars and did not roll properly, so I injured my ankle.

I have also been in a vehicle stopped by soldiers armed with automatic weapons. We had just crossed one hundred yards of ground between barbed wire fences separating communist Eastern Europe from the West. The soldiers had our papers, and we had waited many minutes when two of the men with AK-47s slung across their backs marched stiffly up to the van, loudly called my name, and demanded that I identify myself. It was an exciting moment. But they were just handing back passports, and mine happened to be the first.

Finally, I stayed at the Meurice Hotel when I was a child. I did not know its history then—only that it was a big, fancy hotel.

But all descriptions of interstices are conjecture. I cannot say for sure that there is a rabbit run across the Rue de Rivoli.

W. F. Rogers

ABOUT THE AUTHOR

W. F. Rogers is a spacecraft systems engineer and program manager. He loves history, and he loves his two daughters. He wrote The Mirror and the Prism series for them.